## HIGH MARKS FROM FELLOW PROFESSIONALS
### for
### *Manhattan North Narcotics: Chasing the Kilo Fairy*

"This book captures every nuance of the surreal, sublime, grit, charm, and danger of being a narcotics detective in Manhattan North, which figuratively speaking is about a million miles from Midtown. Jake McNicholas takes you on wild ride in this wonderfully unique, engaging, illuminating and frightening tale of what it really means to chase the kilo fairy – one vial at a time."

—Robert Mladinich, author or co-author of four books, including *From the Mouth of the Monster: The Joel Rifkin Story* and *Undisclosed Files of the Police: Cases from the Archives of the NYPD from 1831 to the Present.* He is also the writer and editor of *Frontline*, the publication for the NYPD Sergeants Benevolent Association.

"Jake McNicholas brings the dangerous world of narcotics enforcement in New York City to life like no other. The cops are gritty, witty and sometimes giddy. Readers tag along with main characters, Detective Jimmy McTigue and his partner Bobby Washington onto the narcotics sets, the borough office and afterhours hangouts feeling as if they're part of the team. The banter between the cops, who simultaneously seem to love and hate their job, is brutally honest. McNicholas knows their work as well as anybody, and politics be damned, does not hold anything back. It might be fiction, but one thing is for certain, McNicholas give readers an insider's view of the "God's" work being performed everyday by the brave men and women assigned to the NYPD's Narcotic Division."

—Bernard Whalen, NYPD Lieutenant, is co-author of *Justifiable Homicide; The NYPD's First Fifty Years—Politicians, Police*

*Commissioners, and Patrolmen;* and *Undisclosed Files of the Polilce—Cases From the Archives of the NYPD.*

"Jake McNicholas has hit it out of the park with his first novel about the gritty and violent world faced by NYPD narcotics detectives. He shows his detectives to be as I know them to be: ordinary, yet dedicated, working men and women who reflect, in their war-zone humor and personalities, what it's like to work almost daily in an atmosphere besieged by crime. The plot is intriguing, the characters are well developed, and the writing style makes for engrossing, difficult-to-take-a-break-from, reading. It brought me right back to my days 'on the job!' I look forward to future writings by Mr. McNicholas."

—Christopher J. Freitag is a retired Captain, Fair Lawn, NJ, Police Department (27 years service). He was organizer and commander of the Fair Lawn Emergency Response Team (SWAT-type unit) for 15 years; an FBI Certified Firearms Instructor and firearms instructor at the Fair Lawn Police and Bergen County Police Academies. He is also co-author of the State of New Jersey Auxiliary Police Firearms Course.

# Manhattan North Narcotics

*Chasing the Kilo Fairy*

## Jake McNicholas

Manhattan North Narcotics: Chasing the Kilo Fairy
Copyright © 2016 by John F. McNicholas

Published in the United States of America by
Escarpment Press, Hendersonville, NC

www.escarpmentpress.weebly.com
Hendersonville, NC

First Edition: October 1, 2016
10 9 8 7 6 5 4 3 2 1
Cover Photo © Copyright: Georgijevic, iStock.com

ISBN: 978-0692778708 (Escarpment Press)
ISBN: 0692778705

For My Mom and Dad

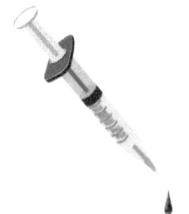

# Prologue

"Do you know who the fuck Ethel Mertz is?"

"Not a clue."

They were sitting across from each other in a dark corner of Ruth's Chris Steak House on West Fifty First Street, Artie Levin, agent, eating the Cowboy Rib Eye and washing it down with a Fireball, and Meg Cassidy, actress, picking at the Wedge Salad with Bleu Cheese and drinking a club soda with a splash of cranberry.

Artie was 45 years old, 5'10" and about 180. He kept in shape with a former Army Special Forces personnel trainer, one of those guys that ran a boot camp exercise class for young Upper Eastside mothers who drank red wine in the afternoon and talked about their nannies. He had a large nose and was losing his hair. He was thinking seriously about going with a little hair transplantation, the procedure that took a strip of hair off the back of your head and stuck it up front. In the interim, he went everywhere wearing a baseball hat; most times backwards, sometimes sideways—his "ghetto look." He was loud, annoying, and obnoxious to a fault.

Artie had three clients in what he called his stable. He represented—or repped (as he liked to put it)—Dexter Spencer, an all pro wide receiver playing football for the Detroit Lions. He crossed over into the entertainment field with Howard

Chance, who was playing Richard in ABC's hit *The Transgendered Butler*. And then there was his "big money" client, Meg Cassidy.

First time he saw Cassidy was at the Hooters in the shopping center behind the AMC Loews on the Horace Harding Expressway in Fresh Meadows Queens. She was coming across the floor with a tray, carrying glasses of craft beer, some buffalo chicken nachos and a couple of Big Baja Burgers and wearing those skin tight orange shorts and the white tank top. Gave him a woody! She was working a couple of shifts a week and studying English at St. John's. She was tall, with long legs, long brown hair, deep blue eyes, a few freckles on each side of her nose. It was the smile though, God the smile. Artie thought *that*—more than anything else—was his ticket.

He struck up a conversation, threw her his business card, and pretty soon thereafter got her a spot eating a Nathan's hot dog and they never looked back.

She was 30 now, and had just finished starring in two big hit movies. She debuted as a bikini-clad terrorism fighter, "Denise LaPiece," in a flick by the same name. In her second movie she played a runway model "P.I.," who took down rogue ICE agents who were actually locking up illegal aliens on the Southern Border. That beauty was called *The ICE Men Cometh*.

But now, Artie had gotten his hands on a script that he thought was going to raise Meg's game, a serious role as a teacher in the inner city. It wasn't glamorous at all—she'd even be a little overweight—but a real meaty role that Artie thought, with a little help, could get her an Academy Award nomination.

"You know who Lucille Ball is?"

"Sure, Artie, I've heard of her," said Meg.

"You see, Ethel Mertz was Lucy's sidekick on the show, *I Love Lucy*, from the fifties. Lucy was hooked up with Ricky, a 'spic' bandleader who ran a nightclub and talked with an accent. Lucy and Ethel got into all kinds of shit at home. Ethel was married to this old fuck named Fred, so Vivian Vance, who played Ethel, had to change her look because she was considerably younger and not a bad looker in her own right. I got to be honest with you, the thought of Fred pounding Ethel gives me the willies. Anyway, she wound up gaining twenty pounds or something and changing her hair—and *that's* what *you'll* need to do for this movie. You read the script. I think you can do it, and I think it will be great for your career."

"I *did* read it and I *did* like it. Who's going to be directing?"

"Fred Meunch. You can't get better talent than that. Once his name's attached to a project it gets instant credibility. They haven't even considered who else is going to be in it. What, you worried about putting on the weight?"

"Really, Artie, you don't know me at all do you? In fact I'll think I'll have a steak right now," she laughed. "*And* a Budweiser, too!"

"Another good thing," said Artie. "Looks like all the filming will take place here in New York—they'll shoot the interior shit at the Silver Cup Studios in Long Island City, and use the real gritty atmosphere of the five boroughs, with locations all over."

"Would be *real* nice to stay home," sighed Meg. She took a long drink of her club soda and sat back in her seat and closed her eyes. She had been living out in LA, but had spent the last three weeks back in New York, down at Breezy Point with her mom and dad, relaxing, unwinding—getting the Hollywood "germs" out of her system. She hated the West Coast—couldn't even find a decent slice of pizza.

Artie finished his steak and was eying one of the waitresses, while Meg had her eyes closed.

Meg came to. "Let's do it Artie, I trust you."

"Want to come back to my place?"

"No thanks, I'm meeting my Dad after he's finished work."

"Call you in the morning," said Artie, giving her a kiss, and watching her leave.

And then he gave the waitress his business card.

* * * * *

Artie lived on the sixteenth floor of Liberty Green, a brick and glass tower located at 300 North End Avenue in Battery Park City. He was paying ninety-two hundred a month for a three-bedroom, and for that he got the high ceilings with the water view and a half-assed suburban way of life. He was making money pretty much hand-over-fist and he was now into the world of art: the up-and-coming modern painters—and that's how he decorated the place. He liked American Blake Daniels and his out there, purely vivid shit, and he had recently fallen in love with the stuff that Australian Marc Freeman was producing. Most recently, a girl he had hooked up with turned him on to Japanese painter Akira Ikezoe. The guy was living in Brooklyn, so Artie took a ride over there one day and gobbled up some of his latest work. He figured it was an investment.

He was definitely getting into the whole scene at Battery Park. He hadn't been there when the Towers fell, nor for the damage it caused, nor the chaos that had ensued. Things were back to normal, and Artie was even taking sailing lessons at the North Cove Marina at the Manhattan Sailing School.

He took one of the bedrooms and made it his "man cave," with a seventy-five inch flat screen, a fully stocked bar, and a two-person sauna. He watched a lot of *The World Series of Poker* and any and all sports—and, shit, of course porn. He liked to walk over to Chambers and Church Streets to the Pioneer Bar and drink shots. It's also where he picked up his weed from Linda, a daytime bartender at the joint.

He was banging a Latina law student named Gladys, who lived on the Upper East Side, above Ninety Sixth Street, so he found himself up north quite frequently. He wasn't concerned about driving his bright red Escalade up there to "get a little."

Jake McNicholas

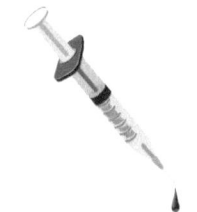

# Chapter 1

There is a building that sits on Fifth Avenue that is bounded by 142nd and 143rd Streets in upper Manhattan, which is a monument to the brave men of the 369th Regiment, better known as the "Harlem Hellfighters."

The U.S. Army was segregated during World War I and the years prior. In 1913, New York established the 15th New York Infantry Regiment, a "colored" outfit, as they referred to it back then. It was a unit of the National Guard, and reported for duty in France in 1917 as the 369th. It was during the Meuse-Argonne Offensive in 1918 that they earned their title and continued their record of bravery and valor in the bloody Pacific on Okinawa in World War II and later in Korea and the Persian Gulf. The unit proudly serves to this day.

The building sits just off the Harlem River and, in many ways, is a throwback to other armories built earlier that dot the landscape that is New York. There are actually two structures that make up the site, and they were built in two stages: the Drill Shed, constructed between 1920 and 1924; and the Administration Building, built between 1930 and 1933. It is the latter building that is most interesting.

Stand in front of that edifice with your back to the river and the Harlem River Drive. Off to the left is Harlem Storage, and in front of that and across the street, at the tip of Fifth Avenue, is a small patch of grass with a granite spire that asks you to remember the service of the 369th during the Meuse-Argonne Offensive. The Armory itself has two steps that lead to the circular slab of concrete where the flagpole is, and then seven steps that lead up to the front of the building. Take in all of its magnificence: the wrought-iron gates that dot the entire façade; and then follow the architecture further up to the two glorious eagles on the edge of the top facing outbound that appear to be standing guard for those within. The stone steps lead to the four-paneled, wood doors, which are stunning in their own right. Above, in gridded green iron is the address, 2366, and then above that, etched in sandstone, is the inscription "369 Infantry NYNG." It says it all and takes one's breath away.

It was through that entrance and into that building that the men and women of Manhattan North Narcotics proceeded.

And, even after all this time, it gave Detective Jimmy McTigue chills just walking through those doors.

\* \* \* \* \*

"All right, who's getting on?" asked Sgt. Matt Quinn.

They were in a good spot in the office, located where they were, in the corner with two walls making up the back of what they called their "cubicle." On each of the remaining sides was a wooden partition that came up about four feet and an opening that was opposite the back wall. There were ten desks in the section, which served as the home for Sgt. Quinn's team, along with Al Gavin and Jack Clint from Sgt. Lewis's crew.

"I don't care who's making the collars, but somebody best be buying me lunch," said Detective Bobby Washington. "I'm

8

making you crackers enough money in O.T. Least you could do is buy a brother a sandwich."

"That mean I'm a cracker, too?" asked Tommy Bell.

"You just a dumb ass," said Bobby Washington. "You and that big donkey, McTigue."

"Easy Bobby," said Jimmy McTigue. "I'm very sensitive."

"At least he didn't reference your incredible love for beer," said Detective Santos Cruz.

"Take it easy Puerto Rican," said Bobby Washington. "I'm still trying to figure out you, Defranco, and that fuckin' bullfrog of his."

"Pay day Thursday tomorrow and I'm getting old Rudy a mouse for lunch," said Detective Charlie Defranco.

"Fuck the mouse," said Washington. "Just get me a hero from one of your *Eye-talian* delis."

"Hey Bobby, what's black and doesn't work?" asked Defranco.

"Fuck you, grease ball!" yelled Bobby Washington.

Charlie laughing, "Decaf coffee, you raciest bastard."

"I'm getting on Bobby," said Detective Richie Whalen. "And I'll be happy to go over to the KFC on W155th Street and pick you up a bucket. I know how much *you people* dig chicken."

"*You people* is it, Whalen? You and the rest of you Irish pricks ought to try sobering up for a day or two. Do yourself some good. Besides, if I'm eating chicken, the only place I'm going is Popeye's."

""Richie, you sure it's your turn?" asked Detective Frank Martin.

"Holy shit, Martin speaks!" screamed Washington. "I haven't heard him talk this much since his promotion party and all he said was 'Thanks a lot, guys.' And please, Frank, remember, I'm your friend, so don't shoot me."

"I don't know why I bother," sighed Sgt. Quinn.

"Because you love this shit," said Sgt. Lewis.

"What a fucking team you guys are," said Detective Jack Clint.

"I'll second that," said Detective Al Gavin.

"And don't you fuckin' forget it," said Bobby Washington, standing and looking around the cubicle. "I might be on a team with some crazy white boys, Irish stew balls, a spic and a spook, but I ain't going out the door with nobody else. You my brothers and you got my back and yeah I love you fuckers for it."

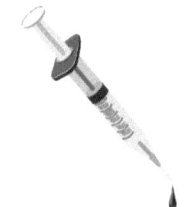

# Chapter 2

Tommy Bell had previously worked in the 10th Precinct on the west side of Manhattan. There were cops that didn't even know the place existed, nestled like it was on Twentieth Street between Seventh and Eighth Avenue. The command covered Fourteenth Street to Twenty-Ninth Street from Seventh Avenue to the river, and Twenty-Ninth Street to Forty-Fourth Street from Ninth Avenue to the river.

First day there, Bell couldn't find a locker. Second day, he was in the basement looking around when an old lady came shuffling up to him out of nowhere and asked, in a real Southern drawl, "Hey cotton picker you need a locker?" She must have been 75 years old, and was wearing a housecoat and a pair of Hush Puppies. Tommy said, "Sure," and the women took a lock off one in the corner and there you had it.

Her name was Millie, and she lived in the precinct. She had a rocking chair to the right of the desk, where she slept, and she had the run of the entire building. Years ago, there had been an incident up the block, in her apartment, a break-in while Millie was home. She got spooked, had no one else, and before you knew it she was "camping out" in the Command. Bosses visiting the precinct would go behind the desk to make an entry in the command log and would always say, "Hello Millie." She was acquainted with all of them. The prostitutes knew her, and she knew them, and even though the candy machine was supposed to be for police personnel only, Millie would collect money from the girls and supply them with sweets if they had a hankering. She called everyone "Cotton Picker." She was from Baton Rouge, Louisiana.

She had a couple of favorites in the command, and Tommy was one of them, though it didn't start out that way. One day, an intoxicated livery driver "took out" three cars on the station house block, and Tommy wound up making the arrest. He took all the Miller empties from the floor of the car and laid them on the table in the muster room for vouchering. The only problem was that Millie grabbed them when Tommy was in the basement and brought them up the block for the deposit.

But she was funny and sweet, whether cooking food on her hot plate, or checking on the male prisoners on the second floor by the lounge. A couple of times a month, she would head up to Port Authority and take the bus to Atlantic City. If Tommy was working, he'd give her a ride in the radio car, and she would always call the telephone switchboard when she returned looking for a ride back. She'd say to the cop manning the phone, "If that cotton picker, Bell, is working, tell him I need a lift. I'm at the Terminal."

Tommy was enjoying work, liked the guys, and was having laughs, but, as with so many cops, there came a time when he realized that a change was in order, so he submitted a request to be transferred to the Organized Crime Control Bureau. The CO was a little short on manpower and was reluctant to sign off on the paperwork at the time.

The collar that got Tommy Bell's Captain to sign his "fifty-seven," the transfer paperwork to go to narcotics, went down like so.

Tommy and Mike Hyland were working "Boy/David." The 10th Precinct was overflowing with prostitution, so much so that the command turned out a "pros" car on both the midnight and four-by-twelve tours. They were easy collars, though you had to take four. The girls got in the car unless they had a property slip issued by Central Booking that verified they had been arrested recently. If so, that was kind of a "get out of jail free card," and another gal would take her place. Get back to the arrest room, fill out an online booking sheet that detailed the circumstances of the arrest with a complaint number of 999999 and the ladies would print themselves. Then they would put together a food order, call the deli and, on the way down, the radio car would stop and pick up the chow. The girls would sit in the back seat, front-cuffed, gorging themselves on Snickers bars, sandwiches, Fritos, Milky Ways, Mountain Dew, and the like. They were also known to have an occasional beer.

Tommy and Mike were doing a four-by and had asked the boys from "Eddie/Frank" if it was okay if they went into their sector and hit Pete's Deli on W29th Street and Tenth Avenue. That's the way it used to be. You ate in your sector, or you got permission. They were dying for one of Pete's famous burgers, all grease and onions and government cheese. Nothing quite like it. "Sure thing," the boys had said. "Help yourself."

So they got their burgers and were heading back to "Boy/David," with Hyland driving and Tommy as the recorder, when Hyland spotted the bartender, Javelin Jack, from McManus's Bar on W19th street and Seventh Avenue. Jack had gone to Brooklyn Tech years ago and had been struck in the head with a javelin at the indoor games at the Washington Heights Armory. The nickname stuck. Anyway, Jack was drinking a "skirtless" quart bottle of Bud and heading to the tavern when the boys rolled up.

"Jack, you want a ride, pal?"

"Sure thing, Tommy."

The radio car made the left on W29th Street off Tenth Avenue, and headed west toward Eleventh. Tommy recognized prostitutes "Ralph" and "Ruth" on the corner, looking southbound. Ralph was almost "complete," had had breast augmentation, was taking hormones, and was saving up for the trip to Denmark. Ruth was his best friend—all ass, tits, and legs—who thought every cop in the command looked like someone famous.

She called Lt. Fine, "Mick Jagger-looking motherfucker"; called Larry Havenick, "Skelator-looking motherfucker"; called Jack Marsh, "Barney Rubble-looking motherfucker."

The radio car rolled up to the light and Ruth looked at Tommy and screamed, "Hey, Curtis Granderson-looking motherfuckah, that black limo just snatched my wife-in-law, Hazel!"

"I don't think you look like Curtis," said Hyland.

"Forget it Mike. Look."

Sure enough, at that very moment, the back door, passenger side, of the limo heading south, opened and a female tried to exit the moving vehicle—*until* a huge hand came flying out of the door, yanked her back in, and closed it.

Tommy got on the loudspeaker and told the limo to pull over.

Hyland hit the turret lights and gave a "whoop whoop" on the siren.

Javelin Jack took a sip of cold beer and got comfortable.

The vehicle sped up and made the quick left on W28th Street, went half a block and was now stuck in traffic. Tommy hadn't even had time to put anything over the radio. He told Javelin Jack to sit tight and stay low, they were going to roll up and take the limo before the light changed. But just as they were opening the radio car doors, the limo mounted the sidewalk on the south side and headed to Tenth.

"Ten Boy to Central," said Tommy.

"Go Boy."

"Got a pick-up of a possible kidnapping. In pursuit of a black stretch limo traveling eastbound on W28th Street toward Tenth Avenue. He's up on the sidewalk Central and just took out a mailbox."

"Got a plate number, Boy?"

"Standby . . ."

Hyland driving the car. Tommy up front with the radio. Javelin Jack in the back seat leaning forward, between the two, drinking his beer.

"Central NY plate William Oscar," and then Tommy stopping the transmission.

"Shit, I need glasses. I can't read the fucking plate."

"I got glasses and *I* can't read that fucking plate," said Hyland.

And then, Javelin Jack in the back screaming, "*I* can read that fucking plate. Double-you, oh, three, four, three, one."

"Central, be advised NY plate William, Oscar, three, four, three, one, north bound on Tenth Avenue and now heading west on Thirty Third Street."

"Ten four."

"Jack, we owe you big time," said Tommy.

"Make sure it is reflected in your nightly gratuities. Any chance we can stop? I'm just about out of beer."

The limo blew past the stop sign on W33rd Street, and then it headed south again on Eleventh Avenue, Tommy keeping Central apprised. They could hear sirens off in the distance; the cavalry was coming, and there was chatter on the radio from different units. At 29th Street, the limo made a right, hit Twelfth Avenue, and headed north.

"Central, Northbound on Twelfth," said Tommy.

And as luck would have it, just past West 34th Street, behind the Jacob Javits Convention Center, the limo found itself in the middle lane, cars on each side and stopped dead in traffic. With the radio car some ten feet behind the vehicle, Hyland came to an abrupt stop and said, "Scram, Jack, we will see you later." They ran up on either side of the limo, with Tommy screaming, "Shut the car off and open the fucking doors," before putting his Glock 9 through the passenger side window. By then, additional units were on the scene.

Turned out it was a kidnapping all right, some wanna-be, organized crime guys from Easton Pennsylvania thought Hazel had stolen some jewelry during a previous encounter. They collared the two, plus the limo driver, and recovered a P226 Sig Sauer, a .45, and an M84 stun grenade.

They took Javelin Jack out for a steak at the Old Homestead on Tenth Avenue, even though the place was on the "corruption prone" list due to its practice of offering free and discounted meals.

Months later, and after five days of narcotics training on a barge within the confines of the Fifth Precinct, Tommy Bell found himself standing in the hallway of the Armory with three other new guys for four days. On the final day, a big white guy, well over six feet tall, and two hundred and forty pounds, easy, with brown hair and unshaven, came down the hallway, laughing, joking, play sparring with guys and greeting the ladies. He walked up to Tommy.

"You Bell?" he asked.

"Yes, Sir."

"No *Sir*. I'm not the boss. I'm Jimmy McTigue. You like buffalo wings and cold beer."

"Well . . . yeah."

"Okay, you throw your junk in my locker. We're heading down to Brother Jimmy's. Welcome to Narcotics."

Jake McNicholas

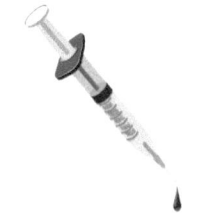

# Chapter 3

Charlie Defranco got to Narcotics after spending eight years in the One-Oh-Five (105th Precinct) in Queens. For close to six years he was on patrol, a slave to the radio in the largest precinct geographically in the five boroughs. For the last year and a half before he had made the move, he had been a member of the SNEU Team (Street Narcotics Enforcement Unit).

And it had been good. The sergeant was great, the rest of the guys wonderful, and they were doing good work and making money. Then one day, it all changed. The boss got promoted and wound up heading downtown to the "Puzzle Palace" at One Police Plaza; one guy left for the Emergency Service Unit; a guy to Harbor; and the horse lover on the team went to Mounted. The new boss was in over his head, and Charlie felt a little lost.

It all kind of came to head one day. Charlie had been down at court in Jamaica testifying at the Grand Jury regarding an observation sale case. He never made it back to the command, and the team had hit the streets to do enforcement. The SNEU unit had always been rather meticulous, so much so that even guys that were receiving summonses were brought back to the station house and run for warrants, and were photographed. Charlie kept a binder with the pictures and locations. You never knew when that kind of information would come in handy.

So the next day, Charlie was in the office with the rest of the team, and asked about the previous night's activity. Mike Bruno, a loudmouth new guy, and cock sure of himself, told Charlie what had occurred and handed him four photos for the binder—four photos of guys they had summonsed but cut loose. Charlie took a look and then:

"You take these pictures Bruno?"

"That's right. What about it?"

"You take a good look at them?"

"Yeah, I took a good look at them."

Charlie had one particular Polaroid that he was looking at. It was taken in the muster room, and was of a male black in his twenties with glasses and cornrows. It was taken from the waist up. Above the individual's right shoulder was a wanted photo.

"Take another look at this one, Einstein, and tell me if you notice anything," said Charlie.

Bruno did one of those tongue snaps off the roof of his mouth and had the "Why am I entertaining this guy?" look on his face when he took the picture in his hand and leaned back in his chair. And then he noticed it. The wanted poster was a male, Black, with glasses and cornrows. It was plain as day. The perp was standing next to his own wanted poster!

Charlie figured it was time to move on.

He lived off of Exit 28S on the Southern State Parkway in Wantagh, so he had been hoping to go to Queens Narcotics, which was "turning out" of the grounds of Creedmoor, the psychiatric center over on Union Turnpike and Winchester Boulevard.

He was married to his high school sweetheart and had two twin boys, age 10, and a daughter, 12, going on 19. The whole family liked critters, so the house included two cats, one a

Chausie; a terrier; three parakeets; a forty-gallon aquarium; three hamsters; and a Mini Rex rabbit.

At the work area in Manhattan North, Charlie had shoved two, beat up, old desks together, one with no drawers at all, and on the top, up against the wall, placed two, twenty gallon aquariums, three feet wide and one foot high. In one tank was a Maine Lobster. In the other was an African bullfrog named Rudy.

Rudy lived by himself, where he spent most of his time burrowed under the deep coco husk Charlie had laid on the bottom of the tank. Most days, he was fed earthworms, cockroaches, crickets, or wax worms. But just about every two weeks, on payday, Charlie would treat Rudy to a live mouse. On those days, it was pretty much standing room only in the cubicle for the show. Sometimes there was gambling involved and, on more than one occasion, a video camera from the equipment room was used to film the action.

Jimmy McTigue knew a nun who taught second grade over at St. Rose of Lima on west 164th Street, so, one day, for a treat, he picked up the class and brought them back to the Armory for a field trip. He made sure to tell everyone in the office to watch the language. The kids were amazed. The trip got cut short, though, when the chuck wagon bell sounded.

A few months before, the boys had returned from a "B & B" (Buy and Bust) and found the Maine lobster missing. There was a note Scotch taped to the tank that read: "WE GOT YOUR LOBSTER AND WE ARE HOLDING HIM HOSTAGE. INSTRUCTIONS TO FOLLOW." Charlie figured it was somebody in the Two-Eight (28th Precinct) team, stuffed in the corner of one of the other rooms down the hallway. He knew they had an aquarium. But the lobster wasn't there

A day later, a note on the aquarium read: "LEAVE ONE MEATBALL HERO FROM PARESI'S DELI IN THE REFRIGERATOR BY THE FOD" (Field Operations Desk). Charlie met the demand, and a day later the lobster was back.

"Shit like this," Charlie Defranco would say, "you can't make it up. Man, am I glad things worked out the way they did. Sure, paying the toll sucks, but I love being up here with you guys."

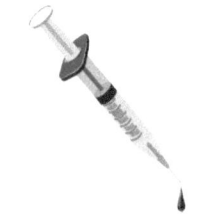

# Chapter 4

One of the legendary undercovers in NYPD narcotics history was Bobby Washington. He could purchase anything off anyone at any time and he had been doing so for over ten years; didn't matter whether it was buy and bust or a long-term, buy operation.

But he was, in every sense of the word, a complete and utter disaster. He was split from his wife and the mother of two of his kids; he had a project girlfriend from the Woodrow Wilson Houses; and he was banging a young, uniformed cop in the Two-Three (23rd Precinct). When he wasn't buying drugs, he spent his time in the office reading the letters in *Penthouse* magazine and Iceberg Slim novels.

He gave strict instructions to everyone in the cubicle and surrounding area that under no circumstances, whether he was there or not, was anyone to pick up the phone and acknowledge that he was present. He was *always* in the field, no matter who was calling. Santos Cruz took a call one day from an unidentified female. Told her Bobby was out in the field.

"I don't know where that motherfuckin' field is, and I don't know what that motherfuckah is doing in the field, but you tell that nigga, field time be over, or I'll be burying *him* in the field."

"Bobby, I think your girlfriend called," said Santos later.

"Girlfriend, shit, that was my mother."

Bobby was looking to "ride the wave" in narcotics, stay as long as he could, because he had absolutely no appetite for real police work and he needed the OT big time. His check was being garnished for child support. Got so bad that he was a beer vendor up at Yankee Stadium on his off days to help make ends meet, and he was doing odd jobs in Glackens Bar & Grill—the cop, letter carrier, bus driver, domino player joint—on 149th Street and Walton Avenue in the Bronx.

But everyone, to a man, loved him because he made you money, he was absolutely fearless, and because of an incident that had occurred a while back.

Some years ago, when prisoners were still allowed to smoke cigarettes down at Central Booking, the team was asked to head over to the vicinity of Yeshiva University.

"We just got this from Lieutenant Bilge, guys," said Sgt. Quinn. "Seems there is a rash of weed transactions over by Yeshiva. We're going to head over there, make some observations, maybe grab a few bodies."

Jimmy McTigue asked out of nowhere, "What did they call Jerry Tarkanian's team out in Nevada?"

"The Running Rebels," said Richie Whalen.

"Okay, then what do they call the team at Yeshiva?"

"Got me," said Charlie Defranco.

"The Running Rabbis."

And then Tommy Bell in that singsong voice like the whore in *Full Metal Jacket*, "Jimmy, you so corny."

Sgt. Quinn couldn't help but laugh. "I swear, sometimes it's like working with Abbott and Costello. For you younger guys, they were a comedy team. Bobby, take Sgt. Lewis's tinted-out, UC vehicle and park up there in the V/O." Tommy and

Jimmy, grab the prisoner van, and me and Charlie in Five Eighty Two. Are you still going to court, Richie?"

"Yeah, from the Audubon search warrant."

"Ten-Four."

Bobby wasn't out there ten minutes when he spots a male doing a hand-to-hand.

"You guys on?"

"Go Bobby," said Quinn.

"Got us a male Hispanic, approximately twenty-five years old, blue jeans, Hawaiian shirt, just hit off . . . shit . . . looks like a male Indian in Bermuda shorts."

Jimmy looking to have some fun, "What tribe?"

"What you talking about?" asked Bobby.

"The tribe, the tribe. Was he Apache, Comanche?"

"Could be Hikawi," said Tommy.

"Tommy, you got to stop watching WE television and that old stuff—*F Troop*?"

"You boys crazy," said Bobby. "Not *that* kind of Indian— Seven Eleven Indian."

Jimmy and Tommy wound up grabbing the kid a couple of blocks off the set. Nearly shit his pants and started crying, saying his old man would kill him. He had Hawaiian Shirt's cell number, so they chucked his weed down the sewer and told him to take a hike and don't come back. Last they saw of him, he was sprinting down Broadway toward the bus depot.

"Hawaii is definitely *doing* Bobby," said Tommy.

The prisoner van was back in position in two minutes when Bobby comes up on the air again. "Got a white boy in his thirties, tweed jacket, dungarees, brown hair and glasses. Just got done and is headed westbound on One-Eight-One, smoking a cigarette. Shit's in his jacket pocket."

In the annals of the history of Sgt. Quinn's team and their arrests, this very well could have been the most obnoxious individual to ever have had the cuffs slapped on him. Jimmy and Tommy grab the guy, and the first thing out of his mouth was, "You have no right to stop me, you ignorant stewards of oppression."

Tommy and Jimmy looked at each other.

"Unhand me and allow me to go about my business. I have done nothing wrong. I am just another victim of a lawless police state. Unhand me, I say."

It was Jimmy, almost laughing, who asked, "What's up with that zip lock bag of weed hanging out of your tweed jacket pocket, Sherlock?"

"That constitutes an illegal search conducted by fascist members of the NYPD."

Tommy said to Jimmy, "Who's he calling fat?"

"Must be me," said Jimmy. "I *have* been putting on the pounds lately."

This went on for the better part of an hour, Yeshiva professor Neil Simon breaking balls from the back of the P van, while the boys conducted further observations. They got no other bodies and lost Hawaiian Shirt when he jumped in a livery and headed to the Bronx. But they had his cell phone number.

Bobby parked his car by the Two-Five (25th Precinct) and identified Neil Simon when he exited the P van. Tommy brought him in. Jimmy approached the undercover.

"We gave the Indian a pass, Bobby. This other guy, the professor, a real ball breaker. Had about ten, nickel bags on him in a zip lock. Hasn't shut up since we collared him. A real Occupy Wall Streeter."

"That his envelope there?" asked Bobby, pointing to the yellow manila under Jimmy's arm with the prisoner's property. "I saw him puffing. He got smokes in there?"

"Yeah, he does."

"Give them to me."

Jimmy handed over the smokes and watched as Bobby went into his shirt pocket and pulled out one of those slim boxes that rich people use to hold cigarettes. He reached in, grabbed one, and placed the smoke in the pack of Kools that belonged to Neil Simon.

"Whatever you do Jimmy, don't let that asshole light up here. It's a dummy smoke, going to explode. Fuck this guy!"

Jimmy McTigue and Tommy Bell drove Neil Simon down to be "lodged," after he was processed, the professor from Yeshiva yapping away through the entire trip. Some time later, he got a call from an old friend in Central Booking.

"Some shit, Jimmy."

"What do you mean?'

"The white guy in the sports jacket. Making all kinds of trouble in the holding cell with his big mouth. Anyway, he decides to sell one of his smokes to this head-shaved, neo Nazi, biker dude. Guy lights up and the thing exploded in his face. We just transported Neil Simon to Downtown Beekman."

"Beautiful, just beautiful," Jimmy said, and pretty much, from then on, Bobby Washington could do no wrong.

# Jake McNicholas

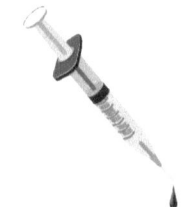

# Chapter 5

Up until some years ago, there were police precincts in this city that still existed in a virtual time warp.

The One-Ten (110th Precinct) was one of those commands.

Maybe it had to do with its location in Elmhurst Queens on 43rd Avenue, off Junction Blvd. Maybe it had to do with Stanley's Deli, or the Donegal Tavern up the block. But there was no mistaking the fact that things were a bit different there.

Where else would the midnight tour finish up work on a Saturday morning, get their bacon, egg, and cheese sandwiches at Stan's, and then walk a couple of doors over to the Donegal. Soft toss some pebbles at the second-story window of the bartender, Desie, have him open the window and throw down the keys to the bar, and have the lads go in and help themselves, while he ate breakfast and took a shower.

Or how about the bar itself, hopping and crowded on a Friday night, the juke box blasting, and guys throwing darts at the far end by the pool table and kitchen. Detective Mike Clifford, from the squad, walks in with a prisoner, front-cuffed, and gets a couple of stools in the corner, with their backs to the window facing the street, and then patrons asking Hughie, behind the stick, to get Mike a drink and the prisoner, too, because apparently he's going away for a long time. Pretty soon, the prisoner is drinking his Bud from a frosted glass and has six coasters lined up in front of him.

Where else might there be a retirement party upstairs in the Squad, and guys heading up there past the desk, cops and civilians alike, with cases of beer and bottles of booze and food? The coolers were laid out in the holding cell, and the prisoner inside, waiting to go down to get lodged, was having a drink and eating a sandwich just like everybody else.

That is the place Richie Whalen came from before he arrived at Manhattan North Narcotics, and it suited him. *He* was a bit of a legend. It certainly had something to do with the shootout he had gotten into one November night.

He had been walking a foot post up by Lamont Avenue and Case Street when he got into it with a burglar exiting a private house. He was on the other side of a Voyager, parked in a driveway, when a three-time loser started letting rounds go, firing under the vehicle and trying to ricochet them into Richie, who was trying to: find cover; return fire; and combat unload and load his Smith and Wesson .38—all at the same time. Finally, there was a lull in the action, which gave Richie a chance to sneak around by the street side, come up behind the guy, take him down, and cuff him.

But it was more than that. It was just the way he operated.

No one called him Richie; it was always Whalen, whether it was cops at the Command, patrons at the Donegal, local storeowners, or people in the neighborhood—and, oh the stuff Whalen got himself into.

One time, a sector car wound up stopping a Chevy pickup with a trailer and a 1991 Chris Craft Crowne on it. Nice little boat.

The driver took a collar, so the vehicle and boat had to be vouchered for safekeeping, and parked down the block from the precinct. Whalen figured that would be the closest many of them would ever get to a pleasure craft, so he stocked the boat with food and coolers, and the boys, off-duty and in shorts and T-shirts, spent a few hours onboard the vessel, which was still up on the trailer, on 44th Avenue, overlooking the Long Island Railroad.

Or one of the great parties of all time, the "Richie Whalen is Leaving CPOP Going Back to Patrol Party" (Community Police Officers Program) in the backyard of the Donegal, a dozen of the boys in full uniform, except Mike Coulter on the grill, with his apron on over his gun belt.

On this one occasion, they had a single police van at the One-Ten in service, and the ICO (Integrity Control Officer) needed it to transport some radios and equipment to the radio repair shop over by the LIE. He assumes it's parked in the garage, and comes out there to get it—only it's nowhere in sight. Turns out, Whalen packed it up with nine, senior citizens and drove them down to Rockaway and 108th Street. Brought blankets and chairs for the old-timers to relax on. Last anyone had seen of him, he had his gun belt and shirt off, and was laid out on the beach working on his "savage tan."

Then there were the shopkeepers in the neighborhood: the pharmacies, tailors and the like, the establishments lining Broadway and Roosevelt Avenue with the signs in the windows, and the people, too, with the bumper stickers on the car: "I (with a heart) Whalen."

One day, Whalen and his partner kidnapped Desie and had him committed to the psychiatric ward of Elmhurst General for the day. Later, when the Irish bartender began his torturous journey to citizenship, it was Whalen who provided the necessary, fabricated paperwork.

But there came a time when Whalen's wife, Rose, told him she was expecting again (that would make five) and their three-bedroom apartment in Woodhaven would no longer be an option. Rose's sister had spotted a nice house on Turner Road in Pearl River, only blocks from where she lived.

Word traveled fast in Elmhurst, and there was much sadness in the neighborhood. Whalen was heading north, and he couldn't deal with the commute and paying the toll, so he weighed his options and came to the decision. "It's time for me to get out of the bag and get a little serious."

Next stop: Manhattan North Narcotics.

The ICO was happy. The time warp was over.

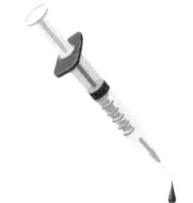

# Chapter 6

Santos Cruz was born in the small fishing village of La Parguera in the town of Lajas on the Southwest coast of Puerto Rico. His dad was a fisherman, and it was easy pickings. The waters of the Caribbean were teeming with blue marlin, barrel snapper, groupers, mackerel, tuna, and many other fish. His family, his parents and three sisters, lived comfortably, but it was his mother who dreamed of a different life for her children. So, years ago, they made the move, came to New York, and settled in the Morris Park section of the Bronx in an apartment on Bogart Avenue.

Santos fell in love with the city. He excelled in his studies and, when it came time to go to high school, joined a few of the neighborhood kids and attended Mount Saint Michael's, an all boys academy on Murdock Avenue in Eastchester. He became very involved, but was most proud of his football career there, and returned every year to watch the Mount play Cardinal Hayes in the Turkey Bowl.

He headed off to Fordham University, but there was always something else that called him. In the days of his youth, there had been a particular neighborhood cop, who used to chase the bullies who would beat up his friends and him. And one day, he had to admit to himself that he wanted "to be just like him."

He wound up heading to the Four-Oh (40th Precinct) on Alexander Avenue and, after a couple of years, he was riding in a steady sector with his partner, Dave Jarrell. And they were taking care of business, these two, hard-working, conscientious cops, who were making a difference. They treated people right, which often times was half the battle.

One day, they were on patrol, when the dispatcher asked them to respond to a "difficulty breathing," an infant at the Brook Houses off East 135th Street. Santos was driving, Dave the recorder, and when they got to the scene they could both see that the baby was turning blue. They threw the mother in the back seat, and headed over to Lincoln Medical, Dave cleaning the airway and giving whispers of breath to the little girl. The mother was in the back wailing, and Santos was driving, the sweat pouring off him. They had advised the 911 dispatcher that they were on their way, so when they pulled up to the emergency room there was a team waiting for them, and they whisked the mother and infant inside. Santos moved the radio car. Ten minutes later, they were told that the girl had died.

Dave Jarrell took it especially hard. He had flown an AH-64D Longbow, Apache helicopter with the US Army as part of Operation Anaconda in support of Operation Iraqi Freedom in Afghanistan in 2003. He always knew that sooner or later he would be putting in for the Aviation Unit, but the death of that little girl accelerated his decision.

"I'm making a move, Santos. It's time."

"I'll miss you, Dave, but go for it bro'."

So he put in his "57." Aviation knew where he was, and had been waiting for him, and so, a couple of months later, he found himself out at Floyd Bennett Field.

Santos figured to hang in a little longer. He still liked patrol. But one day, he was in the radio car waiting for a roll call change and his partner to show up, when a tiny, little girl lugging her equipment and carrying a telephone book, walked out of the front door.

"What's the telephone book for?" asked Santos.

"To sit on, just in case I have to drive," said the gal.

The very next day, Santos Cruz put in for OCCB (Organized Crime Control Bureau) and narcotics.

Second week up in Manhattan North, the team realized who they were getting. You see, Santos was one of the most meticulous cops these guys had ever come across. He had been called down to traffic court for an old moving summons from nine years ago. Pretty much *absolutely* no way one could testify with an independent memory of an event that long ago. But what the driver didn't know was that Santos would include certain facts in his memo book in connection with car stops, including weather *and* a physical description of the driver. And in his memo book for this occasion, Santos had noted that the driver, Roberto Sanchez, had an eyeball earring hanging from his right lobe.

And sure enough that is how Mr. Sanchez arrived at traffic court—wearing the fucking earring!

"Un-fuckin'-believable," said Bobby Washington.

"Santos, please, you are absolutely welcome to do my 'onlines' whenever I get on," said Jimmy McTigue.

"Shit, if you're doing the vetting, I'd rent my basement apartment to a Syrian soccer team, no problem," said Richie Whalen.

Jake McNicholas

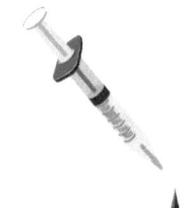

# Chapter 7

"Can you believe this nonsense?" said Bobby Washington. "Some security. Got a Chinese delivery guy up here in the office probably dropping menus under the doors. Some shit."

"That's not a Chinese delivery boy, Bobby," Sgt. Quinn said. "That's our new undercover."

His name was Wenjain Wong, and he had transferred in from the One-Oh-Nine (109th Precinct) in Flushing—or "Frushing," as some referred to the neighborhood, since it had such a large Asian population. His parents had emigrated from Fengau, China, the "Ghost City" on the banks of the Yangtze River, when he was four years old, and settled over in Bayside. Now, they ran a dry cleaning operation in the Bay Terrace shopping center in Whitestone. He went to St. Francis Prep off the LIE and Springfield Boulevard. The school had history. Vince Lombardi and Joe Torre went there when the school was in Brooklyn. Wenjain played running back on the football team. He was going to Queens College when 9/11 hit, quit school, headed to the recruiter, and joined the Marines.

Got out of boot camp and they gave him his MOS (military occupational specialty). They made him an office, clerk typist. He requested Mast to see the Colonel, and next thing he knew he was in 29 Palms at infantry training—MOS 0311. He was assigned to the First Battalion, Fifth Marines of the First Marine

Division. November 2004 he was on Operation Phantom Fury, the second battle for Fallujah.

Sgt. Quinn does a hand wave and he comes over to the cubicle and introduces himself.

"What's up guys, I'm Wenjain Wong."

Everybody makes their introduction and handshakes and Wenjain spots the Eagle Globe and Anchor on Jimmy McTigue's forearm and says, "Semper Fi."

"Ooh Rah. Who were you with?" asked Jimmy.

"One-Five."

"Where in Iraq?"

"Second battle of Fallujah."

Jimmy said, "God bless you. Love that tee shirt I seen. Makes me proud. "U.S. Marines. We Were At Iwo Jima. Fallujah Ain't Shit."

"Who were *you* with?"

"One Eight."

"After the Beirut bombing," Wenjain acknowledged.

"Yeah. But it still pisses me off when I think about it."

Everyone in the cubicle was watching Jimmy, and what they saw was such an overwhelming look of sadness that it scared them.

Tommy Bell had seen that look before and, trying to break the mood, said, "Not another Marine. I can barely handle this one."

Things went back to normal.

Then Bobby Washington, trying to pronounce Wenjain, said, "It ain't going to work—the name. From now on, you're Wally."

That was that.

"We're heading out the door to do a little B and B," said Sgt. Quinn. "It's up to you, you want to stay back and get settled, Richie can help you—he isn't going out—or, you want to come out with us, get your feet wet, your call."

"Let's get to it."

"You have any problems ghosting?"

"No, I think I can do it."

It was Sgt. Quinn, Jimmy, and Tommy, with Frank Martin and Santos in the P Van. Bobby Washington said, "Let's go, Wally, me and you," and they got their transmitting devices and headed to the tinted-out, undercover car.

The set was a crack spot, "purple tops," on E122nd Street between Second and Third Avenues in the Two-Five (25th Precinct). Bobby was going to do the buy and Wally was ghosting, hanging back, giving Bobby room to play, but eyeballing him at all times and giving the play-by-play, if at all possible. It would come up on the kell, the oversized, briefcase that picked up the transmissions from the undercovers. Let the field team know what was happening.

So the boys were set up, Jimmy driving, Sgt. Quinn up front, and Tommy in the backseat fooling with the kell.

"Seems like a lovely guy," said Jimmy.

"You are the only guy that can get away with that, Jimmy," said Tommy. "Lovely guy? Shit, doesn't matter. He was in the Marines. All you jarheads stick together. What do you think, boss?"

"I think he'll be fine," said Sgt. Quinn. "I talked to an old buddy of mine used to work in the One-Oh-Nine. He says deep down he thinks the guy is Irish. He wants to take care of business, drink beer, and have some laughs."

"Please, Sarge, don't tell me that," Tommy laughed. "I have enough on my hands with this potato eater," and he head nodded Jimmy.

They could hear Bobby and Wally moving around in the vehicle, over the kell, and they could hear Bobby say, "We're stepping out," and the car door open and close. A couple of minute later, they had an eyeball on the two—Bobby on the south side of 122nd Street, and Wally on the north, about fifty feet to the rear. They were crossing over Third Avenue onto the block and out of sight.

And then Bobby saying, "Yeah dog, give me two. Those purple tops do it for me. Hook me up brother."

Wally saying, "Male Black in an Oakland Raiders hat, dungarees and orange sneakers."

Sgt. Quinn saying, "Wally's doing good."

Bobby saying, "Thanks dog. You see me back here."

Wally saying, "He's stepping off."

Bobby did the "I just got done ditty bop" and headed across Third Avenue, all happy and shit, giving the description all the while. Wally laid back a bit on the corner of E122nd and Third. Then, two Black males approached, a Mutt and Jeff team, and the boys could hear this on the kell. They still had an eyeball on the corner.

"Hey gook motherfuckah," from Mutt.

"Ching Chong man, what's you got on you?" from Jeff.

The hairs on the back of the necks of Sgt. Quinn, Jimmy McTigue, and Tommy Bell were raised now—raised big time. There was absolute silence in the car, except for the measured breathing of the three. And then . . .

"Give it up, motherfuckah, or I'm slicing you," from one of them.

Jimmy was just about to floor it, when, over the kell, he heard new guy, Wally, say, "Is that right, shit head."

His first right hit Mutt full flush in the jaw and knocked him over a parked Volvo. His second right hit Jeff full flush above the left eye and knocked him into a mailbox.

There was complete silence in the car, and then Jimmy McTigue looked at Sgt. Quinn and Tommy Bell, and said matter-of-factly, "I think the new guy is going to work out."

\* \* \* \* \*

They didn't bother with the collar that day. Leave him out there for the next time. The boys headed back to the office and told the story, and Wally admitted that he had done a little boxing in the Marine Corps. Bobby Washington took it all in and then said rather sheepishly, "Hey Wally, you *are* okay with me calling you Wally, ain't you?" That got a laugh out of everyone, and then, they headed downtown to The Parlour on West 86th Street. Happy Hour—two for one.

Jake McNicholas

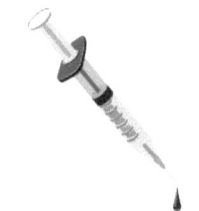

# Chapter 8

**Even before 9/11,** Aiman Qantan's grocery store down the block from Manhattan North Narcotics was called "The Terrorist."

Things were changing in New York. Where once all the corner grocery stores that were located in the inner city neighborhoods were run by Puerto Ricans, now they were likely owned and operated by Middle Easterners, all or most all of them Yemeni.

Aiman had emigrated from the quiet, little Red Sea town of Hababa in 1994, worked at a relative's location in the confines of the 73rd Precinct for close to six years, and then opened up his own place on West 139th Street and Fifth Avenue. He put in sixteen-hour days in a store that was open 24/7. Took himself a Puerto Rican wife, and had three kids. He attended the mosque on 96th Street and Third Avenue, but wasn't "crazy" Muslim. He sold beer and loose cigarettes. In fact, he had been selling untaxed smokes and expired baby formula, but someone up at the Armory had laid down the law, and told him to cease and desist if he wanted to stay in business. It was time to shut down that aspect of the free enterprise system. He heeded the advice.

The store was small, but he had a Mexican on the grill, so he was serving up enough sandwiches to pay the rent. Fridays after paydays were especially profitable, because the boys went out after work, south of 96th Street, and drank copious amounts of alcohol. Nothing like a bacon, egg, and cheese sandwich off the greasy grill of "The Terrorist" to fix you up the next day.

On the Plexiglas, off to the left of the front counter, were three pictures, old time Polaroids, of Aiman back in the old country sporting traditional garb and an AK-47.

Aiman didn't particularly like cops, but he loved Jimmy McTigue.

It was late one night a couple of years ago, and Jimmy had walked down from the Armory to get a breath of fresh air and a "cold one" while the team finished up paperwork in connection to six arrests they had made up in the Three-Four. Aiman was doing the overnighter, knew Jimmy when he walked in, knew he was heading to the corner in the back of the store to have two Bud tall boys. Jimmy always paid and he always made a point to ask Aiman how he and his family were, in a nice, quiet, sincere way.

Aiman was busy conducting business with a female buying smokes, and Jimmy was in the back enjoying the Bud. The lady left, and in walked two gangbangers in uniform: baseball hats on sideways, gold chains around the necks, long T-shirts outside of the low hanging dungarees—*and*, as always, those stupid looks on their faces. They were acting like fools in front of the counter where Aiman was, and Jimmy was in the back looking at the two homeboys in the mirror in the corner behind the cash register.

Jimmy was raised up, and his neck hair went haywire as he waited with his Smith & Wesson .38 five-shot in his right hand.

"Yo, motherfuckah, how 'bout a couple of those Phillies you got back there?"

44

He was probably around thirty, wearing an LA Dodgers baseball cap, thin—*real* thin—but with definition to his arms, which was probably the result of a previous incarceration. He kept looking around and kind of did a dance in front of the register, his larger friend, with the KC Royals lid off to the side, watching the street through the front door, watching his buddy in front of the register, watching Aiman turning around to get the Dutch Masters for the blunt. By then, as Aiman turned around, "LA Dodger" had pulled out his "jammy," a Glock 9, from his waistband, and had it pointed sideways at Aiman and was screaming in his best idiotic, gangbanger voice, "Give me the motherfuckin' money and a carton of Kools."

Jimmy was in the back, taking it all in. Aiman was playing the game and waiting for the show to start, this not being the first time he had been robbed. He reached for the smokes and was now at the register, opened it, and handed over about eighty dollars in cash.

LA Dodger said, "And that secret stash you gots in the cigar box underneath, motherfuckah."

Aiman reached way down below the register, and Jimmy watched in the mirror, and then came down the far aisle, tiptoeing. He paused and grabbed a box of *Cap'n Crunch* and launched it into the area just short of where LA Dodger and Aiman were dancing, and came out of the far aisle with his .38 in his outstretched hand about two feet from the head of LA Dodger, and said, real cool-like for full effect, "Hey, homey, drop the piece, or the game's over and your friend there is attending your funeral."

# Jake McNicholas

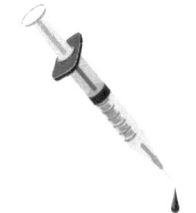

# Chapter 9

One might think that a guy who lived through the horrors of Vietnam would learn to appreciate and savor those little joys that made life worth living.

Not so with the head of Manhattan North Narcotics, Inspector Norman Lucas.

He had always been good with his hands, a born carpenter, so in February of 1967 he joined the Navy Seabees to get away from home and to serve his country. That October, he landed in Da Nang, which wasn't a bad place to be if you were "in country." Later in the year, though, he and three of his buddies got word that they would be heading up to I Corps, which was no fucking joke, because the Marines were up in I Corps. Next thing he knew, he was up at Phu Bai and then on a CH-46 heading to the Marine Combat Base at Khe Sanh. He celebrated Christmas there.

There was an airstrip and six thousand Marines, and come mid-January the place was surrounded by some twenty thousand NVA regulars, and the siege was on. Seventy-seven days of some of the most brutal, hair-raising conditions of the war. Lucas got lucky and was sleeping in the fortified bunker the Seabees had built called the "Alamo Hilton." That was okay for nighttime, but by day he was out on the airstrip with the rest of the construction battalion trying to repair the aluminum runway that was being torn apart by "incoming."

But he survived, came home, and joined the NYPD. Used the GI Bill to get a bachelor's degree in Public Administration from Manhattan College, up in the Bronx. Now he was an inspector and had recently been transferred out of the Warrants Division, where he kept a lid on overtime. He had absolutely *no* experience in narcotics and wasn't real keen on asking for advice.

When word came down that Lucas was coming to Manhattan North, Jimmy made a phone call.

"If you don't mind working for a complete and utter scumbag, who thinks he knows everything, you won't have a problem," one of the guys said.

"No shit," the guy said. "I wouldn't have believed it if I hadn't seen it with my own eyes. Lucas lives upstate, I think maybe Garnerville. Anyway, he ends his tour and heads home. The Yankees are in the playoffs a couple of years ago, that series against the Orioles, and there was a big detail from Warrants had a bunch of us back in uniform. Lucas decides to stop at the detail before heading home, and has inspections take a serious look as to whether we're carrying our whistles and reflective belts. The guy's a bigger asshole than Alec Baldwin and Howard Dean combined."

But the guys figured how bad could it be? Manhattan North was separated into two buildings: the Armory; and the Northern Manhattan Initiative, which was located on the eastside, way south on 106th Street and Park Avenue. The inspector's office and his administrative staff were located there.

It was a payday Thursday, when the Armory denizens first realized what dire circumstances they now faced. It was a down day in the office for just about everyone, only a couple of teams heading out the door for enforcement, and the guys who still didn't have direct deposit were sitting around waiting to get their pay. McTigue, Bell, Defranco, Whalen, Santos, and Sgt. Quinn were going to cash their checks and then head down to the Kinsale Tavern on 94th Street and Third, and have a burger and a couple of beers. They sat in their area watching an old episode of *The Sopranos*. Charlie had just fed Rudy, the bullfrog, a live mouse, and the crowd had moseyed back to their cubicles. Guys were typing, and reading newspapers.

And then, before anyone knew what hit them, Inspector Norman Lucas walked in unannounced.

Jimmy saw him first, all six-feet, three-inches tall, and a hundred-and-ninety pounds, with a full head of dark hair and a handsome, familiar face. Where had he seen that face? He walked right over to the television and shut it off, had everyone's attention and then, at the top of his lungs, screamed, "I am Inspector Lucas. From this day forward, do not *ever* let me see this TV on *unless* it is for training purposes. I don't ever again want to see newspapers on a desk, nor do I expect to see members of this office sitting around and bullshitting. Supervisors report to the conference room. Oh yeah, I had better start seeing an increase in search warrants." And then he stormed out.

"Is that guy for real?" asked Tommy.

"I'm just glad he didn't come in when I was feeding Rudy. I'd be walking a foot post in Staten Island—shudder the thought," added Charlie.

"He looks like somebody, though, and I can't quite place him," said Jimmy. "I think a movie star or something. But I can't put my finger on it."

"Yeah, you're right," said Tommy. "I can see the guy too. Man, going to bother me. Call you tonight at around three AM when I think of it. Shit, wait, I know. That moron from *Dumb and Dumber*, the guy that broke balls on an old and feeble Charlton Heston."

"That's it, that's it," said Jimmy. "It still amazes me, the stuff rolling around in that huge head of yours, Tommy. Can't remember how to voucher property but you come up with Jim Carrey."

"But he ain't no comedian, that dude's *vicious*," said Charlie.

Santos laughing, "Okay, from now on he's 'The Vicious Jim Carrey.' "

\* \* \* \* \*

Next day, Captain Sink ordered up a Lodge A5-5, Original Finish, Chuck Wagon Dinner Bell—with striker—from Amazon, and had it mounted by the FOD.

"I got a confidential informant in the other building. Lucas comes over here, we get a phone call, we ring the bell. Then we run for our lives."

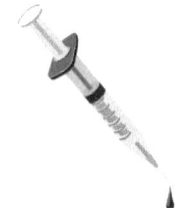

# Chapter 10

**Most guys go** their entire careers without ever firing their weapon except at the Outdoor Range in the Bronx. Frank Martin wasn't *most* guys. It must have been in the DNA. Back in 1968, with gunpoint robberies of liquor stores, delis, and mom and pop groceries, skyrocketing out of control, the NYPD created a forty-man unit of hard men with sharpshooting ability, whose mission was to put a dent in the mayhem and pistol-whipping that had become so widespread. They called the team the Stake Out Unit.

What they did was this: choose a location that was particularly susceptible to a robbery, place a two-man team in the back of the store, and wait for the fireworks to start. Most times, the cops would be armed with their .38 Smith & Wesson service revolvers, or five-shot, "off-duties," and an Ithaca 37, 12-gauge, short barrel shotgun. Some guys also carried a Colt 1911, .45, with hollow points.

Frank Martin's dad Luke was a member of the unit.

It was widely successful. They made hundreds of collars and, at the same time, put the fear of God in the heart of every stickup man in the city. Between 1968 and 1973, when the unit was disbanded due to political pressure, the men of the SOU shot forty-three, would-be, holdup men, killing twenty-four and wounding nineteen. Trouble was, all the perpetrators were Black and Hispanic. Said one member of the unit, "I ain't prejudiced. Send in a white guy and I'll light him up too. An asshole's an asshole."

Luke Martin had three kills.

Frank was like his dad in this way, too; he was a quiet sort. He lived in the Isaacs Projects on E93rd Street and First Avenue, where he grew up with his wife and daughter. Housing cops called the place the "Budweiser Projects," because it still had a sizeable Irish population. Frank attended mass at Saint Elizabeth of Hungary every chance he got, and he liked to have a beer at Ryan's Daughter on E85th Street, because it had a pool table in the back.

Trouble always followed Frank Martin. In that sense, he had already equaled his father.

Early one morning, after drawing up a collar, Frank left 100 Centre Street through the back entrance and walked across Baxter Street and then into Columbia Park to get to his car.

The park was empty at this time of night, none of the Tai Chi and Kung Fu guys, the Falun Gong women, or the old-timers playing chess, were around.

He was just coming across the concrete softball field when two Asians opened up on each other with automatic weapons. Frank would later learn that a new gang, "Born to Kill," made up of ethnic Chinese from Vietnam, were warring with long established elements of "The Flying Dragons" over territory and the heroin trade. Two in the morning, Frank in "short centerfield," right in the middle of the shootout, crouches, grabs his Glock in his right hand, brings his left arm across his chest and fires one round that hits "BTK guy" square in the forehead. Kill number one.

Frank lived near the top of the Isaacs, the twenty-fourth floor, and he was sleeping-in after a midnight, one morning. His wife and daughter were shopping in Yorkville, when he heard a commotion outside his place. He opened the door to see a lone housing cop heading to the far end of the hallway, and then he saw the cop drop down into a prone position and heard the unmistakable sounds of shots being fired.

The guy in the last apartment was firing from inside his door. Frank had always known he was trouble, and now the cop was hit in the shoulder, and Frank grabbed him by the ankle and dragged him into his apartment. He had his off-duty in the pocket of his shorts. He grabbed the department radio and shouted, "Ten-Thirteen, shots fired, officer down," and gave the location. Then he peeked out the door and saw the guy heading for the staircase or elevator, and he squeezed off a round and hit the guy right above the heart. Kill number two.

He was up on Amsterdam Avenue and 173rd Street, walking a foot post, across the street from the Highbridge Pool, one November evening. He was tucked into a doorway, trying to stay out of the cold wind that was blowing. Not much activity on the street, little pedestrian traffic, but a lone male Hispanic on the corner. Then out of nowhere, a late model Ford Explorer, heading southbound and stopping, and then gun shots from the driver struck the male and dropped him. Frank stepped out of the doorway, and, as the vehicle began to drive off, put one into the driver's temple, through the open window. One boss responding to the scene actually said it was a bad shoot, because the vehicle was moving, but everything worked out in the end. Kill number three.

"The Job" had been asking Frank from the beginning where he wanted to go, but he kept saying he enjoyed patrol and liked the guys he was working with. The higher-ups wanted to see him up at the Outdoor Range, but Frank didn't like the commute and there was no overtime. After the last shooting, he finally asked if he could go to Manhattan North Narcotics.

Word spreads quickly when you have killed three guys. Leave it to Bobby Washington to make the point.

"This narco team is really coming together. Now we got fuckin' Wyatt Earp working with us."

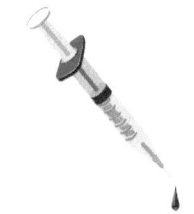

# Chapter 11

**Artie figured it would be a good idea** to get together with Fred Muench and Meg before filming started. Fred's New York office was in Midtown, and Meg was doing something in Soho, so he reckoned he'd invite them over for lunch. But at the last minute, Fred got called out of town, so he sent his assistant, Kurt Norris, in his place.

He called up one of those off-the-grid maid services that was happy to send over a piece of ass that had no problem going topless while she was cleaning. She was an Asian chick with a sizable rack who spoke little English, and she spent the better part of two hours doing away with the beer bottles, pizza boxes, overflowing ash trays, empty tuna cans, old newspapers, and the like. Artie left a couple of copies of *Hustler* around just to see if he'd get a reaction. Right before she left, she looked at Artie and pumped her fist.

The hand job cost him an extra two hundred dollars.

Artie got some overpriced deli on Sixth Avenue to cater the affair. An hour after the maid split, a young Mexican rang the bell, carrying a tray of wraps and some salads.

Sometime later, Meg and Norris were in the doorway. Norris was 40, completely bald and a bit overweight. Meg had met him on the set of *Denise LaPiece* and liked him.

Meg came in first and she looked absolutely stunning in her Vince Camuto ensemble: the off the shoulder, blue blouse; the skintight, white slacks; and the heels. She gave Artie a kiss, looked around the apartment and said, "Looks nice Artie. Who cleaned it for you? Yeah, and don't tell me *you* did. And will you *please* take off that hat."

"I've been slaving all morning," Artie said, as he adjusted his Yankees cap a little further askew.

Meg watched him and began to have some serious doubts.

Norris was inside by now, and said, "I got to agree with Meg, Artie. No way you could have accomplished this on your own. I've seen you in action. Nice place, though—and I dig the art."

Artie led them to the sunken living room and took the drink orders. Meg was going with a Diet Pepsi, and Norris had a white wine. Artie was drinking a Bud out of the bottle.

"Now remember Meg, you are going to have to put on some pounds," Artie said. "Easy on the diet soda!" He gave her a wink and handed her a new script with some revisions.

"Fred and I are really looking forward to this project, Meg," said Norris, munching on a ham and Swiss. "I mean it. We both think you are perfect for the role."

"Thanks, Kurt. And don't worry. I got a plan to put on some weight. And I think I'm going to enjoy the process," and she started laughing.

Artie said, "Feel free to start now if you like. Some of those wraps are pure fuckin' fat. I was thinking of you when I ordered."

"Thanks Artie," she said, shaking her head.

Norris laid out Muench's vision for the picture; told them who else was on board; detailed some of the locations and the shooting schedule; and answered questions. Meg was all ears and watched him intently. Artie was texting and slugging down Buds.

"Filming will start pretty soon, Meg," and he gave her a tap on the knee.

"I'll be ready," Meg laughed.

"I got a car downstairs. Do you need a ride anywhere?"

"No thanks, Kurt, I'm meeting some friends."

They were all out of the sunken living room and nearing the door when Artie's phone rang. He took the call and waved to both of them.

Meg was just about in the hallway when she heard Artie say, "Yeah Sweet Pea, that's some good shit. We'll talk about it later."

Jake McNicholas

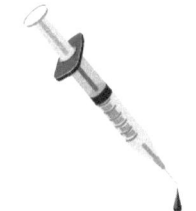

# Chapter 12

The latest "flavor of the month," when it came to ignorant, hypocritical, and corrupt black ministers in New York was Chester Skinner.

Skinner cheated on his former wife. Skinner cheated the United States Government on his taxes. Skinner spent most of his time, when he wasn't shaking down corporations, ginning up the assholes in the Black community, whose sole purpose in life was "What's in it for them, how can I get mine, and who cares if the brothers are slaughtering people of color in the community as long as the pigs aren't using excessive force when stopping and arresting the shitheads?" He was a frequent visitor to the White House, and he had his own television show on a cable network nobody watched called *Right Back at You*.

His church and congregation were located in Jamaica, Queens, but old Chester lived in a leafy suburb in New Jersey with his girlfriend and three young children who attended private school and were driven there by the nanny, an illegal immigrant who was being paid *below* minimum wage. You get the picture. Skinner came into New York, most days, in his late model BMW.

His best friend in the entire world seemed to be the mayor, Mike Caruso. Certainly it could have had something to do with the fact that Caruso had needed the Black vote and a large turnout to get elected. The mayor pretty much gave the good reverend the run of the city, including undue influence on police policy.

So the cops hated both of them, and Tommy Bell had a special brand of hatred for Skinner, because his own dad was a real-life preacher, a good and noble man, who tended to the poor, comforted the sick, and *never* got an invite to City Hall—much less the White house. He was caring for his flock from a small church on Sutphin Boulevard.

"I hate that fucking guy, and excuse me, but I just can't help it," Tommy had said on more than one occasion. "I hope he chokes on a KFC chicken bone. Best thing the Colonel could ever do for the city."

"Why don't you say what you *really* mean, Tommy? Stop holding back. Get your blood pressure up. I couldn't survive you having ulcer problems again, and watching you eating yogurt and downing Pepto Bismol." Jimmy was laughing.

"Easy, boys," said Charlie. "Just accept the fact that the whole system and the administration, from Obama on down, is corrupt. That's all the President talks about, doing your fair share, and he invites that tax-evading asshole over to the White House for lunch. And don't get me started on the Clintons, as they wallow in corruption like pigs at the trough. While fuckin' Hillary does whatever she wants, the slugs from our Justice Department, from the Eastern District here in New York, go after regular Joes using structuring guidelines that were meant to be used against terrorists and organized crime. You deposit under ten grand on multiple occasions, a red flag goes up with the Feds, because they think you're hiding something. Got a buddy of mine, owns his own company, told his delivery guys to make cash deposits to avoid carrying money around and getting robbed. They went after *him*. Had to hire a lawyer, of course, a former assistant US Attorney. At the end of the day, they took a four hundred thousand dollar fine."

"Fuckin' Defranco, take it easy. You're watching *way* too much FOX. You need to alter your viewing habits," said Bobby Washington.

"What, and watch what you watch *Jerry Springer, Maury*, and an occasional episode of *Bait Car*, to see your relatives? Remember, guys, we work for a department that went after a female cop years ago for paying for one scoop of ice cream and getting two. Kind of puts the corruption of the White House and the Clintons in perspective."

They all had a laugh, because the only alternative was to cry, when you realized what mischief Skinner, the Mayor, and the clueless members of the City Council were up to.

You see, "the brothers" were smoking weed and nothing was going to stop them. Couldn't get an NFL player with a million dollar contract to stop, what hope would you have of getting a young guy in the neighborhood to give it up? Cops just shook their heads. They'd smoke right in front of you, in building lobbies, on subway cars—on school property. No one was doing time for it; most cases, you showed up, you paid a fine, and you were on your way.

But they were *not* showing up, and they were *not* paying their fines, which meant a warrant was issued. They could do everything, short of parting the Red Sea, to find marijuana and purchase marijuana, but they couldn't respond to court to settle the matter. That and the fact that apparently no one had cash to pay the fine. And, somehow, that was the *cop's* fault?

"How come no one asks this question of the Mayor and Skinner and these other assholes?" mused Jimmy one day. "How come all these guys got money to buy weed and smoke weed every day of the week, but nobody has money to settle up down at court after they get collared?"

So the "higher-ups" decided it was a good idea that the NYPD would go easy on weed. The City Council was on board, and the Black and Hispanic Coalition were on board. Got so crazy that a Polish Coalition was on board because two Polacks had been bagged smoking weed on the handball courts at McCarran Park in the 94th Precinct, and one of the kids had a father on the City Council. Sale and possession in small amounts would be no big deal. And the city was told that.

Only someone forgot to tell the Jamaicans, who were making huge amounts of money distributing marijuana. And it was starting to get hard for the police department to ignore, regardless of what the Mayor and Skinner were trying to peddle, because the Jamaicans were whacking people at a horrible rate.

Three males butchered and set on fire in a stash house off Fourteenth Avenue in College Point in the 109th Precinct; a women and an 18-year-old female shotgun-blasted in a beauty salon in the 67th; an infant killed in a drive-by on Roosevelt and 74th Street in the 115th—*all* because of the marijuana trade.

Which meant that after months of telling street cops and the Narcotics Division to avoid making marijuana collars under the threat of an overtime shut down, the lads were informed that "Condor Overtime" was in effect for weed.

"Something like this happened once before," said Sgt. Quinn. "The PC's wife was walking the poodle on Sixty First Street and Central Park West, where they lived, and some numbskull asks her if she needed some good shit. Scared the daylights out of her, especially after the asshole tells her how great she was looking. We shut down for a week and spent our days in and around the Park making weed collars."

So all these events, when taken together, resulted in the boys coming into contact with "Basically Bill."

# Jake McNicholas

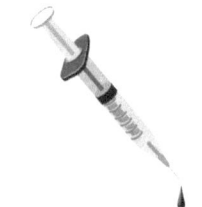

# Chapter 13

"So we're going to do two things today, boys," said Sgt. Quinn. "We're going to make some weed collars and we're going to try and identify JD (John Doe) Redskins."

"I'm sorry, Sarge, I won't be able to participate in this operation if you continue to use the derogatory term Redskin. I find it offensive," said Jimmy.

"I find it offensive, too," said Richie. "But only because Washington beat the Giants last week. Eli threw three picks."

And then this gem of wisdom from Bobby Washington.

"I just wish these fuckin' liberals would get as worked up over savages butchering little fuckin' babies for body parts as they do about a fuckin' football team's name. So many black babies, too. You couldn't do it to baby seals, those crazies from PETA be all over your shit."

"Damn, Bobby, where'd that come from?" Asked Jimmy.

"I've been improving my reading habits."

"But, guys," said Tommy, "we're missing something very important. According to the shitheads on the City Council we will have to give JD Redskins a receipt explaining the reason why we stopped him and asked for identification."

"Just put down 'Long Term Buy Operation. See You On Take Down Day Asshole,' " said Charlie.

"Say this for the City Council, though," added Sgt. Quinn. "They don't let the fact that they haven't got a clue when it comes to law enforcement get in their way when it comes to making our job tougher."

"They're 'bout as useless as a bunch of vegetarians at a pig roast."

"Fucking Bobby, you are on today," said Tommy.

The plan of operation was this. The team was going to head up north to the vicinity of Broadway and Isham, address a weed condition, and, as long as they were out, come back down south and take a look for JD Redskins, a male Hispanic who wore a Washington Redskins baseball hat and had sold heroin multiple times to Wally Wong, who was posing as a tough-guy member of the Ghost Shadows. JD Redskins was the last guy who needed to be identified in connection with Richie Whalen's case. Wally and Bobby had bought into seventeen guys—sixteen had been identified—and Richie was looking to tidy up this last matter before the case was taken down.

So the gang headed uptown to the Piper's Kilt, everyone except Wally and Bobby, who couldn't really sit in the middle of Washington Heights with a bunch of white boys and Tommy eating burgers. Most guys went with the Bronx Burger, the one with the side order of chili. They finished up and then set up for the weed spot, and it was easy pickings. They grabbed a couple of buyers, got the seller, the whole thing wrapped up in less than an hour and a half, and then headed south to set up around West 145th Street between Broadway and Amsterdam, by the library. Jimmy and Santos in the P Van, Sgt. Quinn and Tommy in 582, and Charlie and Richie in the Impala. Wally and Bobby were relaxing in the tinted-out U/C vehicle.

Sure enough, JD Redskins was out there in his hat, wearing dungarees and a black and red bowling shirt, all 5'8", and 110 lbs. of him. Charlie and Richie got out of their vehicle, strolled up to him with their shields out and Charlie said, "Warrant Division, you're John Best." Well, of course he was *not* John Best and JD Redskins was happy to say that. "Shit no, you got the wrong guy. I got ID." So he handed over whatever—his new city ID, or his food stamp card—and Charlie recorded the information and said, "Sorry pal, we made a mistake. Our bad. Have a nice day." Then they headed back to the car, with JD Redskins, a.k.a. Domingo Villa, thinking, "Those are some dumb motherfuckahs."

It went off without a hitch. But then, Charlie and Richie had barely driven off when Wally got on and said, "Boys, you are not going to believe this shit. He certainly got balls. He just did a hand-to-hand. Male Black, twenties, five eight, a hundred and sixty pounds, wearing a Batman shirt, heading to Broadway. Put the shit in his right pants pocket."

"We're down on Broadway, Boss," said Jimmy. "We'll snatch him up."

"Batman" hit Broadway and went North, Santos driving the P van, and Jimmy in the passenger seat, the van inching behind Batman until the corner at 148th Street. Jimmy got out, tiptoed up and grabbed him, turned him around and said, "Listen pal, we know your holding, so make it easy on yourself and just hand me the stuff you got in your right pants pocket."

And he did.

Jimmy noticed, too, while he was cuffing him that Batman was considerably older than the description. He had an envelope out and took everything out of Batman's pockets—ChapStick, condoms, house keys, wallet, package of Horny Goat Weed, tissues, and the decks of heroin stamped ISIS—and stuck the contents inside. Then, "What's your name?"

"Guillermo Sinclair."

"Your date of birth?"

"Nine, sixteen, seventy-three."

"Okay, Bill, hop in the van and just relax. I'll talk to you when we get to precinct."

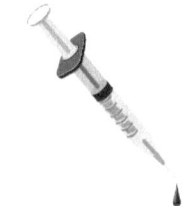

# Chapter 14

The Narcotics Division of the NYPD is comprised of seven, separate, geographical entities and the Drug Enforcement Task Force.

Queens, the Bronx, and Staten Island each had one operation to cover its respective area. Both Brooklyn and Manhattan had a pair, in each case, signified by splitting the borough in two and distinguishing them as North and South.

Manhattan North Narcotics covered all the precincts that were situated north of 59th Street and included the 19th, 20th, 23rd, 25th, 26th, 28th, 30th, 32nd, 33rd, and the 34th. With regards to narcotics enforcement, the boys went where the drugs and the activity were, so they were rarely conducting operations in the 19th or 20th precincts.

In an effort to streamline the arrest processing for Manhattan North, and to keep narcotics and their collars from invading precincts, the muster room and the arrest processing areas, an intake area was constructed in the alleyway of the Two-Five on East 119th Street. Make collars up north, and you'd head to the building in the Two-Five alleyway to conduct the strip searches, do paperwork, fingerprint, and debrief prisoners. It was a good deal, too, because across the street and up the block on Park Avenue was the bar, Raggs. It served cold beer, was air conditioned, and was usually populated by cops, detectives, guys from the Liffey Moving Company, and some locals. The female bartenders were generous and *occasionally* built. If you had collars and had the prisoner van, you were responsible for driving the "perps" downtown for lodging; and you couldn't make the trip without the arrest numbers coming up. So, on a hot summer day, one could take a walk up the block and have an ice-cold beer and listen to Frank Sinatra singing *The Summer Wind* on the jukebox, while waiting for those numbers.

The lieutenant who ran the operation on the "four by twelve" was Aloysius Boylan, a twenty-eight year veteran, who had gotten jammed up some years back. What had happened was this: Boylan had been a boss in the Special Victims Unit, which "turned out" of 3280 Broadway. He and his associates investigated the most heinous of crimes imaginable: sexual assaults and child abuse cases. Boylan was an extremely religious man, and everyone agreed he was a good soul.

One day, he and a detective from the office responded to an apartment in the Three-Oh. Uniform was already there, and what they had was a three-year-old boy stuffed in a cooler; a female beaten, bruised and crying; and the boyfriend sitting nearby, rear-cuffed. When Boylan entered the apartment, the boyfriend began screaming at the mother, "You fuckin' bitch I should have killed you too, you fuckin' cunt!" After years of such horror, Boylan had a tired, weary look about him, almost like the "thousand yard stare" combat Marines and soldiers get. He asked the boyfriend a simple question, after he took off his hat and coat.

"Did you do that to that little boy?"

"That's right, motherfuckah."

There were a number of uniformed cops and detectives in the room at the time, but Boylan was the senior member on the scene, and they all knew of him. And now, they watched as he slowly walked over to the boyfriend, gently placed his hand on his arm, and stood him up. He was a big, young guy, prison-built, and maybe thirty years Boylan's junior. Guys who were there in the apartment that day still say they couldn't believe how quick everything happened. Boylan turned the perp around, uncuffed him, and said, "Excuse me," and began to beat the living shit out of the prisoner. Took four cops to pull him off the screaming asshole.

Sometime later, he was assigned to the arrest processing building.

And there he worked, always smiling as if the weight of the world was off his shoulders. He sat behind that raised desk with his big, fat, red Irish face and his huge handlebar mustache, making small talk and welcoming the cops and the prisoners alike. Even the guys who'd been arrested liked him.

"Be nice lads, it's over now. Nothing can be done till you see the judge. You cooperate, we'll make sure to treat you right," he would say. And he was true to his word.

There was only one thing: Operations were pretty much shut down nightly at 7:00 PM, because Lt. Aloysius Boylan would be watching *Jeopardy*.

Jake McNicholas

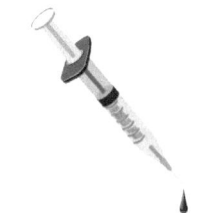

# Chapter 15

They rolled up to the Two-Five a little after seven. Wally was already on the block in the undercover car with the tinted-out windows and had confirmed that the weed seller was *the* "weed seller," and that Batman, a.k.a. Guillermo Sinclair, was the guy who had gotten done by JD Redskins. Richie Whalen and Charlie Defranco had already parked their car and escorted the first three collars into arrest processing. Jimmy brought up the rear with Batman.

Timing is everything in life and in police work. There was another team inside: Sgt. Hammond and his guys; and things were going to start moving again because *Jeopardy* was just about over. In fact, at that very moment, there was an eerie silence. Even the prisoners knew to stop the chatter. On the television, Alex Trebek had just read the Final Jeopardy Answer from the category, "The Character and the Novel."

Alex Trebek said, "Ignatius J. Reilly."

You could have heard a pin drop. Lt. Boylan was back behind that raised desk of his, staring at the TV, his massive head resting on his two fists. It seemed like an eternity had elapsed before the silence was shattered by Lt. Boylan and another individual off to the side screaming, in unison, "What is A Confederacy of Dunces?!"

Jimmy turned to Guillermo Sinclair and said, "I got to tell you, Bill, I'm really impressed."

Up on the desk, Lt. Boylan was flabbergasted—beside himself. "Nice to see we are getting a higher caliber of prisoner here. Mr. Batman, I salute you. But for the love of God, how'd you come up with that one? No matter. A soda and a snack from the candy machine inside the station house and it's on me. Jimmy McTigue, make sure you take care of it, and I will give you the money."

"Will do, Boss."

Pretty soon, Sgt. Hammond's team, with six collars from the Three-Two, had finished its paperwork and vacated the small area to the left of the entrance. Charlie Defranco was the arresting officer, and he was working on the online booking sheets, acquiring most of the information from the pedigree sheets off the prisoner envelopes. Occasionally he would ask more detailed questions, which the sheets on the envelope hadn't covered. Tommy and Jimmy were breaking down the envelopes, separating personal property from arrest evidence. They also counted everyone's money and indicated the amount on the Prisoner Property Form. Everyone would be getting their money returned *except* the guy who sold the weed; the three hundred and fifty dollars he had on his person would be vouchered as proceeds from drug transactions.

Sgt. Quinn stepped behind the desk and entered the names of those arrested in the logbook, making a special note that said all the prisoners were in good physical condition. Lt. Boylan sat there still amazed; nothing like that had ever happened before.

"A quick question, my friend, how did you know that answer?"

Guillermo Sinclair was a mere five feet from the desk when he said, "Basically, sir, I was an English major at Baruch. I basically loved English, ever since I went to school, and that was one of my favorite books—that and John Steinbeck's *Of Mice and Men*."

"Baruch was it? ' UCLA,' University on the Corner of Lexington Avenue. I guess you're living proof that it is possible to get a decent education in New York *regardless* of what the Teachers Union does. More power to you."

Jimmy said, "You sure like to use that term, *basically*, Bill."

Hammond's team had already finished its prisoner search and now they had them by the fingerprint scanner, a machine that looked much like a copier. For Narcotics, gone were the days of ink and cards, when arresting officers took prisoners downtown and anxiously awaited the decision of the desk sergeant as to whether the prints would be accepted or kicked back. Now, the prints went down via the scanner, and once an arrest number was produced, the prisoners could be taken down and lodged at Central Booking.

Jimmy and Tommy led their four to the long room that stretched out behind the desk. There were five cells there, and all four prisoners were put in the cell closest to the entrance to the station house. There was a cell attendant on duty, who kept an eye on them. One by one, each prisoner was brought to the cell furthest away and searched. They saved Guillermo Sinclair for last.

In the cell, they removed his cuffs.

"Listen, Bill," Jimmy said, "I'm sure you know the drill. This is required."

"I know, sir."

"Let me have your belt and then take a seat and start taking out the laces from your Chuck Taylors. Man, haven't seen *them* in a while. Then bang the sneakers together, turn them upside down, and hand them to Tommy here for a quick look-see."

Sinclair did as instructed. He then handed the belt and laces over to Jimmy, who dropped them in the envelope that would be heading downtown with the prisoner.

"Let me have your shirt, Bill, and you can take off your pants and socks, too," Jimmy said.

Bill handed over the clothing, and Jimmy went through the shirt and pants meticulously and ignored the socks. Tommy had on plastic gloves.

"Alright, Bill, please turn around, bend over, spread your cheeks, and cough." Jimmy felt like a half-assed doctor. "Said that one time, Tommy, and a guy coughed and out flew a zip lock bag with twenty-three crack vials. Guy actually said, 'They're not mine.' Take a seat, Bill, and relax. Bill, let me ask you something. You're a smart guy, respectful, how'd you wind up here?"

"Basically, I have a serious heroin problem."

"I didn't see any tracks," said Tommy.

"No sir, I basically snort and smoke it. Stick the liquefied heroin in a nasal spray bottle and go from there. Call it 'shabanging.' Got hooked a while back, *but* I can function. But I'm afraid I have really basically fucked up, because I'm on probation, and getting arrested again is *not* good."

"What do you do?" asked Jimmy.

"I work for the Post Office."

"That makes sense," said Tommy. "They won't fire you unless you steal the mail or kill somebody, most times. Guillermo Sinclair, you look straight Black."

76

"Basically my mom's Dominican and my father is Black. I speak Spanish."

"Listen, Bill, I'll be honest with you. You impress me. You certainly impressed Lt. Boylan. You're on probation, and possession of ten decks is no joke. Today wasn't the first time you purchased narcotics. You know any places up here that are pitching, locations you can get into? Maybe help us out and help yourself out at the same time? You'd be a dream for us; an intelligent guy that's fluent in English and Spanish."

"Basically I do know of some locations, and I would appreciate any help you could give me."

"Here's my number. You get out, give me a call. You see— and I'll use *your* word—we're basically chasing the "Kilo Fairy," the Big Hit, the Mother Lode. We're going to start the paperwork. Don't mention this to anyone, please. We'll meet with you when you get out. Oh yeah, what do you want from the machine? It's on Lt. Boylan."

"I'll have a Mountain Dew and a bag of Fritos, if they have 'em. And basically, thanks."

\* \* \* \* \*

Sinclair was out in two days, on a hundred dollars bail, part of the new, progressive, criminal justice system, only *this time* it actually worked for the good guys. He lived uptown on Nagle Avenue, so Tommy and Jimmy had him walk over to Dyckman and Tenth Avenue, then took him to a secluded spot by Fort Tryon Park.

They had two pieces of paperwork to fill out in connection to Sinclair becoming a Confidential Informant (CI). The first page was mostly "pedigree" information, but the second page required the subject to write, in his own hand, "My code name is . . ." and then sign *that* name.

"I'm basically not sure what my name should be."

"I got it!" Jimmy said. From this day forth, you are 'Basically Bill.' "

They got a couple of pictures of him to attach to the paperwork (they had already conducted a Triple III check and settled everything with Probation). Jimmy told Basically Bill the rules of engagement: this wasn't a license to be partaking in criminal activity.

"But, shit," Jimmy said, "we don't expect choirboys to be helping us out. You get collared again, call me immediately. Now I'm sure you have a few go-to guys on the street, but how 'bout an inside location?"

"Basically, I've been thinking about that. I get detailed occasionally to a different post office. I'm a mail handler. Basically, I know of this place on West Hundred Thirty Eighth Street."

"Got an address?" asked Tommy.

"No, but I'll get it. It's between Amsterdam and Riverside Drive."

"What do they sell?" asked Tommy.

"Basically coke and heroin."

Then Jimmy taking over, "Any brand name?"

"TRANSFORMER for the heroin."

"When was the last time you were up there?"

"Two weeks ago."

"Any guns or dogs?"

"Basically no."

"And you have no problem getting in?"

"Never. They basically know me."

"Anything else?"
"I basically think I saw that 'Kilo Fairy.' "

## Jake McNicholas

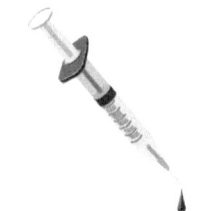

# Chapter 16

Up on the roof of the old armory, with the smell of the meat from the Weber grill and the soft breeze coming off the River, if you closed your eyes you could surely forget you were up in Harlem.

There were lights on all over, and city sounds—horns and sirens, and an occasional gunshot off in the distance. Looking northeast from the roof, you could see Yankee Stadium. The Bombers were home against the hated Red Sox; the ballpark packed and lit up like a birthday cake.

Earlier, Jimmy had borrowed a hundred dollars of buy money (the cash used by the undercovers to purchase narcotics) from Sgt. Quinn, and he had headed over to Western Beef on 128th Street. He bought burgers, dogs, some Johnsonville sausages, potato salad, coleslaw, pickles, and knishes; he also bought a half-gallon of milk and some Ring Dings for Captain Sink and came back to the car with it all—plus a watermelon. He pointed at the melon in the basket, and told Tommy, "got something for the brothers."

Now, they were up on the roof, with ice-cold beer from Hector Garcia who ran the *bodega* across the street from the Three-Oh Precinct, Sgt. Quinn's team, and Sgt. Lewis with Al

Gavin and Jack Clint. Captain Sink and Lt. Bilge were up there too, as was Alba Castro from the Two-Five team.

It was a down day, so everyone was pretty much dressed in shorts and relaxing.

Bobby Washington was standing by the grill in Bermuda shorts and a green Izod, smoking a large cigar. He wore his pants like a retired supervisor from the Garment District who was living in Florida—high at the waist.

Wally Wong thought he reminded him of someone. "I got it now, Bobby. I know who you look like—that guy Urkel from the old TV show, the nerd with the glasses."

"I'll tell you what, Chinaman. You be starving today 'cause I don't see no cats on the grill. And, Jimmy, who do you think you are with that Hawaiian shirt, Jack Fuckin' Lord? I get it. You McGarrett, and Bell's Danno. We get Defranco to be Don Ho."

Bobby was on a roll.

Off to the side, sitting on the beach chairs, were Capt. Sink and Lt. Bilge, their feet spread out on top of Richie Whalen's blue cooler. They were talking shop. Bilge ate a hot dog and drank a cold Bud from the can, and Sink had a large, plastic cup of milk, and was eating a burger, eagerly eyeballing the box of Ring Dings alongside the salads on the table. There was a time, some years back, that that wouldn't have been the case. But then, Robert Sink had made a trip to "The Farm."

It wasn't the kind of farm with John Deere tractors and crops and such. *This* farm was an alcohol and drug rehab facility located out in the Hamptons, where cops with a problem were sent to get healthy. And there was a time when Robert Sink would rather *drink* than get laid.

Used to be, in the old days, the Department Chaplain, Monsignor Dunn, would kidnap guys that needed help. That didn't happen much anymore, but The Job was keenly aware that cops had problems, and would send a person in need off to the facility by showing cause. Or a cop could realize he or she had a problem and volunteer to go. Sink realized he had a problem.

He was working in Uniform at the time, living in an apartment off Victory Boulevard in Staten Island, and he had headed up to Pearl River for a 10-13 party for a guy in his command, the Ninth Precinct. He wasn't familiar with the area, and this was before GPS, so he had enough trouble getting to the Knights of Columbus in daylight. But he got there, none the less, and met the lads from the Third Squad and started "pounding," because back then Sink always had "the taste."

He spent five hours drinking, and, at about one in the morning, decided it was time to head back to Staten Island, driving one-lane blacktops in the dark of night, looking for home. He spent hours in an alcoholic haze, barely remembering the details the next day, but recalling one especially important incident. At about five o'clock in the morning, he approached a tollbooth out of the fog and asked the female toll collector if that was Staten Island up ahead.

"Staten Island? Honey, you five miles outside Philadelphia."

Next day Robert Sink went "farming," and he hadn't had a drink since.

\* \* \* \* \*

Richie worked the grill and was wearing an apron that read,

"Rugby Players Eat Their Dead," a gift from Jimmy. "Yeah it's a reference to the team that crashed in the Andes, years ago," he explained. "They were forced to look into *alternative* eating practices."

Bobby had heard the explanation and said, at the time, "What a fuckin' team. Got a cannibal lover on it, too."

Alba Castro was the only female up on the roof, and she looked wonderful. The breeze coming off the river played a magical game with her long, black hair. She wore a pair of blue shorts and a T-shirt that read: "Michael Buczek Little League." Buczek had been killed in 1988 in the Three-Four Precinct, and now the organization provided baseball to the youngsters in Washington Heights. Forty-three kids who had played ball up there had gone on to become cops. Alba was grinning and enjoying the show and said, "Thanks, Jimmy, for the invite," and then to Bobby, who was looking her up and down with his tongue out, "Bobby put some ice down your shorts before you hurt yourself."

Jimmy got a kick out of her. One day, he had found himself alone in the cubicle after he had returned from court, the team out doing B & B without him. He only had a couple of hours remaining on duty when he heard the chuck wagon dinner bell signifying an impending visit by The Vicious Jim Carrey. He headed for the door to get lost until the end of tour. His Jeep was parked in the back by the basketball courts, and while he was walking back there, Alba Castro, who he didn't know, was approaching the entrance to the building.

"I wouldn't, if I was you. The wagon bell sounded. Lucas is on the way . . ." Then, with his hand outstretched, "I'm Jimmy McTigue."

"Thanks, Jimmy, nice to meet you. I'm Alba Castro. What now?"

"I was going to head down to the Kinsale for a burger. You want to join me?"

"Sure."

They headed down south to 94th and Third in Jimmy's Jeep, and he liked her immediately. She didn't have the rough edge to her that so many of the female cops acquired after some time on The Job—and she had a great laugh. She looked right at Jimmy while they were talking, so much so, that it was a little bit intimidating. Alba had been down at court on a trial, and was wearing a dark gray pants suit. She had her jacket off, draped over the seat, sitting there in a white blouse with the fabric stretching in all the right places and her off-duty strapped on her left hip.

They managed to park in a spot out front. Jimmy held the door open for her, and Alba flashed a grin and actually said, "Thanks, pal." They went past the bar, off the wall on the left, and found a table in the back near the kitchen.

"This is a nice place, Jimmy. First time I've been here."

"Great place, Alba. Used to be a time, you didn't have direct deposit, you could cash your checks here. Nine-Eleven changed that. I've had some great times in this place. If laughs were money, I'd be a millionaire."

They ordered a couple of Diet Cokes and cheeseburgers, and then Jimmy, "Where'd you work, Alba?"

"I did ten years in the Four-Two, up on Washington Avenue. I loved it. It was a great place to learn, and it had a special feel about it. One of the reasons is the Communion Breakfast every year. They've been running it close to seventy years, and all these retired guys come back. Wonderful men, a testament to this job. Nothing nicer than to sit at a table with them and hear their stories."

"You know, years ago, I made one," said Jimmy. "I'll never forget it. Snowing out and we got out of mass and then we mustered up in front of church, guys in uniform and the old-timers, and we marched behind the Pipe Band, to Alex and Henry's, the catering place. Never forget, early Sunday morning and the roosters stirring. Did you know Mike Higgins from the squad, when he was there?"

"Just to say hello."

"He's got Stage-Four Cancer from the Trade Center."

And then silence from both of them—and the realization that it would never end.

The girl brought the food, and Jimmy said, "Best burgers up here . . . you didn't come from the Four-Two to Narcotics, did you?"

"No, I had a friend in Applicant Investigation. He said come over. You'll get the shield. Be a nice break from patrol. I worked out of the Academy. Gramercy Park was nice and the commute wasn't bad, because I'm living in Throgs Neck. Turned out to be a horror story."

"How come?"

"You have to realize that what the powers that be, in the Department and in City Government, are saying is *completely different* from what is actually happening. Don't believe that nonsense that they haven't lowered standards. I try to close out cases, because people have taken multiple collars, and I can't. They are using all sorts of schemes to recruit cops that the mayor and the City Council want. Face the facts, Jimmy. They're looking to cut down on you white boys." Her eyes twinkled when she said it. "Personally, I'm getting kind of partial to some of you," she laughed. "I had one girl locked up three times for shoplifting. Think about that. If they managed to catch her *three* times, how many times was she doing it? She's in the Academy now."

"Don't worry about it, Alba. Applicant Investigation's loss is Manhattan North's gain."

"Well, thank you, Jimmy."

The waitress had returned, and Jimmy got the check.

"I've done all the talking. What about you?" as she reached into her pocket for money.

Jimmy avoided the question and said, "Don't worry about it Alba, it's my treat."

"Thanks very much," and she was smiling. Then, she reached across the table, patted Jimmy on the head, and said, "You're a good guy. What do you comb that with, a firecracker?"

And they both laughed.

\* \* \* \* \*

By then, the boys and Alba were standing in a big semicircle, laughing and giggling; telling stories; and bullshitting ("cop talk"—all of it—and spanning the ages). Then, Mattie Quinn jumped in and said, "Listen to this one."

"I heard this from an old-timer from the Three-Oh, a cop by the name of Mike Donnelly, who worked in the old Eighteenth, which is now Midtown North. Anyway, he's working the pier on the West Side, one day, over where the Intrepid is berthed, and he's got 'the taste,' and a bunch of people getting ready to shove off ask him if he wants to come aboard for a bon voyage party. They're heading to the Bahamas in a few hours. 'Well, yeah!' he says, and he gets blasted and passes out, and by the time he wakes up, the ship is five hours out to sea—and this is before cell phones and all of that shit."

"What'd he do?" asked Wally.

"What could he do? He wasn't worried so much about The Job, but his wife would surely kill him. The passengers wound up chipping in and provided him with some cruise wear, and the Captain wound up finding out and secured him a spot downstairs with the crew, which really turned out good for him, since there was a Crew Bar that was very inexpensive. He had gotten word back to Command, and Roll Call covered for him, and his partner told his wife he was sitting on a hospitalized prisoner. The trip to the Bahamas took two days, and then he flew home."

They drank more cold beer and laughed more, and Whalen asked them if they wanted cheeseburgers. There was a radio on, with the game playing, and someone had just blasted a homer for the Yankees. It felt almost like, up on that roof, that you could hear the crowd from the Bronx. Captain Sink had heard the story and got out of his beach chair and walked over to the circle.

"I got one for you," the Captain said. "It's not as funny, or as rich as my nineteen-year-old son going to Cornell and telling me that the campus doesn't feel safe because a couple of girls are walking around in sombreros on Halloween night—but it's still good.

"Now remember, boys, I'm older than you, so old that I remember when stewardesses used to be good looking. I was working in the Ninth Precinct in 1976, tough, dangerous times, when the Black Liberation Army was assassinating cops. There was this guy in the Ninth by the name of Mike Perkins, old-timer, and he was coming to the end of his career. Mike had been a waist gunner on a B-17, Flying Fortress with the 'Bloody Hundredth' of the Eighth Air Force in World War Two. 'Alice from Dallas' was his ship's name. He had been on the Schweinfurt, ball bearing-factory raid in Nineteen Forty-Three, when they lost sixty planes, and he had been shot down and captured by the Germans. Never spoke about it. A good-natured guy. He had an edge to him, though, and he was out on patrol, one day, and he was loaded for bear. Carried a sawed-off shotgun under his choker, had it this one winter night. Guy gives him some shit on Avenue C and East Third Street. Makes a move to his waistband, and Mike whacks the guy across the bridge of the nose like he's John Wayne in *Rio Bravo*. Turns out the guy is the son of some mover and shaker, and he had come down to Alphabet City to score some heroin—in fact, Mike recovers ten decks. Internal Affairs gets involved, and they wind up bringing Mike in.

"So, Mike's sitting in his chair at some undisclosed location, when these two college boys in nice suits walk into the room and actually try the 'good cop-bad cop' routine. Mike's got this puzzled look on his face, lights up a cigarette, and the two guys give him the third degree on a whole host of shit, and Mike blows huge smoke rings from his mouth, looks these two up and down and finally says, nice and easy, 'Listen, I didn't give up anything to the fuckin' Nazis, so what makes you two assholes think I'm going to give anything up to you?' "

Everyone had a laugh and, then, Captain Sink said, "Raise your drink, boys, and a toast to old Mike Perkins, one of the Greatest Generation."

Jimmy McTigue's phone rang.

"Hey Jim, it's Basically Bill. I think I've got something for you."

Jake McNicholas

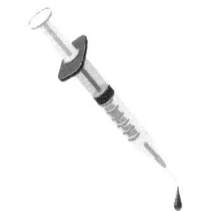

# Chapter 17

Jimmy and Santos picked up Basically Bill up on Broadway across from Good Shepherd Roman Catholic Church and in front of the Piper's Kilt. They were driving the unmarked Chevy, Jimmy lowering the window a bit to give Bill the heads-up that it was them, and Bill sliding into the back seat.

Basically Bill had gotten into 606 West 138th Street again. He had entered the apartment with a friend, a guy known to the dealers, who was up there to purchase some coke. Bill told them he was broke and was waiting for payday and was just along for the ride. Maybe share some. They were good with that—which changed everything for Jimmy.

It wasn't necessary to send Basically Bill into the location with buy money to make a purchase. He had seen product and was familiar with the location; that itself was enough to get a search warrant, as long as the judge was on board. So, they had to take Bill to 100 Centre Street, have him articulate to the judge what had actually occurred during his visit to the apartment, and the judge would decide whether that was enough to sign the warrant, all of this a necessity since Bill was a new confidential informant with absolutely no history.

Jimmy knew the Honorable Tommy Flynn was available that day. He had a familiarity with Flynn, had gotten an emergency search warrant some months back that had resulted in five collars, an AK-47, two bulletproof vests, four hundred decks of heroin stamped "SNOOPY," and eight thousand dollars in cash from an apartment within the confines of the Four-Six in the Bronx.

"Just don't bullshit the Judge, Bill," Jimmy said. "And please try to leave the 'basically' out. The Judge doesn't want to hear *basically*. Now go through it again."

"Well I basically knew . . . sorry . . . I *knew* that 2B in 606 W138th Street was selling heroin and coke. I had been in there before. It's between Broadway and Riverside Drive, lots of Jersey people going in and out, and there is always a guy on the front stoop, basically watching, but whoever is there, they know me. This time, I was with another guy, a steady customer, and by the time we get to the front door they got it open for us."

"Good, Bill, very good, just like that," Jimmy encouraged.

"Go in the front door," continued Bill, "up the stairs—I never take the elevator—and on the second door on the right, got a big B over the peep hole."

By now Jimmy knew all about the spot. He had run the apartment for collars, and there was history, three Dominicans providing that location as their address on online booking sheets. There were two current "kites" on the location—both for narcotics sales. Jimmy had called his friend down at Con Ed, who had provided him with the name Kiko Rivera as the tenant with a turn-on date. The building was run by a management company over in Borough Park, Brooklyn, and he had called and gotten a tenants list. Kiko Rivera in 2B. Jimmy and Santos played anti-crime, one day, drove up the block in the beat-up Chevy Impala (obvious cop car), shields around their necks and radios in hand, entering the front door by pushing random bells until someone rang the buzzer. They took the elevator to the second floor, spotted 2B, with the B above the peephole, and walked to the far end of the hall. They knocked on the door and asked the elderly female if everything was all right, because they had gotten a report that somebody was screaming. It was all bullshit, but they had verified apartment 2B.

""Good, Bill, you're doing good, now just get to it," Jimmy encouraged.

"My buddy basically just knocked on the door around two p.m. We walked in, and he asked the guy I know as Bolo for an eight ball. There was stuff out all over the table, decks of heroin, and packets of coke, scales—the works. Thought I saw what looked like a kilo. The guy gives him the money, and we were basically on our way."

"That's good, Bro', real good," added Santos.

They were heading south on Broadway, listening to music, and watching the city life. Jimmy pulled over on West 100th Street, went into Columbia Bagels and came back with coffee and buttered corn muffins for everyone. They sat at the corner, facing southbound, Bill in the back seat still rehearsing, Jimmy and Santos taking turns telling him that everything was going to be fine. Then they finished up and took the West Side highway south to 100 Center Street.

Jimmy pulled over on Lafayette Street, where Family Court was, where Judge Judy used to work, double-parked and jumped out. Santos got in the driver's seat and said, "Knock em dead, Bill." Then, Jimmy and Bill headed across the street, then across Centre, past the long line of civilians waiting to be screened through security, Jimmy flashing his gold shield to the court officer and saying, while he nodded toward Bill, "he's with me."

They headed up to Judge Flynn's second-floor courtroom via the stairs. Bill waited outside.

The room was full: family members of the recently arrested, who were about to appear; district attorneys; uniformed cops and those in soft clothes; lawyers for Legal Aid; and private practice. Jimmy let the court officer know he was there regarding a warrant, and, twenty minutes later, during a lull in proceedings, he and Bill were escorted into Flynn's chambers.

Judge Flynn was, by then, sitting behind his desk, hunched over paperwork with glasses on the tip of the nose. He looked up at McTigue and Bill and said, "How's it going, detectives?"

"Fine, sir." Jimmy was looking at Bill now, and said, "Got a new CI here who's been in an apartment we are especially interested in. Doing a booming business pitching coke and heroin in the Three-Oh."

"You confident that this is the location and that the gentleman is being frank?" asked Flynn.

"Absolutely, sir."

Flynn did a cursory review of the warrant application, signed it, stood up, shook both Jimmy's and Bill's hands and said, "Good luck."

"Thanks, sir."

They took the stairs down and headed out the door, across Centre Street. They could see Santos still parked in front of Family Court.

"Good job, Bill," Jimmy said. "We're all set. Stay away from there. We'll be hitting it, and I sure as hell don't need you in there.

"Okay."

"You *basically* did alright. We'll see how it turns out." And they got into the car.

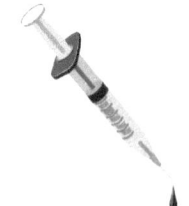

# Chapter 18

**What they decided,** Jimmy McTigue and Sgt. Quinn, was this: Hit 606 West 138th Street on a Friday at six o'clock. They figured that would be a time with the most product at the location, and there might be a bunch of bodies on the scene— Jersey assholes and the rest looking to "get done" before the weekend.

They were going to use two teams: theirs and Sgt. Lewis's. They needed guys in the backyard, which meant entering from the alley of the building behind 606, on West 137th Street. They needed the entry team; they needed hallway security; and they needed security in front of the building.

What worried Jimmy the most, besides the players getting raised up, was entry to the apartment building itself. The door opened outward and was laid out in such a way as to make it virtually impossible to use a pry or a crowbar to open it. But he knew the Three-Oh beat cop who covered the block, Willie Gonzalez, who had actually scored a front door key from the Hasidic management company over in Brooklyn. He decided to ask Alba if she wanted to make some money, do some overtime, and have some laughs. What she was going to do was hit a *bodega* up on Broadway, buy some groceries, then walk to the location and open the front door with the key when the boys were rolling up. She was all in.

That was the plan: two teams and Lt. Bilge, but then an unexpected addition in the ICO—Lt. Joyce.

Joyce was a bit of a pineapple. He had come to Narcotics from Community Affairs with nineteen years on the job and all intentions of retiring at twenty, using his last year to maximize his overtime.

He spent most of his tour in the office, though: monitoring the sign-in sheets; reviewing court slips; cracking down on overtime; and, his pet peeve, eliminating the cigarette smoking in the building, which made him especially annoying to Quinn's team. Tommy Bell, Charlie Defranco, and Bobby Washington all enjoyed an occasional smoke, and they weren't averse to lighting up in the cubicle. Shit, no one cared *and* it didn't even bother the pets. But Joyce had caught them a few times, and he wasn't immune to breaking balls.

The teams did a "ten by six" that Friday, some of the guys playing basketball on the courts in the back of the Armory, near where the department vehicles were parked.

At approximately three o'clock, everyone was in the general area and set to go. Jimmy went down to the equipment room and signed out radios, the kell, a crow bar and pry, bolt cutters, and some lights. He signed out the hydro, the *Ghostbusters-*looking device that was comprised of a metal box containing a motor attached to a hose and metal rod, which expanded and would destroy a doorjamb. They didn't need the ram; *that* was already in the van, as was the milk crate containing flex cuffs, manila envelopes for prisoner property, and assorted tools for an apartment search. He set all the gear down on his desk and then made notifications. He called IAB, the Borough, and the Narcotics Division. He made multiple copies of the TAC plan and the apartment layout he had gotten from the Department of

Buildings and then ordered up five pies from Patsy's on First Avenue and 118th Street.

Jimmy said to the team, "Okay gang, Sgt. Lewis and Richie Whalen are Team One and are leading us in. They got outside security. They're the hospital car, and they'll be in Eighty Six. Me, Sgt. Quinn, Santos, Lt. Bilge, Charlie D in the P van— Team Two. Charlie has the ram, I got the Hydro, and Santos will be the recorder. Team Three is Lt. Joyce, Frank Martin, and Tommy Bell. They got hallway security and are in Five Eighty-Two. Team Four—and, guys, this is important—is Al Gavin and Jack Clint. You guys got the rear of the building, so make sure you take the bolt cutters because you will have to snap the lock on the fence leading into the alley that leads to the rear of the place. I don't have to tell you to watch out for shit flying out the window. Gavin, that big head of yours is sure to get nailed with something coming out."

Al Gavin said, "Fuck you, Jimmy."

"I'd say that you could roll right down Broadway and make the right when we're on the move. We got no indication of weapons or dogs—but who knows. Guys in the Three-Four, the other day, shot a pit bull with the voice box removed. Wally and Bobby will be our eyes and ears on the set."

Jimmy went into his pocket and pulled out twenty dollars in cash and handed it to Alba—Alba, lovely in a flowery dress she had gotten from Target, and a pair of Skechers, Glock 9 in her black handbag. He smiled, saying, "You could buy some rice and some Goya beans and cook us up a meal," and Alba responding, "That's why I love you Jimmy, you're so politically correct." She half meant the "I love you" part.

After he had eaten, as five o'clock rolled around, Bobby Washington, dressed down and looking homeless drinking a can of Bud Lite out of a brown paper bag with a straw, arrived in the vicinity of the location. He had checked his communication device with the kell earlier, and he carried a Ruger LCR, loaded with five, .38 specials, plus P hollow points, his off-duty weapon of choice.

They sent Wally Wong, carrying the same firearm, out to the vicinity of the location on a bike with a basket on the front, looking like any other Chinese delivery guy. Just for the laughs, Wally attached an Alex Rodriguez baseball card to the rear wheel of the bike with a clothespin. He was a diehard Mets fan.

They came out of the front of the Armory laughing and giggling, without an apparent care in the world, carrying various pieces of equipment, everyone in blue NYPD raid jackets with narcotics or police emblazoned on the back. Everyone, that is, except Alba. They were in various modes of dress: slacks, dungarees, or cargo pants; sneakers or timberlands; and baseball hats—and carrying assorted firearms. Jimmy had turned down the automatic weapon, comfortable with going old school, so he wore his .38 Smith & Wesson service revolver in a swivel holster on his gun belt, the holster hanging downward like some sort of western gunslinger. Everyone else carried their department-issued Glock 9s in holsters under their jackets.

Alba used Jimmy's Jeep and headed up to a secluded spot on Convent Avenue near City College, where she parked. Then, she took a leisurely walk down to Broadway.

The rest of the team headed to the fenced-in lot behind the Armory where the vehicles were parked. They took a slow crawl onto the street and lined up in the exact order for the search warrant.

Santos drove the van, with Lt. Bilge up front fooling with the radio, looking for 101.1 FM, playing The Supremes. Mattie

Quinn and Charlie D were sitting in the second seat with Jimmy, who was opening up the kell and placing it behind them on the third seat. On the floor of the van, right by the sliding door, were the ram and the hydro.

They took a slow ride through upper Manhattan, north on Lenox Avenue to 145th Street, and then west, the vehicles lined up and running caravan style, everyone making small talk and bullshitting, not really nervous or worried, but eager to get there and get it done. Maybe there were just a few butterflies in the pits of the stomachs.

"Hey, Lt. Bilge, one question," asked Jimmy, "who's keeping an eye on Lt. Joyce?"

Bilge laughed. He took off his Doolittle Raiders baseball hat, ran his hands through his thinning hair, and said, "Geez I don't know, Jimmy. Hope he doesn't hurt himself. I'll say this, though, if he is as determined at taking police action as he is at breaking balls on office cigarette smokers, we are going to have a superstar on our hands."

"I'll try to keep him out of trouble, boys," Sgt. Quinn said. "Let's just get this thing done, get back safe and sound, and make some money. I was eying that outfit Santos wore at the Ten-Thirteen party a couple weeks ago at Gaelic Park, and it's obvious to all concerned that he needs to spend some cash on some new threads. Where the fuck did you get that get-up?"

Santos laughing, "That's from the new Sinbad collection. It ain't much, but it's all I got."

Jimmy shaking his head and saying, "He got it from that old department store, Robert Hall. Robert *threw* it out and he *hauled* it in."

They passed Amsterdam Avenue and the McDonalds on Broadway, and they made the left on Riverside Drive. They passed the entrance to Riverbank State Park and then Riverside Park off to the right. South of 135th Street, the park on the right ended and a beautiful view of the Hudson River opened up. They "slow drove" all the way down to Grant's Tomb and made a U-turn, then came up just south of 135th Street and parked by the storage facility.

Quinn said, "Alba, you on?"

"Yeah, boss," Alba sounding lovely on the kell. "Done my shopping and set to go. Rice and beans for everyone."

"Wally, you on?"

"Four, Sarge. Got a great view of the block—all good. Up on the stairs, male Hispanic—thirties, five six, one forty—wearing a Yankees hat, what else."

"I'm on, Sarge," added Bobby. "Got the eyeballs on the set and it's all good. Awaiting your arrival."

By now, Al Gavin and Jack Clint were parked and facing southbound on Broadway, also, south of 135th Street. Days before, working a midnight, the two had checked out the location and the locked gate that lead to the rear of 606 West 138th Street. They might not even need the bolt cutters after all, because, when they had "reconned" the spot, the gate was wide open, the alleyway cluttered with numerous garbage cans and tied-up paper products, but with clear access to the back of the search warrant location. Three windows faced the rear courtyard of the apartment—one small, the bathroom's, and the remaining two covered with ratty, dark curtains. One had an air conditioner. Since the rear of 606 wasn't that far off Broadway, what they had decided to do was just walk north on Broadway, sans raid jackets, wearing Verizon hard hats and carrying the bolt cutters. Piece of cake.

What the teams needed now was perfect timing. The caravan had to come up West 138th Street from Riverside Drive unobstructed. They needed to reach the location just short of Broadway with the hospital car out front, free and clear, and the rest of the vehicles lined up behind it. They needed Wally and Bobby to make sure there was no possibility that the light on Broadway would go red, with civilian vehicles in front of the search warrant teams.

So they were ready—*really*. Bilge lowered the van's radio, and Quinn checked his watch. Then, Quinn asked Wally and Bobby how everything looked. All was good. They headed north and idled between West 136th Street and West 137th Street with Quinn on the department radio.

"Al, Jack, you on?"

"Yeah, boss."

"Time to make the donuts."

"Ten-Four."

"Alba, you on?"

"Yeah, Sarge."

"Time to go home and start cooking."

"Ten-Four," said Alba. "Be reaching the door in about two minutes. I'll sing 'There is a Rose in Spanish Harlem' when I'm heading up the stairs."

"Ten-Four, my dear."

Bobby standing on the corner of West 138th Street with a clear view of the entire block all the way down to Riverside Drive said, as if talking to himself, and heard clearly on the kell, "Baby, it's all good, all good."

By now, Alba was heading up the steps singing "Spanish Harlem." They started to roll. The three vehicles made the right onto West 138th Street, the block sun drenched and clear all the way up to Broadway. Alba had an eyeball on the lookout in front of the door. He obviously had done this before, because he got raised up immediately when he spotted the vehicles heading east bound, and opened the front and headed into the building and up the stairs. Alba never even had to use the key. She just held the door open and waited for the boys.

By this time, Al and Jack were already in the back. The gate had been wide open when they arrived. They had their shields out, attached to chains hanging around their necks, and their heads were arched upward toward the three windows in the back that belonged to 606. Nothing yet.

Richie, driving the black Chevy Impala, had made the right and was flying up the block toward Broadway, the two other vehicles close behind. Mid block, he noticed the steps empty and the door ajar. He continued past the location and left the vehicle in the middle of the street just short of Broadway. Santos and the boys in the P Van were now able to roll up right in front of the location. Whalen and Sgt. Lewis were out in front of 606, watching.

The show was about to start. Santos had rolled right up in front of the building, and Jimmy whipped open the sliding door to the van, the hydro in his hands, and was heading up the stairs—Alba, with a big smile on her face, at the entrance. Charlie had the ram, and, before you knew it, the three of them and Lt. Bilge were taking the stairs to the second floor, with Frank Martin, Tommy Bell, and Lt. Joyce close behind. Jimmy wedged the hydro's metal rods between the doorjamb, hit the "On" switch, and watched the rods expand outward. The wood and metal surrounding the door began to splinter and warp, and then, in his best Jack Nicholson, loud and booming, Jimmy screamed, "Heeeeeeere's Johnny!" Charlie was more direct.

"POLICE, OPEN THE FUCKIN' DOOR, YOU FUCKIN' ASSHOLES."

Out in the back, Al Gavin and Jack Clint could hear the hydro *and* Jimmy, and hear people in the apartment yelling and screaming. They figured if there was product in the apartment, someone would be heading to the bathroom to flush the shit down the toilet. But then, all of a sudden, the bathroom window opened and out came flying what looked like a brick, a kilo, into the courtyard, almost hitting Gavin in the head.

"We got incoming, Al, so keep that helmet on," laughed Clint. "Can't let anything happen to that *cabeza*."

And then, two more! Gavin went over to recover the packages, his head down, when, all of a sudden, Clint yelled at the top of his lungs, "Hey asshole, what do you think you're doing?" to the guy who had just climbed out the window that had no air conditioner and was hanging off the sill in blue shorts, black loafers, and a black, short-sleeved, collared shirt, which was buttoned down the middle. The boys could hear the lads in the apartment screaming various commands.

Jimmy had removed the hydro, and Charlie had used one shot with the ram to completely take down the front door.

Everyone from Team Two was now in the apartment, Frank and Tommy watching the hallway, but in all the excitement, Lt. Joyce had entered the location and headed to the rear bedroom—and that's when he spotted "Pablo" hanging out the window.

"Holly shit," Joyce said.

Out in the back, Al Gavin looked at the perp hanging out the window and yelled, "Please don't fall down and kill yourself. That's way too much paperwork to deal with."

Back in the apartment, the team had conducted a search and had two individuals handcuffed, lying face down in the foyer just off the kitchen, all of them with a clear view into the bedroom, when, all of a sudden, Lt. Joyce charged toward the window, grabbed the hanging perp by the shirt, and screamed, "Hang on, hang on. I got you."

Only he didn't.

Because, by the time Joyce had grabbed the guy by the shirt, he had grown tired and slipped out of his cabana wear, and fallen the two stories, yelling in a heavy Spanish accent, "Oh, nooooooooooooo!"

Jimmy said, to no one in particular, "Oops."

Clint looked up at the window, and Lt. Joyce holding the empty black shirt, looked at the ground and then over to Gavin, and said, "Sometimes, it's good to be rear security and *not* the entry team."

He then got on the radio and said, "Narcotics portable to Central K."

"Go ahead, Narcotics Portable."

"We're going to need a bus at Six Oh Nine, West Hundred and Thirty-Seventh Street, the backyard."

"What's the condition, portable?"

"We got an injured male, Central, took a bit of a fall."

Inside the apartment, by the entrance to the bedroom, Lt. Bilge looked at Jimmy and said, "If this isn't a fine 'How do you do?'"

Jimmy smiled and said, "I thought you were watching him."

Joyce had his head stuck out the window and could see Gavin and Clint kneeling over the moaning perp. He actually looked okay, moving his limbs and all, but when Joyce yelled down and asked how he was doing, Al Gavin looked up and, in all seriousness, yelled back, "He looks all right, Boss, but his upcoming appearance on *Dancing with the Stars* is probably out."

By now, Lt. Joyce was by the window, pacing back and forth and muttering, "It wasn't my fault, it wasn't my fault." The boys were in the back bedroom. Tommy had come in from the hallway just in time to hear Joyce say, "It was an accident. Shit, the guy slipped out of my hands. Nothing I could do, right?"

Tommy said, "Don't worry Loo. Seems like it is all good, and you didn't toss the guy out the window. Shit, all this excitement got me *Jonesing* for a smoke."

"I think I'll wait till I get back to the office, and have a nice cup of coffee and a cigarette while I'm doing paperwork," said Charlie.

"You guys certainly deserve it," added Bilge.

"Seems fair to me," said Jimmy.

"Okay that's enough," yelled Joyce. "I guess I'm picking up what you're laying down. I get it."

\* \* \* \* \*

It turned out to be a monster hit. They had found "The Kilo Fairy," and it was good. The boys wound up recovering five bricks of coke; ten thousand, three hundred and seventeen dollars in U.S. currency; one hundred decks of heroin stamped "TRANSFORMER"; a .357 magnum with a defaced serial number; and had three collars.

Basically Bill had been right on.

And Lt. Joyce *never* broke balls about smoking in the cubicle again.

Jake McNicholas

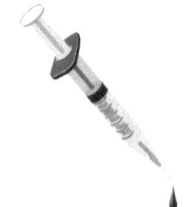

# Chapter 19

Here's what Meg Cassidy had done. Filming was to begin in three weeks, so she rounded up some of her old girlfriends and spent her days eating big lunches and drinking pints of Guinness. They would hit Kennedy's in Breezy Point or cab it over to the Rockaways and spend a leisurely afternoon talking girl talk and laughing like high schoolers at the Wharf, The Bungalow Bar, or Healy's. Often times they would head back and sleep at Meg's house for an adult pajama party her mom and dad loved to host.

The twenty pounds came fast. It was funny, though, because it was noticeable mostly in her face. Her cheeks were definitely fuller and there seemed to be a glow about her, like she was with child, and everyone remarked about it. Meg thought it was a couple of things—*besides* the weight. She was really enjoying being home with her parents—it was great seeing her old friends and being in the neighborhood—and *she* was seeing Artie, and though her Dad wasn't a fan, she was satisfied the way things were going.

It was great news, too, when she learned that the bulk of the location filming for *These Bells Toll* would take place in Elmhurst, Queens. Monarch Studios had bought the rights to a short story that had been published in *The Catholic Writer* about a young woman with health issues teaching inner city children in a Catholic school. Fred Meunch was to direct, and Meg already knew him to say hello.

Meunch was a perfectionist, had read the script, and had known immediately what kind of school would best serve his artistic vision. The head of location scouting was Tom Rye, and Tom had a good feel for what the director needed. There were two major requirements for the school in the movie: a long staircase at the entrance and inside the building; and a small, ratty gym. It took him some time, but he found the spot at St. Bartholomew's in Elmhurst, Queens.

The church on Ithaca Street was beautiful, a testament to the Irish and Italians who had populated the area years ago. Now the parish conducted masses in English, Spanish, Indonesian, and Tagalog, the language of the Philippines. The school itself was on Judge Street, between 43rd Avenue and Ithaca, and, back in the day, was just for girls, the boys attending in a different building on 43rd Avenue. But things had changed, that building being sold off to the city years ago, and now the school on Judge was co-ed and taught approximately three hundred students. There were two Dominican nuns left, but the rest of the staff were mostly young, single women. They loved their jobs—and the kids learned.

Meunch figured they could get the filming done at the school in two weeks, then back to the Silver Cup Studio in Long Island City for interiors. The crew had taken over the entire block, had it lined up with the Marshshark Craft trucks, The Movie Kitchen, Budd Enterprises LTD, with the theatrical lights and equipment, and the movie/TV set, medic vehicle. Meg had a Winnebago parked on 43rd Avenue, adjacent to the park that was across from the school. It wasn't Will Smith's 2.5 million dollar trailer, but it was nice and comfortable.

Meg was playing Lori Wilson, the dedicated teacher who loved her job and the kids, but had suffered a serious illness and could never have children of her own. Harold John was her boyfriend, Pat White, a Wall Street hedge fund guy who was stringing her along while he played the field and cheated clients—cheated them *big time.* In the end, that would be the "ace in the hole" for Lori. She had some evidence linking Pat to a Wall Street Ponzi deal that she never realized she had.

They filmed Meg's big scene, the one that would get her Oscar consideration, according to Artie, at the start of week two. She'd be acting on that big staircase, three quarters up on it and shouting down at Harold John; yelling that if he couldn't understand her passion for the job and her love for the kids, then maybe he should just leave.

Meunch had an easy way about him, and Meg liked him.

"You ready, Meg?" Meunch asked.

"Sure thing. Let's do it."

Meg was dressed in a dark blue pants suit and she mounted the stairs in a pair of shower shoes. At her mark, she put on her black heels, not too high, received a last bit of makeup, and then spotted John at the bottom of the stairs, who smiled and gave her a thumbs-up.

Meunch actually said it, because he liked saying it, "Quiet on the set. Take one. Action!"

Meg: "I have asked you, Pat, to be patient. You know what these kids mean to me, know especially how close I am to them, knowing that I'll never be able to have children of my own. Yes, in many ways it is a calling, but one I wish to share with you for the rest of my life.

John: "I'm moving on, dear. Honestly, I'm pretty tired of your martyr attitude. Never really suited me."

Meg: "You say that to *me?* You say that *now,* after I opened up to you. It was all lies, wasn't it? Your interest in my teaching and sympathy about my health—just some sick method to woo me. Isn't that right?"

John: "Pretty much, honey. I figured you were a real challenge. I was getting laid every night, but I couldn't wait to get into your pants. Take care. You were worth the wait though."

Then Meg looking down, not as a victim, but defiant, hand on her hip and a smile on her mouth, saying in a strong, firm voice echoing off the walls and the staircase: "Shit, Pat, then be off. But remember, I know about the *Corporate Fund.* You mentioned it in your sleep one night. It didn't dawn on me till the other day when I read in the newspapers about the investigation by the US Attorney's Office into Ralph Wilson."

John: "What are you talking about?"

Meg: "Save it, my friend. It really is time to say fucking goodbye."

Oh yeah, it was some hokey shit, but this was Hollywood and, in the end, the whole scene was almost *Gone With The Wind*-ish.

Meunch said, "Absolutely beautiful. That's a wrap

\* \* \* \* \*

The staircase scene was toward the end of the movie, where Lori gets the dump but then finds love with a student's father who just lost his wife.

It was noon, and Meg didn't have to be back on the set until three. She could head back to the Winnebago and relax, or head over to the Movie Kitchen truck and lunch on salad and tuna wraps, but she was actually dying for a slice of pizza. She had a new outfit for her afternoon shoot: shorts, sneakers, and a Mets jersey, so she headed to the Winnebago, made the early change, and told her assistant that she would be back in an hour at the most. Gaining the weight was great, because, unless someone was a rabid fan, no one really recognized her. So she began to take a slow walk down 43rd Avenue, with the park on her right, past Neufeld's Funeral home, crossing Macnish Street, and then coming upon Dandy's Pizzeria, just short of Broadway, opposite the Long Island Railroad.

Jake McNicholas

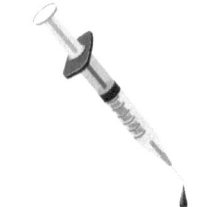

# Chapter 20

What brought Jimmy and Tommy into Corona, Queens was something that had been picked up during a conversation.

The boys were up on a wire, working it from the Drug Enforcement Agency building on 10th Avenue and 17th Street, almost right behind Chelsea Market. It was Tommy's case and the DEA's REDRUM (murder spelled backwards) team was involved, so it was a pretty good deal. DEA had plenty of cash to throw around and access to more equipment and gadgets than you could imagine. They were also providing the Spanish translators monitoring the conversations from the DEA building itself. Someone from the team was occasionally required to spend the tour down there, when the Feds weren't providing coverage, just in case something interesting came up on the wire that required immediate action. If you caught the four-by-twelve tour, you could start work from the field, drive your own car in, and head home from there at the end of the night after you made copies of the call sheets. Or you could go across the street to the Red Rock Tavern, a Hogs and Heifers knock-off, and watch scantily clad gals in boots dance on the bar and pour various shots down the throats of Feds, cops, bikers—and some yuppies.

Marie, the translator, was listening to a conversation between one of the subjects and an unidentified male Hispanic. It wasn't like she could just sit there and listen to *everything*, either. If it didn't involve criminal activity, personal in nature, say, she had to shut it down and come back in later. Minimization. All the time hoping not to miss anything. The subject and the unidentified male Hispanic, JD Cigar, were talking about the Yankees, the pussy on *Telemundo*, and their wives. It wasn't quite as funny as an Organized Crime wire, with the "goombahs" talking about whacking guys for putting too much oregano in the tomato sauce, but it was funny enough.

When Marie started listening again, they were talking business and mentioned a location in Lefrak City. It wasn't time-sensitive, so, when Jimmy and Tommy had a chance, they were going to head into Queens to the building and maybe knock on a door or two. Definitely check the mailboxes and sit on the place for a while.

So, one day, they took a ride out there in the beat-up Chevy, Tommy driving and Jimmy in the passenger seat, over the RFK Bridge that everyone still called the Triboro, and onto the Grand Central Parkway eastbound toward the 108th Street, Long Island Expressway exit. Traffic was moving smoothly past LaGuardia Airport and then came to a complete and utter standstill just past the exit for the Whitestone Expressway.

"I think it's something in the right lane, Tommy," said Jimmy.

"Yeah, it looks like FD."

The Fire Department had two rigs on the scene off to the right, had the trucks angled to block the entire right lane and any room off to the shoulder. Jimmy and Tommy moved slowly now in the first lane parallel to FD that was not blocked. When they got near, Jimmy could see the problem. It wasn't a grass fire, or an overturned vehicle, or even an accident. There were about six guys changing the tire for a twenty-something blond in Daisy Duke shorts, a white halter-top, and killer high heels.

"You got to love these guys," said Tommy.

"I'm actually shocked they're up this late in the afternoon," added Jimmy.

As they rolled slowly past, Jimmy eyeballed one of the firefighters—the most animated one, who was chatting up the blond—and recognized him.

"Ernie Fussell. I should have known. How you been, my friend?"

"Jimmy, God bless you. Living the dream. All is good. Still have the pillow you gave me when I left."

"Be safe, lad, and don't hurt yourself. I know work is hell for you guys."

"Will do."

Tommy eased the car past, and Jimmy filled him in.

"Before you got up to Manhattan North, Tommy, Ernie was on our job and had come up as an undercover. Shit, plenty of white guys getting done, but poor Ernie couldn't fool anyone. Got so bad, he'd be on the set, dealers would actually say 'Hello, officer.' He was about as useless as a female reporter on an NFL sideline. His observation skills were even worse. We're out one day and he's swearing that he just saw a hand-to-hand involving a kilo. Turns out it was one homeless guy handing another homeless guy one of those single-portion, cereal boxes of Fruit Loops. After that, people started calling him *McGoo*."

"Now *that's* some funny shit."

Tommy got off at the LIE exit and now was proceeding on the service road.

"Take a left on 108th Street and then bang your first right. We'll park on this side of the LIE and take the foot bridge over the expressway," Jimmy said. "Won't raise anybody up with the car."

And that's what they did—parked the vehicle, crossed over, and split up. Tommy entered the building, was challenged by the "rent-a-cop," security guard in the lobby, and ID'ed himself. Told the brother he needed to check something out on one of the floors. He took the elevator up to nine, got off, and then came down to the fifth floor and checked the doors of two apartments. He stopped for a smoke up against the window in the stairwell and then returned to nine and took the elevator back down. Who knew what the security guard was up to? Back down in the lobby, he looked at the bank of mailboxes and the building directory. He noted the phone number of the building's management company in his reporter's notebook.

Jimmy was outside, strolling the full block in front of the building. One of the shitheads on the wire had alluded to a bright green, Ford Edge with Jersey plates that was always parked somewhere in front of the location, and, sure enough, he spotted the vehicle close to Junction Boulevard and got the registration information. Twenty-five minutes later, they were heading back across the footbridge to their car.

"You hungry, Tommy?"

"Hell yeah."

"You good with Italian?"

"Sure thing, Jimmy."

"I guess it's Italian."

Jimmy knew Queens. He knew if you were looking for sandwiches, there was only one place to go, and that was Mama's on 104th Street in Corona by St. Leo's. Turkey and mozzarella, or a Mama's Special. Had his mouth watering. If it was pizza you wanted, it was over at Dandy's on 43rd Avenue. The owners were Albanian, but all the food was still authentic Italian.

"Pizza or hero Tommy?"

"Let's go pizza and a cold beer."

Jimmy drove now, and took the scenic route heading over to Queens Boulevard. He made a right and drove westbound past the Queens Center Mall and the White Castle, past the old Macy's, and to Broadway where he made a right. Off to the left was the Post Time Pub where he had had a drink on more than one occasion, and now coming up on the right was the library. Approaching the Long Island Railroad underpass, on the west side, two Asian restaurants, Thai and Chinese; and then, on the opposite side of the street, a 99 Cent Store that was once an old German deli. They drove under the trestle and made the first right onto 43rd Avenue, against the one-way, because there was no traffic. As luck would have it, there was a spot a couple of doors off the front of Dandy's, so they made the U-turn and parked. They went in.

Dandy's was "old school," hadn't been altered in fifty years. There were two huge windows on either side of the door facing the street. The counter and the oven were on the right as you walked in, with a single row of five tables hugging the wall on the opposite side. There was an old painting of Bari, Italy up over the tables, leftover from the days when *real* Italians ran the joint. But the Albanians kept the recipes, and the pizza and meals coming out of the place were still spot on. Once past the front, there was a small back room with a couple of tables before you hit a small prep kitchen.

"Yes sir," Jimmy said. "I'll have two Sicilian, corners please, and a Coors Lite with a cup. What do you want, Tommy?"

"Couple of slices with sausage. Same beer and a cup, too."

The old guy placed the slices in the oven for a couple of minutes to warm up. Then he went back to what he was doing when the boys walked in: making pizza boxes and stacking them on the shelf on the wall to the right of the oven. He had plenty of time—the place was empty.

They took their trays and their beers and walked back to the small room. They sat and faced each other at the table closest to the prep kitchen. Tommy's back was toward the door and Jimmy faced forward to the street. He could see the front door and counter area and most of the tables on his right in front of the restaurant. It was nice and cool in the back, and quiet, just some faint sounds from the Mexican working in the kitchen.

"I'll say this, Tommy. You're the case officer, and this case with DEA works out like we think it will, you're liable to get grade. This whole thing is pretty involved. Got to give credit to Lt. Bilge coming up with the idea and selling it downtown, and it never hurts having the Feds on board—as long as *we're* taking care of our own shit."

"It is a pretty novel approach and nice having you as the assistant case officer," said Tommy. "I mean, opening up our own money order and transfer service operation, *Dinero Mandar*, right up in the Heights, have Dominican UCs from the office run the place, and just sit back and see what happens. 'If you build it, they will come.' Shit, right now we got the money-laundering case with the El Dorado Task Force, multiple subjects involving narcotics distribution—including the Dominican with the kilos from Seaman Avenue. We got the guy trapping-out cars, and, last-but-not-least, the double homicide the Feds are particularly interested in."

"*Plus* the other smaller stuff coming in," added Jimmy. "We'd be looking for an easy twenty-five subjects, if tomorrow was take-down day. That guy from Seaman, I think his name is Acosta, he turned out to be a real pain in the ass to ID."

"You used a radio car, didn't you?"

"Yeah, me and Charlie. We borrowed one from the Three-Four, got some collar brass and headed over by Seaman. Charlie had me laughing. Said as long as we were in uniform it would be a complete and utter waste if we didn't head south of Ninety-Sixth Street and go for a sit-down."

"And the free—or *discounted*—meal," laughed Tommy."

"If you remember, we had information that the Domo would exit a particular building on Seaman at approximately thirteen hundred."

"I think my CI gave me that."

"Well, this day, he comes out, jumps in a livery, and we're able to pull over the car on Tenth Avenue. Told them we were investigating a gunpoint robbery. He had a piece of mail on him with his name and apartment number. It was as easy as that."

Tommy finished his slices and beer. "I'm heading down the block, see if I can't find a store for my smokes and Lotto numbers. You need anything?"

"No, I think I'll go for another slice. The sausage you had looked good. I'll meet you by the car."

He got another slice and sat back in his seat, when the bell on the front door gave a little ring and a pretty girl in shorts and a Lucas Duda Mets jersey walked in. Tall glass of water, with long brown hair tied up in a ponytail that came out of the back of the hat where you adjust it. Deep blue eyes he could see from his seat. In her late twenties maybe. She ordered up a slice and soda from the fountain and sat facing the street, back to Jimmy, with her cell phone on the table in front of her.

Then, the door opened again and in walked a couple of twenty-year-old white boys, low slung pants, and sideways baseball hats, "wiggers," what some people call them. Being loud, pushing and shoving. Couple of assholes, Jimmy thought.

"Hey, old man! How 'bout a couple of fuckin' slices?" said the shorter of the two, wearing *The Walking Dead* T-Shirt.

His partner in the "Video Games Are My Life, Get Over It" shirt said, "Sometime today" and then fixated on the girl and continued, "What do we have here? Like Duda, do you? I got a little *Duda* for you."

She had her head down, trying to ignore them, but now that the other guy was in the game, they were double-teaming her, hovering and being stupid—and then Jimmy was in the doorway with his arms folded.

Walking Dead guy said, "What do you want, asshole?"

And then Jimmy said to the old-timer behind the counter, "Sir, would you please dial nine-one-one, and have them send two ambulances to this location? Have them put a rush on it."

Walking Dead and Video guy didn't know what to do. They looked at each other and mumbled something under their breath, all the swagger gone now, gave Jimmy the finger, and then left. Jimmy walked over to the table and said, "You okay? They were a couple of jerks, weren't they?"

"Sure were," the girl said, and smiled this big, wonderful smile that lit up her face. She looked beautiful just sitting there, looking up at Jimmy, a bit of tomato sauce on the corner of her mouth, and Jimmy did the "finger gesture" indicating something was there. She smiled again, then giggled and reached across the table for a napkin and said, "You just can't take me anywhere. Thanks again."

"My pleasure," said Jimmy, and he could see Tommy outside leaning up against the car, on the phone.

"I'm Jimmy McTigue." He put out his hand and she took it in hers, soft and warm with a firm grip, and she said, "Glad to meet you, Jimmy McTigue. I'm Meg . . . Wilson," and smiled again.

Then, Jimmy looking down at the remnants of her pizza and surprising himself by saying, "A Sicilian corner. I *knew* you were special," and Meg Wilson coming right back with, "My hero wouldn't be eating anything different."

And then he got that funny feeling deep down in his stomach.

He carried business cards on him at all times indicating that he was an NYPD Narcotic's Detective, but, instead of handing her one of them, he reached across the table, grabbed a napkin, and wrote down his name and phone number.

"If you ever need a helping hand," and gave it to her, and she said with that smile again, "Thanks, Jimmy."

They walked out the front door together and Jimmy asked, as he gave Tommy a head nod, "Can we give you a lift anywhere?"

"No thanks, Jimmy. Just heading over a couple of blocks."

"Well, see you, Meg Wilson," and Jimmy threw Tommy the keys and walked over to the passenger side. Tommy dropped them and reached to pick them up, and then Meg Wilson turned to give Jimmy McTigue one last, little wave, still sporting that smile, the freckles dancing on her face.

In the car, Tommy said, "She looked familiar. Did you give her your phone number?"

"Yeah, what's the big deal?" replied Jimmy. "I've done it before."

"Nuns don't count," Tommy laughed, and they were off.

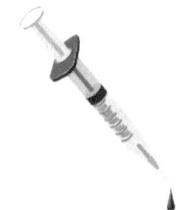

# Chapter 21

She saw the old man behind the counter making pizza boxes and putting them on the shelf behind him.

"Can I have a Sicilian, corner please, and a Diet Pepsi from the fountain?"

"Just a moment, young lady," as he opened up the oven and checked the contents. "Fresh pie will be out in a minute. You want ice in the soda?"

"Yes, please."

She checked her phone and saw a text from Artie asking how the filming was going. She tried calling back, but it went straight to voicemail. That had been happening a lot lately. The pizza man took the fresh Sicilian out of the oven, cut it in squares and put the slice and soda on a tray and said, "Enjoy, young lady, there are napkins on the table" and went back to folding boxes. Meg walked over to the table and sat down.

Then two guys coming in, loud and cursing, giving her a hard time and making here feel really uncomfortable. She was trying to ignore them, her head bent down to the phone, when a sudden change in attention and the voice of someone else; and then looking up and seeing this big guy, sandy hair and a three-day growth on his face, with arms folded, in the back doorway, telling the pizza guy to call an ambulance; and Meg figuring out immediately what he meant—and relaxing.

The two guys went out the door, and the guy came over and put her at ease, and she laughed when he pointed out that she had sauce on the side of her mouth. He introduced himself and they shook hands, and hers felt comfortable in his, and then she said to this Jimmy McTigue, "I'm Meg Wilson"—not sure at first why she used her character's name, but then thinking, yeah, it would be nice not to be "The Movie Star."

He gave her his number on a napkin and she remembered him saying, "If you ever need a helping hand"—corny, but Meg Cassidy liked him right off the bat.

They walked out the front door together and he asked if she needed a ride. He was with a black guy leaning up on a car, and she said "No," and then he said, "Well I'll see you, Meg Wilson."

She headed toward the school, glanced back and saw this Jimmy McTigue toss the car keys to the black guy, saw the black guy drop them, and then watched as he bent down to the sidewalk, the momentary glimpse of handcuffs hanging off his belt.

*Is Jimmy McTigue a cop?* she asked herself.

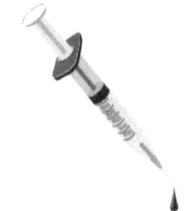

# Chapter 22

Some years back, when Jimmy McTigue first got to Manhattan North, he participated in the search warrant that resulted in Earl Hogan getting shot.

It was, up to that time, the most incredible thing he had ever seen since becoming a cop. What the operation consisted of was the simultaneous execution of some twenty warrants on West 161st Street between Broadway and Amsterdam Avenue.

Billy Gallagher was the case officer, and his preparation practices were legendary. Of course, surprise was the key because the block was full of lookouts, both on foot and riding bikes, so Gallagher's plan had to be creative. And he had a flair for the dramatic.

Dave McMahon was working in Manhattan North at the time and he was a member of the NYPD Pipes and Drums, the largest police pipe band in the world. Their job was simple enough—send members of the service that have been killed in the line of duty home to be with God. No band did it better. Gallagher asked Dave if he wanted to do something special during the search warrants, and he said, "Anything you want."

So McMahon and Earl Hogan get a couple of Con Edison helmets and some blue shirts and they got into the building on the corner of West 161st Street and Broadway from the back entrance. McMahon is toting his bagpipes in a big black box that can easily pass as some sort of tool carrier. They get up there and wait for the word.

And while they were getting in place, just about every member of Manhattan North Narcotics was mustering up in front of the Armory. It got so crazy that a few guys who were on limited duty, and were limping around on canes, were out there in their raid jackets, too.

They had Tommy Santiago and Oscar Triago dressed-down and in the cab of a U-Haul truck, and they stuck about twenty guys from the office in the back, armed with firearms, rams, crowbars, and other equipment. They closed the door and then packed a regular city bus with the rest of the crew.

Right about when the U-Haul was ready to make the turn off Amsterdam and head west on West 161st Street, McMahon hit up his pipes and started playing *Garryowen*, and every swinging dick on the street looked toward the heavens. The truck stopped at the end of the block and the door flew open, and then right behind it, a city bus full of guys and gals from the office. The block didn't know what hit it.

McMahon and Hogan were heading down the stairwell when the cavalry were eighty-four, on the scene, and taking over the block, when they surprised a dealer heading to the roof carrying a "Saturday Night Special" in his hand. He panicked, the gun went off, and Earl gets shot in the leg. But they collar the asshole and walk him down the stairs anyway.

The Job asks Earl where he wants to go, and he says the Joint Terrorist Task Force.

* * * * *

Jimmy was sitting in the cubicle typing up a DD-5 in regards to a kite that described narcotics activity on the corner of West 145th Street and St. Nick. He had conducted surveillance on the location during various tours, and, on several occasions, had an undercover make a couple of buy attempts with negative results. So, he was closing out the kite as unfounded, when he heard his name called.

"Jimmy McTigue, how are you, my dear friend? Still banging away as a Narco Ranger, aren't you?"

"Earl, my God, how are you?"

Jimmy got up and they embraced, and then he made the introductions to the crew in the cubicle.

"How's the leg?"

"It's okay. No more running for me. And I miss the basketball. We used to have *some* games in the back on down days. You couldn't shoot for shit, but you were an animal on the boards. How are things here?"

"Good," Jimmy said, waving his hands to encompass the boys. "Got a great team, having laughs, and we're taking it to them. And we're still chasing the Kilo Fairy. How's JTTF?"

"Busy, bro'. Just got back from Africa. And I have to admit that I didn't know anything when I got to the unit. I have learned *so* much. Of course there is shit I can't talk about, but that doesn't matter. Early on, I had to do a presentation regarding some activity in Brooklyn, and all I used was public information, stuff you get from the papers—or Googling. You listen to the President or Joe Biden—or anyone in Homeland Security—and all they do is lie to you. I still get crazy every time I think about these assholes trying to tell us with a straight face that some Middle Eastern shithead, screaming *Allahu Akbar* and mowing down our troops, was pissed off at work because he didn't get a full hour for lunch. Work place violence my ass."

He was actually getting a little worked up, and Jimmy could see it. The typing in the cubicle and area around it had stopped now, and guys from Sgt. Lewis's team and some other detectives came over to listen. Jack Clint and Al Gavin were already there.

"I read an article in the *News* by this guy Awad, from CAIR, attacking Peter King, and I find out that this shithead used to be associated with the Islamic Association of Palestine. FBI and Treasury linked the outfit to Hamas. In ninety-three, Awad was in Philly exchanging pleasantries with big-time leaders from Hamas and the Holy Land Foundation."

"I seem to remember the Feds going after the Holy Land crew."

"Right you are, Jimmy. Glad you're keeping up. Still reading the *Wall Street Journal* and *National Review*? Anyway, they were convicted in oh-eight of plotting to send millions to Palestinian terrorists. But forget about *that* shit. Just look at a couple of spots in Brooklyn. The *Daily News* had a piece. In two thousand ten, before our beloved Seal Team Six whacked Bin Laden, he had named this fuck, Adan Shukrijumjan to be his number-two man. And that guy's old man used to be an *imam* at the Al Farouq Mosque on Atlantic Avenue, over there by the new Barclays Center. And the scumbag also served as a translator for the blind fuckin' Sheik Omar Abd-Al-Rahman. Shit, you remember that crazy Jew, Meir Kahane? Well, this guy, El Sayyid Nosair, shot and killed him in nineteen ninety, and *he* had an office at the Al Farouq.

"The government doesn't want you to know any of this shit," said Richie Whalen. "As long as nobody out there is wishing anybody a Merry Christmas, they're happy."

"You guys need to be careful and need to be vigilant," said Earl. "You remember that poor Yeshiva kid in the van got blasted on the Brooklyn Bridge? Turns out the 'camel jockey' who did the blasting was at the Islamic Society of Bay Ridge earlier in the day, where the *imam* was talking smack about the Jews. And the Al Taqwa Mosque over on Bedford and Fulton— the *imam* over there was a character witness for the blind sheik."

"Man, thanks for opening our eyes, Earl," said Jimmy. "You know how it is, got a bit of tunnel vision in Narcotics."

"Just be safe. I don't have to tell you that if it wasn't for us, the cops, the savages would win whether it's terrorism *or* crime. That's the god's honest truth, no matter what the asshole mayor says. And we certainly can't depend on the Feds. I mean, who they going to send to help us, *Lois Lerner*? You guys need anything, let me know. Don't ever hesitate to ask. Square shit . . . working up here was still the best time I ever had on the job."

"Where's the next trip?" asked Jimmy.

"Heading to Gitmo Wednesday to conduct some interviews."

"So long, Earl, and God bless," said Jimmy.

"Give em hell." said Charlie Defranco.

"Fuck that waterboarding, Earl. Just make those crackers watch a couple of hours of *The View*, and they be giving up *everything*," said Bobby Washington.

And then Earl limped off.

Jake McNicholas

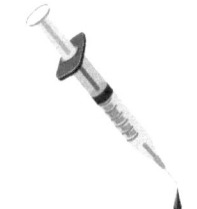

# Chapter 23

**For four Fridays in a row,** Artie found himself in a makeshift music studio, off the corner of Farmers and Guy Brewer Boulevards, and down the block from the old Owl Tavern where airline employees, ZMT operators, and mail handlers from the air mail facility at Kennedy used to drink, and eat pizza.

It was on the second floor of a two-story building, the first floor occupied by a cargo outfit that was doing business out at JFK. There was a parking lot for the premise, off to the right, with a high, wooden fence that obstructed the view of the vehicles inside—meaning the cops from the One-Thirteen couldn't see in.

What brought Artie out there was the latest gangsta rap "phenom," who he wanted to be "representing." Oh yeah, he was going to be making money, but he was also into the whole scene: the pussy, the brothers, and the weed. By the second Friday, he had the contracts drawn up and signed, and everyone at the studio was referring to Artie as "my nigga."

The studio itself was wide open on the left, once you came up the stairs to the second floor. There were tables laid out with all sorts of equipment: the MacBook Pro computer; the digital, audio workstation; the audio interface with the digital conversation; mic pre-amps; DI boxes; and the headphone amps. They had two types of microphones: dynamic and ribbon, and three microphone stands set off to the side. There were a couple of studio monitors, and audio cable was everywhere.

Tucked in on the right side of the floor was a large, windowed conference room that had a long wooden table smack down the middle. Off to the sides, up against the walls, were couches and cushioned chairs.

The table was a mess. It was covered with ashtrays and half-smoked joints; bottles of cognac and *Dos Equis*; cans of Red Bull; buckets of KFC; half-eaten cartons of Chinese food; boxes of Dutch Masters cigars; bags of Lays potato chips; and Cheez Doodles. The smell of marijuana was overpowering.

Artie had signed up the "new gangsta," Terrance Byrd, on the second Friday. He knew Byrd was on the verge of a big offer from Columbia, the same outfit that had just signed LA rapper, "Homey Jones." Byrd's latest was being played by all the Hip Hop stations across the country. His gangsta rap name was Sweet Pea Poon.

Street-cred-wise, he was from the Polo Ground Projects uptown. He had been collared twice for pitching yellow-top, crack vials in "the 'hood," and had done a two-year stretch up in Shawangunk Correctional in Wallkill, New York for a second robbery with a gun.

Artie was no expert, but he figured there was a gang affiliation with the Crips, the studio accommodating twenty or twenty-five "homeboys" every Friday, all wearing something blue. Most times, it was baseball hats turned sideways.

But Artie was digging everything. The brothers were treating him real good after contract time, and the weed was absolutely spectacular. And the broads. He had already taken a shine to a Beyonce lookalike named Tabisha. First Friday out, she had taken his hand and led him to the ladies room, where she sat on the toilet and had Artie face her. Unzipped his Dockers. Just then, the cell rang and it was Meg, and he was about to ignore it—considering the circumstances—when Tabisha whispered, "No, baby I want you to take that call while I show you some of my magic."

He took the call and the whole scenario nearly blew off the top of his head, but shit, a stiff dick has no conscience.

Couple of minutes later, Artie is out by the sound equipment, ready to listen to Poon's latest.

"You gonna love this shit, my man. Some of my best stuff. Calling it 'Never Enough Hair Pie.' " And then the microphone up sideways to his mouth, Poon with his Giants baseball hat sideways, and his hand squeezing his balls singing:

> *"I bees rich,*
> > *With my go to bitch.*
> *Please, nigga, please,*
> > *Ain't no steady squeeze.*
> *Got to much dough,*
> > *For just one ho.*
> *I be pimping and dealing,*
> > *Offing and stealing . . .*

"What you think my man?"

"Shit sounds good to me," replied Artie, firing up another Philly blunt.

"Make us plenty of scratch," said Poon. "I be needing just as much as that West Coast gangsta, Homey Jones, be making."

"I'll be sitting down with Columbia in a couple of days," Artie said. "It's going to be *all* good."

All the hangers on, all the comings and goings, Artie had a hard time figuring out who was who. Shit, they were all dressed in the same uniform: the hats; the oversized T-shirts; the low-riding jeans; the "monster gold" around the neck. Early on, Poon introduced him to one particular brother, though, stockier than the rest, only guy wearing a Kansas City Royals baseball hat.

"This here be Slice," Poon said. "This is my brother, my main nigga, Artie. He speaks for me. What's mine is his and what's his is mine."

Artie could tell right off the bat that Slice had "juice," and he appreciated the way he was treating him.

So it wasn't crazy when, one Friday, Slice came to Artie and asked, "Let me hold onto your wheels for a bit. No need to be worryin', ain't transporting anything, and no other niggas in the car 'cept me. Taking a quick trip to Brooklyn."

"Just be careful," said Artie, and he lit up another joint.

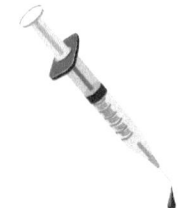

# Chapter 24

One Friday, Aiman Qantan decided to leave Juan, the Mexican, running the grill, in charge of the store, and take a trip over to Brooklyn and help celebrate his cousin Salah's birthday.

He didn't get to see his first cousin much, but he was always fond of him, and so he drove over to Salah's one-bedroom, basement apartment near Bedford and Atlantic Avenue, not too far from the Men's Shelter.

The two of them would have a feast on this Friday. Salah had spent days purchasing the traditional food from various *Halal* stores in the neighborhood. They spread out, facing each other on either side of a small, area rug, and began the meal with *maraq*, the lamb broth soup that Aiman had missed so much. His Puerto Rican wife wasn't making any of this. They shared salad with yogurt and tomato dressing, and feasted on *salta*, the brown, meat stew with chilies, garlic, and tomatoes that was served in a spice-rich salsa, all the while washing it down with red tea made from ground cardamom. There was the wonderful Yemeni restaurant on Court Street, across from Trader Joe's, called Al-Wahda, where Salah purchased the *malawah* bread, layered and folded in butter, and used to eat the meal.

They reminisced and talked of home and family and this strange country where they had settled. Aiman had roots here now and it pleased him to see his young children thriving in school.

The day went quickly, and soon it was the call for evening prayer, and so Salah suggested the small mosque not far from his residence.

The *imam* was an African-American gentleman, fluent in Arabic and knowledgeable in the *Koran*. But he troubled Aiman. He began to speak of the terrible tragedy that had been Katrina years ago, but rather than lament the loss of life, chose instead to blame the people of New Orleans, to call the victims infidels and rage that the death and destruction that had they suffered was deserved. He said all the lands of the Jew and the infidel would someday soon meet the same fate.

After prayer, Aiman and Salah remained in the front of the Mosque chatting. By now, the *imam* had stepped out of the location, and Aiman watched as he went off to the side, near the street, and approached a bright red Escalade. And then he watched as a male Black, wearing a Kansas City Royals baseball hat, exited the vehicle—the same man who had been present at his store a few years ago and tried to rob him.

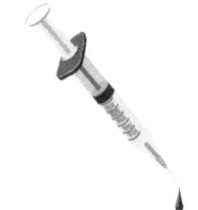

# Chapter 25

"Jimmy."

"Yeah, Tommy."

"What do tits and martinis have in common?"

"I don't know, Tommy."

"One's not enough, and three is too many."

They were sitting in the Cuckoo's Nest, a bar on Woodside Avenue in Queens, past 10:00 AM on a Sunday morning—with the time difference, it was early morning—drinking and viewing rugby at the pub. Ireland was playing England in Aviva Stadium in Dublin, Lansdowne having been leveled years ago.

Tommy was a bachelor for the week. His wife, Michele, and his two daughters had made the trip south to Macon, Georgia to see his in-laws, so Jimmy picked him up at his house in Queens Village and told him they were going for breakfast. They sat down in the diner on the corner of 61st Street and Roosevelt Avenue and went Irish—eggs, black pudding, Irish bacon, and tomato and baked beans. Then they walked to the bar.

Tommy was nursing a Bloody Mary. Jimmy was already on his second Guinness. The place was packed with guys and gals, all rooting for Ireland and a bit dismayed since England scored two quick tries and was up, 14-0.

"Awful lot of white people in here, Jimmy." Tommy was roaring when he said it.

"No problem, Tommy. Anyone asks you, just say you're from the West of Ireland."

"Why's that?"

"Late fifteen hundreds, the Spanish Armada with over a hundred ships was set to invade England. Sir Francis Drake and the British fleet repelled them and sent the fleet back to Spain. The Armada took the route over the tip of Scotland to get back, and heavy storms battered what was left. Some of the ships were lost off the coast of Ireland. Guys swam to shore."

"What's that got to do with me?"

"You're Irish and you're a little darker, hairy like me, they say you're *Black* Irish. My people were from Mayo. Just say that your ancestors were from Sligo."

"And someone is going to *believe* that?'

"Of course not."

"Why?"

"Everybody knows you 'brothers' can't swim. Relax, partner, this crowd is just looking to have a good time. They call it *craic*, like 'That was great craic.' And, no, not *that* kind either. It's all good. It's not like the place is packed with brothers. Five minutes, there would have been shots fired."

They took sips of their drinks and looked at the television behind the bar. Jimmy tried to explain the game.

"All you really need to know is that there are fifteen guys to a side and there is no blocking. And you can't throw the ball forward."

"What I'm really trying to figure out is how you drink that stuff," Tommy said nodding toward the Guinness. "Tried that out of the bottle once, damn near killed me. Give me an Olde English 800 anytime."

Then, Tommy was laughing and pointing to the sign behind the bar by the register, "Will you look at that? Man, that says it all."

The sign read: "*HAPPY HOUR 11:00 AM to 8:00 PM.*"

"We have been known to have a terrible thirst" and Jimmy took a long pull on the Guinness leaving residue in his mustache.

The beautiful County Cavan girl behind the stick, with the dirty blond hair and the lovely smile, came up and asked, "Lads, you need another, it's on me." She used to make Jimmy's heart skip a beat, but who knew what was going on inside her head. Tommy switched to a Smithwick's, after she told him it was light, but Jimmy was sticking with the dark stuff. Just then, the Irish tighthead prop executed a scissor pass with a second row forward that went forty yards for a try.

On the television from Dublin, and in the bar, the crowds were singing *The Fields of Athenry.*

After forty minutes and halftime, England led, 14-7.

Tommy went out to the front to have a smoke and make a phone call.

There was an old-timer in the corner, who gave Jimmy the nod, and pretty soon the Cavan girl was back and said, "Ah, pet, yer man would like to have a shot with you." He went with Jameson, and raised his glass, and the old man looked Jimmy right in the eye and said, "To your Dad. May God bless his soul."

The second half started up.

"Michele and the kids send their love. I will tell you the best thing about being with you. Michele never has a problem with it. Doesn't matter what we're doing, or what time I get home, she knows if I'm with you I'm not chasing tail or getting into trouble. I swear to God, if she had to do it over again, she'd marry you."

"Have another drink and watch the game."

It was an Irish scrum, mid-field—and they won it and pushed the pack some twenty yards. Then, the number eight grabbed the ball and went weak side, split two defenders, executed a blind pass to the wing forward, and it was off to the races. It was tied, 14-14, with the points after.

"You know, this is some good stuff to watch," said Tommy, "*and* I'll be in bed by two PM."

"I'll even tuck you in."

And then Jimmy's cell vibrated, the Kyocera flip phone everyone made fun of. He pulled it out of his pocket and looked at the name corresponding with the number and saw that it was Aiman. That was odd. It had been a couple of years since the incident at his deli, and Jimmy had rarely seen him since. He was trying to keep the Vytorin dosage to 10 mgs, so he had been avoiding the bacon, egg, and cheese sandwiches. He motioned with the phone to Tommy and headed out the door. He had missed the call, but hit "Talk."

"Hello, Aiman, my friend. What's new?

"Mr. Jim, I hope I am not bothering you."

"Not at all."

"I have seen something very strange on Friday, in Brooklyn, and it concerns and troubles me. At evening prayer. I would feel much more comfortable if I could address you face to face. Will I be able to see you?"

"Where are you now?"

"I am at the store."

"Give me thirty minutes and I'll be up there."

"I will be here. Thank you, Mr. Jim."

Tommy came out of the bar ahead of the crowd.

"What happened?" Jimmy asked.

"This medium-sized Irish guy was running in front of the goal posts and he throws the ball on the ground and then he kicks the sucker and somehow the ball went flying through the uprights and the whistle sounded and everyone went crazy."

"That's a drop kick. We win."

"Great, home to bed."

"Not quite. I got a call from The Terrorist. We're heading uptown and you're driving."

Jake McNicholas

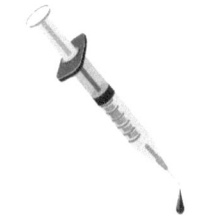

# Chapter 26

They shot across Roosevelt Avenue, Tommy driving, to Queens Boulevard, and up over the 59th Street Bridge—no one, absolutely *no* one, calling it "The Ed Koch," after the former mayor. They were listening to the Jets-Patriots pre-game on the radio.

"Here's the latest, Tommy. Patriots got caught stealing the toilet paper out of the visiting team's locker room."

"I know you're bullshitting, Jimmy, but I wouldn't put it past them."

There was no traffic now, it being Sunday. Tommy hopped on the FDR northbound, then to the Harlem River Drive, and off at the first exit. They were up on Fifth Avenue and The Terrorist in twenty minutes.

Aiman had a small room in the back of the store, with a beat-up, brown desk and a couple of milk crates for chairs. There were cases of soda stacked from floor to ceiling, piles of toilet tissue, and a few cases of baby formula left over from the bad old days. There was a painting of Mecca on the back wall.

On top of the desk, papers, and envelopes, unopened mail, and a checkbook were strewn about. There were also three, framed pictures of children, a girl and two boys, smiling and looking right at the camera, wearing what looked to be school uniforms.

Jimmy was sitting on one of the milk crates. Aiman came in and handed him a cup of coffee and a Bear Claw, and sat on the other crate. The immigrant storeowner and the cop just shooting the shit—and then, they got to it.

"I love it here in my new country, Mister Jim. For my children especially," and he pointed to the photos. "Coming here gave them a future."

"Aiman, you are just like the immigrants of the past. You want to do better for your family. You have much in common with my grandfather, who left his home in Ireland forever and came to America for a better life. You will see it in your kids. And remember this. You got a friend in this department. We are here to protect the *good* people, and that means you and your family."

"Yes, Mister Jim, I understand, and that is why I have called you. I was in Brooklyn for the late prayer on Friday with my cousin at the Suleiman Mosque on Atlantic Avenue."

Jimmy had his reporter's notebook out.

"The *imam*, his name is Rasheed, an American Black man. He blamed that horrible storm years ago, Katrina, on the victims."

"He actually *said* that during prayer?"

"Yes. He said the people of New Orleans were infidels, and they deserved the death and destruction that they suffered. But what was even stranger, Mister Jim, was *after* the service. He met another Black American, and it was the same one who stood by the door in my shop when you helped me—the man in the Kansas City Royals hat."

"You're sure? You are *absolutely* positive? That is strange. I really can't believe the asshole is out on the street."

"Yes, and he was in a car, a bright red Escalade."

"You didn't get the license plate, by chance, did you?"

"No, but if it helps, there was a sticker on the bumper that read 'Hillary Is the One'."

"She certainly is, but one of what? I don't know."

\* \* \* \* \*

Yeah, they were off, but, shit, they were uptown anyway, so Jimmy and Tommy decided to head over to the office. And it was crowded. Some "bean counter" at One Police Plaza had gotten the bright idea in his head that half the teams in Narcotics should now be off on Tuesdays and Wednesdays, in order to increase activity on Saturday and Sunday. The numbers on the weekends didn't change, but the narcotics activity for the middle of the week was now off the hook. The dealers figured Tuesday and Wednesday were now good days for selling, and they took advantage of the opportunity.

First thing Jimmy did when he sat at his computer was run the arrest activity for the address of Aiman's store. There were only two incidents of police enforcement—a collar for domestic violence, six years ago; and the robbery—the arrests that he had handed over to Patrol, a couple of years ago. He scanned the information on the arrest paperwork, and, sure enough, the arresting officer had taken the time to indicate what the perps were wearing—and *one* of them was wearing a Kansas City Royals baseball hat. The arrest sheet read:

NAME: Robert Bolt

ADDRESS: 2975 Eighth Avenue Apt. 2C
DOB: 07/15/77
HEIGHT: 5'10"
WEIGHT: 180
HAIR: Black
EYES: Black
NICKNAME: Slice
SCARS AND TATTOOS: Blue Dog, written on right bicep.

Robert Bolt had quite the criminal record. He had been collared on multiple occasions, but had been clean since he was picked up for the robbery. For some reason, that case was now sealed and Robert was out. He had been arrested three times for drug possession, and had taken two collars for sale in the Seven-Five in Brooklyn North. Jimmy ran him through NYSPIN (New York State Police Information System). No registered vehicles.

He brought up the "brother" with the gun, LA Dodger. *No shit, that's right.* Now he remembered! Un-fucking-believable. Dude's name was actually Winston Salem. But Jimmy found out that old Winston was still languishing out on Riker's Island, lifting weights and getting strong, so no chance he was out and about.

He had a code to enter the database that provided photos of individuals arrested by the NYPD. Gone were days when you had to head down to the basement at One Police Plaza to secure a picture. By using Bolt's NYSID (New York State Identification Number) number he was able to bring up the photo from the robbery arrest.

One down.

Then, he merely went to the Internet and Google. He punched in Brooklyn, Suleiman Mosque, and Rasheed, together. Sure enough, the mosque came up, and it indicated that the *imam* was named Rasheed Abdullah.

He Googled Rasheed Abdullah and came across a *New York Post* article that profiled him. Turns out that Abdullah was once known as Melvin Barnes. He had done time for robbery, upstate at Shawangunk Correctional. During his eleven years of incarceration, he converted to Islam.

"It was one of the most spectacular transformations I have ever witnessed," said Warden Mike Servino in the article. "During his incarceration, Mr. Barnes has learned Arabic, embraced his new religion, and has become a new man."

Barnes' NYSID number provided a photo.

\* \* \* \* \*

Jimmy and Tommy were back in the store, and Aiman took a look at the two photos.

"Yes, Mister Jim, that is them."

And then, in the Jeep, with the music on, and heading back to Queens.

"Listen Tommy, I forgot to tell you. We're golfing at the Brooklyn North Detective's outing at Clearview, Thursday. Me, you, Charlie, and the Sarge.

"I can't golf," Tommy said. "Besides, I don't even have clubs."

"You're going. I'm supervising you while Michele's away. I'm lefty, your lefty. That solves that. You'll see guys you know, and it will be great laughs. I'll drive the cart, you relax. It will be *Driving Miss Daisy*, and you'll be Miss Daisy

"Where to now, Jimmy?

"I'm tucking you into bed, Tommy.  Like I said, Michele told me to keep an eye on you."

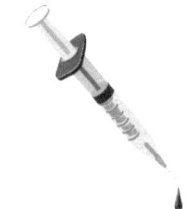

# Chapter 27

The phone rang.

"McTigue."

"Jimmy boy, it's Rick from Roll call."

"I know, Rick."

"How come you always know it's me?"

"Because, as I have told you before, you sound just like Ed Norton from *The Honeymooners*."

"Oh, yeah. Jimmy boy, listen up. I got notifications for tomorrow's Mets game. Yanks are in. You, Bell, Defranco, and Whalen. Sixteen hundred report time."

"That's good," Jimmy said. "Rick, do you know if we can still park up on the grass and under the trees by the service road to the Whitestone Expressway?"

"Hold on." Jimmy could hear him drop the phone and walk away from the desk.

"I just asked Alba, and she says yeah and hello."

He was now thinking of Alba in the flowery dress and her voice over the kell singing "There is a Rose in Spanish Harlem" during the search warrant.

"Okay, Rick, thanks. I'll let the boys know. They're right here. Give my best to Alba."

Jimmy yelled over to Sgt. Quinn, "Me, Charlie, Tommy, and Richie got the Mets game tomorrow." And the Boss waved okay.

"I was there earlier in the season," Jimmy said. "Make sure you got your memo books and a couple of summonses. Inspections have really been breaking balls."

"I was at the marathon a couple of years ago," said Charlie. "Must have been eighty-five degrees. It's Narcotics, Warrants, Manhattan North, and Brooklyn North standing in formation in the hot sun. Two young females from Inspections, black chick, about four foot eleven, and her partner, a white chick, who towered over her at five one. Anyway, they come over to this real hair bag from the Six-Seven, huge guy with time on, looks like he hasn't shaved in a week, and the tiny black chick asks him if he has his orange reflector belt. After a couple of drops of sweat rolled off the front of his hat and onto the pink cell phone she was holding in her hand, the girls thought better of it and did the skedaddle."

"I was up at the Stadium, one year, with Dave McMahon, who's in the Pipe Band," said Jimmy. "He looked like George Armstrong Custer. Monster 'stache. Guy from Inspections told him his mustache shouldn't extend past the corners of his mouth. This was three weeks after the line of duty for Officer Diaz. Everyone knew who McMahon was. Must have been thirty cops that told the guy from Inspections to go fuck himself. Made me proud."

"I ain't never going back in the bag," said Bobby Washington. "Bone smuggling cops sucking dick, guy can't have a decent-sized mustache."

"Tommy, I'll get you at your house. You want to meet there, Charlie?"

Charlie said, "I'll take my own car."

Richie Whalen lived Upstate.

Jimmy went back into the room, which could hold twenty-five lockers comfortably, but was crammed with forty. He got his 2004 Houston All-Star Game gym bag, and placed his shoes, gun belt, and memo book, sans holder, inside. He then took a short-sleeve shirt, already adorned with OCCB collar brass, and pinned his "dupe" shield and nameplate with commendations on it. He grabbed his hat, and hung his nightstick, the old fashioned wooden one he loved to twirl, over the hanger that held his uniform pants. The shield number was that of his father.

Back outside by his desk, he said, "Tommy, I'll get you at twelve thirty. I've got the cooler covered. Richie, Charlie, park over by the tree. Don't worry about food. Me and Tommy will hit Mamma's before we get over to the park."

\* \* \* \* \*

In order to get the good spot by the tree, you had to get there early. Jimmy was off Braddock Avenue by twelve fifteen. Tommy came out of the house in his hat, uniform pants, and a Mets T-shirt, carrying a gym bag in one hand with his gun belt and his shirt, and his nightstick in the other hand. Dressed-down like Jimmy. He put the equipment in the Jeep and returned to the house. He came back out carrying a coffee mug, locked the side door, and jumped in the front seat.

"Here's something Michele and the girls got you when we went to Disney. Keep forgetting to bring it in." He handed him the mug that read, "Uncle Jimmy."

"What's in it?"

"Irish tea. Lyons. Michele thought it would be a treat."

"She's a real keeper, Tommy."

One Hundred Fourth Street and Forty-Sixth Avenue, Corona. Mamma's block was crowded. There were two radio cars, one fire truck, a Con Ed truck, and a couple of unmarked cars, all in the general vicinity. That wasn't taking into account the sanitation trucks and Verizon vans down on the side streets.

Jimmy parked over by St. Leo's, and Tommy stayed in the Jeep with the firearms. There would be four of them plus the boss, to whom they would be assigned at the game. For sandwich purposes, he ordered five Mama's Specials, two meatballs, two turkey specials, three salamis with provolone, and a couple of tunas—plus a couple for after the game and what they would eat now. Tommy, with the gym bags, met Jimmy in the bakery a couple of doors down from the deli, and they ate in the back room with a dozen other guys. Then they iced down the beers and headed for the trees and the grass.

They got lucky. Charlie was already there, sitting in a beach chair, sunning himself.

"Any sign of Richie?"

"He's about a half hour out. George Washington Bridge traffic."

Twenty-five minutes later, Richie rolled up. They got dressed and were down by Gate E by 3:45 PM.

Four fifteen, most of the stragglers had arrived, and an inspector from Queens South addressed the troops.

"We take our jobs very seriously here, officers." He was walking back and forth with his hands behind his back, with a tiny cop walking behind him carrying a clipboard. "This is not a day off, or a tour to be treated lightly. We will be enforcement orientated. There will be absolutely no drinking in the parking lot, *including* beer in plastic cups."

Richie said, "Let me see if I got this straight. They practically ask us to ignore homicides at the West Indian Day Parade, but I'm supposed to look into some old-timer's cup to determine if it's a Bud and then summons him?"

"Relax, Richie," Jimmy said. "It ain't happening. I know, personally, I just lost my summonses."

Charlie was shaking his head. "Insanity. Can't make it up. They don't want me to collar some asshole hanging out on the corner at two o'clock in the morning, smoking weed, but I got to look in some working guy's cup for alcohol at a Mets game. We fought wars for the freedom to drink a cold one at a ball game."

But the boys got lucky when a sergeant from the Four-Four, the boogey-down Bronx, grabbed them. He already had four guys from Midtown South on his roster, and he added Charlie, Tommy, Richie, and Jimmy. They were assigned to the general area around Gate E, and then instructed to "whack it up." That and "let's move the barriers" were the two most common commands at any NYPD detail.

Tommy and Jimmy had their backs to the wall, enjoying the sun and the cool breeze. Nice orderly crowd and pretty girls. Couple of innings went by and Jimmy says, "I'm going inside and hit the head, check the score, get something to drink. You want anything?"

"No, I'm good. I'll get something when you get back."

Jimmy headed upstairs to the mezzanine, checked the scoreboard, and saw it was 2-0, Mets, and then decided to treat himself to a six-dollar pretzel and eight-dollar Diet Coke. It was fucking Grand Larceny. Grabbed the stuff from the counter and then found a spot, off in the corner, with a small table. He took off his hat, placed it down, and relaxed.

And then, out of nowhere, Earl Hogan, wearing shorts and a Mets jersey, and carrying a cold beer. Jimmy gave him a yell, and Earl came over.

"Hey, Jimmy, great to see you again. OT or straight time?"

"Straight time, Earl. How was Guantanamo Bay?"

"It's over, Jimmy. The world as we know it. Mark my words, fuckin' Obama closes Gitmo before he leaves office. He'll transfer these assholes to the supermax in Florence, Colorado, or the barracks at Fort Leavenworth, Kansas. Ask me, you want to put them somewhere, how about off the Cape with John Kerry, or, better yet, in Kenwood Chicago where Obama is from."

"Anything on the Beau Bergdahl exchange?"

"The five they released were stone cold killers. They send them to Qatar. Everybody I talk to at Gitmo assures me that they'll be back in the fight within two years."

Earl was getting amped now, moving his feet and his hands simultaneously, and Jimmy could see it was starting to really bother him.

"They just built an eight-hundred-thousand-dollar soccer field for the inmates, no kidding. Kids over in Jamaica, Queens playing on broken glass and condom fields, and these shitheads are playing like they're on Manchester United or something. You might think that it couldn't get worse, but you'd be wrong. Get this. Khalid Sheik Mohammed of Nine Eleven fame says he's offended that there is a female escorting him to his meetings with his attorney. We don't tell Khalid and his lawyer, 'Too bad, tough shit, go fuck yourself,' we actually tell the female she can't transport anymore. It's sick and it's an embarrassment."

"Face the facts, Earl. We can defeat *anybody* on the battlefield, but we can't defeat the assholes in our own government, who have their heads buried in the sand and haven't got a clue."

"You said it, Jimmy."

"Earl. Got a question. Nothing crazy. More out of curiosity than anything. Something came up during work. You ever hear of Rasheed Abdullah?"

Earl finished off his beer and then chucked the empty five feet into a garbage can.

"If it's the same guy I'm thinking about, black dude got radicalized Upstate. He's bad, if I remember. Plenty 302s on him. That's like a DD-5. Jimmy I got to run to the Shake Shack and get the kids burgers. What are you doing tomorrow?"

"Tomorrow is no good. You know Friday would be fine, Earl. We're heading down to SNC, me and Tommy."

"Good. Meet me in the Paris Café at about one. Give me some time to look at the paperwork on him. Sound good?"

"Great, Earl, see you then."

\* \* \* \* \*

They were up on the hill now, under the trees, sitting in lawn chairs and drinking ice-cold beer. The post game show was on the car radio, Yankees, six, Mets, five. The parking lot was emptying out, with the cars heading to the Grand Central Parkway and the Whitestone Expressway, stop, and go, all brake lights. Roosevelt Avenue was still a mess.

"Something, though," Tommy said to Jimmy, "Earl saying that there was a lot of paper on Abdullah. I'm real interested in what he's got."

"Yeah, me too," said Jimmy, and his voice trailed off. He had his head back, looking up toward the sky, his fingers tapping his near-empty beer can. Charlie and Richie were off to the side arguing over who was better, the Yankees or the Mets. Tommy could see something was bothering Jimmy, all this time, the two together, he knew him like a brother.

"Catherine, Jimmy?" asked Tommy.

"Yeah Tommy, Catherine . . . and now that mosque. They have been both on my mind lately."

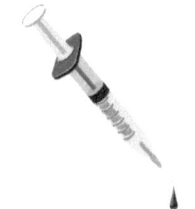

# Chapter 28

It had shaken out this way.

Jimmy McTigue, Charlie Defranco, Tommy Bell, and Sgt. Quinn would be at training.

Santos Cruz and Richie Whalen were going to the Outdoor Range to qualify.

Frank Martin was on a trial with Wally Wong. Wally had bought twenty, redtop, crack vials, in exchange for two hundred dollars in pre-recorded buy money. They recovered all ten, twenty-dollar bills, and an additional forty, redtop vials on the seller's person. But some new attorney from Legal Aid, who had been watching way too much *Law & Order* and *CSI,* had convinced the dealer that the lack of fingerprints on the crack vials was his "get out of jail free" card, regardless of the fact that vials were never ever dusted for prints. So, he told the guy to turn down the plea offer and go to trial. Big mistake.

So, Jimmy was by his desk, with Al Gavin and Jack Klint in the corner feeding the bullfrog some crickets. Bobby Washington had his feet up, reading the newspaper and venting.

"Totally fucked up, and you wonder why I don't read the papers. Says here that *Glamour Magazine* is awarding the Women of the Year Award to Caitlyn Jenner. What the fuck *real* women must feel out there, and what about you Irish boys?

This means the woman of the year got a bigger dick than you guys with that curse and all."

""You really can't argue with that. Bobby, when you're right, you're right," said Clint.

Jimmy typed a little and then asked Al and Jack if they could do him a favor, Al piping up first.

"Sure, Jimmy, what is it?"

"I got training with Charlie, Tommy, and the Boss. The rest of the boys are busy. Any chance you guys could take a trip up to the Polo Ground Projects and check on an address for me? And take a look for a red Escalade with a Hillary Clinton bumper sticker? Don't have a plate. Sit-down lunch is on me, when we can swing it."

"No sweat," said Al Gavin. "And don't worry about lunch."

"Love to," said Jack Clint.

"Fuckin' woman of the year with a dick," mumbled Bobby Washington. "Still can't believe it."

\* \* \* \* \*

Jimmy McTigue liked Al Gavin and Jack Clint. Liked them a lot.

They were members of Sgt. Lewis's team, the sister team to theirs, and the two teams went out and conducted enforcement together frequently.

They were good cops, stand-up guys, and they had great senses of humor, which made working with them a joy. They had both arrived at the office a few years back. Jimmy had gotten on this particular day, and the team was back at the base, with evidence, property, and paperwork covering the desks. There were vouchers for narcotics and money, and a firearm and beepers, lab requests, and narcotics to be tested—and someone was trying to figure out the DAR (daily activity report). *And* overtime slips to fill out. There was even a vehicle to be vouchered that was parked in the back by the basketball courts, and all the property in the car had to be collected for safekeeping. Sgt. Lewis and Sgt. Quinn had met Al and Jack by their desks, and then walked them over to where the teams were working, and made the introductions. Two new guys with absolutely *no* narcotics experience.

Jimmy gave the guys on the team a wink, and then got up and shook Al and Jack's hands and told them to relax. Charlie gave them a tour of the critters, and pointed out a desk that was available.

The team had recovered cocaine packets of tinfoil, which was what Bobby Washington had bought off the dealer, so now, Jimmy walked over to the FOD and grabbed a roll of Reynolds Wrap that was in the bottom drawer, with some eating utensils and old coffee cups. He cut out two squares and filled those squares with a generous amount of Sweet and Low. Folded them up and got them back to his desk, while Gavin and Clint were looking over some paperwork, to get the feel, and trying to figure out who the black dude was with the *Penthouse,* and what his function was. Jimmy got the tin foil on the desk where Charlie and Santos were typing. It was on.

"Wonder if that's coke and how good it is, Santos?" asked Jimmy, as he nodded toward the tin foil.

"Give it to me, and let me see," said Santos. And with that, he opened the packet, took his pinky and dipped into the Sweet and Low, and then brought it up to his mouth and said, "Pretty good shit. I think it's about sixty percent pure."

Charlie snapped his fingers. "Let *me* check it out. My senses are much more active than you guys," and he repeated the process.

Al Gavin and Jack Clint had perplexed looks on their faces. Everybody was watching, and then they saw them look at one another, shrug their shoulders, walk over to the tinfoil, and dip their fingers in and taste it.

Bobby Washington was leaning back in his chair, when he fell backwards and lost the *Penthouse*, the magazine ending up in the lobster tank.

Jimmy McTigue, Santos Cruz, Frank Martin, and Charlie Defranco just looked at each other.

And then a burst of laughter from Sgt. Lewis and Sgt. Quinn.

They had given the new guys the heads-up

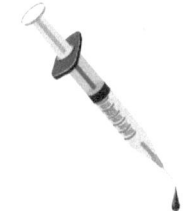

# Chapter 29

There was a magic time in this city when baseball reigned supreme and Willie, Mickey, and the Duke roamed center field.

In Brooklyn, at Ebbetts Field, it was the Dodgers; in the Bronx, at Yankee Stadium, it was the Yankees; and in upper Manhattan, at the Polo Grounds, it was the Giants.

Walter O'Malley was the first to pull up stakes and head west; and then, on September 29, 1957, the New York Giants played their last game at the old ballpark on W155th Street and 8th Avenue, and headed to San Francisco. Soon after, the Polo Grounds would come down.

In 1968, the Polo Grounds Towers were completed. The site was bordered by Fredrick Douglas Boulevard, West 155th Street, and the Harlem River Drive. It consisted of four, thirty-story buildings with over sixteen hundred apartments—and occupied by four thousand people.

It is as hard and as mean a location as there is in the five boroughs of New York.

Jimmy had given Al and Jack the address of Robert Bolt, a.k.a. Slice, earlier. He gave them a picture from his last collar that had taken place at The Terrorist. Maybe they could knock on the door, see what's up. He told them about the red Escalade with the Hillary bumper sticker that Aiman had spotted at the mosque.

They took Sgt. Lewis's cargo van, and headed up to Carrot Top Pastries, the bakery on Broadway, down the block from Columbia Presbyterian, for coffee and a couple of just-baked muffins. Then, they headed over to the projects and parked off the set with a clear view of the front door. They were far enough from the entrance as to not raise suspicion.

They both had their bulletproof vests laid out on the floor between the two seats. The both had department radios lying on the seat in between their legs. Al Gavin had brought his "war bag"—a gym bag containing handcuffs; flex cuffs; Mag light; large, manila envelopes; copy of the Penal Law; Hagstrom Street Atlas; plastic gloves; small billy club; a reporter's notebook; a clipboard; a pair of binoculars; summonses; cigarettes for prisoner negotiations; and assorted, promotional coupons from Dunkin' Donuts. They watched the front door, ate their muffins, and drank their coffee, occasionally using the "binocs" for a closer look. The department radio crackled with jobs from Division. They figured to eat up, and then head into the building and check out the apartment. Do the favor for Jimmy McTigue.

And then, while sitting there.

"This guy, here, Al."

"Yeah, I got him. Wearing the windbreaker . . . little hot for a jacket . . . eyeballing everything."

"Keeps patting the right side of his jacket . . . looks like he's got something under there, little bulky, and walking kind of funny," said Jack, as he watched the "brother" through the binoculars.

"Let's let him walk away from the projects . . . see what's up, stop him when we can."

"Windbreaker" decided to go south on Fredrick Douglas Boulevard until he got to 155th Street. He then headed toward the Macombs Dam Bridge, tapping his right side, looking about, the windbreaker buttoned up front, all the way to the top. The other side of the bridge was the Bronx and Yankee Stadium, a couple of minutes away on foot.

There was very light vehicular traffic on the bridge. There were virtually no pedestrians. Al was driving with Jack in the passenger seat, the cargo van radio off, and one of the department radios tuned to the Bronx and the division covering the Four-Four. They were taking it nice and slow, and then into the Bronx, and now they could see the Stadium.

Al said, "Jack I'm pulling over . . . let you out, and then I'm heading up a block, dumping the van, and walking back toward you. Have him from both sides."

"Great. Sounds like a plan. Even if he gets raised up, I'll be right there."

Windbreaker kept walking and kept patting his right side. Al was up a block, and had exited the van and grabbed an empty pizza box that was lying on top of a garbage can. He had his Glock 19 out, under the box, and was walking toward Jack with Windbreaker tucked in the middle.

Windbreaker walking, tapping, fidgety, all eyeballs, and ears, when he heard the distant sound of the *whoop, whoop* from a radio car. He was really spooked now, and both Al and Jack could see it. Al with the pizza box, closing fast, but still looking like a cop, and then, Windbreaker getting raised up and about to do something, when Jack comes up from behind and puts him in a bear hug. Jack could feel something under the windbreaker, didn't know yet what it was, but had the kid on the floor, face down, and then rolled him over.

"Jesus Christ, Al, what the fuck is that? You're a gun guy, tell me, because I've never seen anything like it."

Dangling over Windbreaker's right shoulder, on a sling, was eighteen and half inches—and almost seven pounds—of pure death.

"Wow, yeah, I know. It's a Kel Tec KSG shotgun. A pump-action bullpup. Two magazine tubes with twelve rounds of three-inch shells. This guy ain't fooling around."

And they cuffed him.

* * * * *

They processed Ordell Mitchell, age twenty-eight, in the Four-Four precinct on East 169th Street. The Command was running prisoners down to court, anyway, and was happy to take Ordell with them.

Jack Clint was taking the collar, so they headed over to Bronx Criminal Court on East 161st Street by Sherman Avenue, parked the cargo van, and went in.

The Assistant District Attorney handling the case was a little cutie named Holly Worthington. She was 26 years old, blond and blue-eyed, and had been working up in the Bronx for a good three months. She grew up Sagaponack New York, Exit 70 on the LIE, where the median price of a house was over four million. She had attended Harvard Law School and required no student loans to cover the $245,000 tuition.

"Tell me again why you followed this young black male from his residence?"

"It's like ninety degrees out, the guys bug-eyed, looking around with what looks like a bulge under his jacket, walking

164

kind of off-kilter," said Jack Clint, eleven years a cop, who grew up in the Fordham section of the Bronx.

"Damn jacket is buttoned almost all the way to the top, and he keeps going to the right side of his body, patting it, like he wanted to make sure whatever was there was secure," said Al Gavin, thirteen years a cop, who grew up in South Ozone Park in Queens.

"You should have seen the guy after a radio car nearby made some noise," said Jack.

"I thought the guy was going to have a heart attack," added Al.

All this time, Holly Worthington had this blank stare on her face. She alternated between looking at Al and Jack, and then down to her yellow legal pad, where she took notes.

"And that is the sole basis for the stop?"

Al Gavin and Jack Clint looked at each other for a moment, and *then*, both knew immediately where this was going. They nodded their heads, yes, and watched as ADA Holly Worthington left the office.

"What are we going to do about lunch, Al?"

"I think a drink will be more in order."

Four minutes later, she was back, after heading down the hall to her supervisor's office and explaining her concerns about the stop. She sat back down behind her desk and had this kind of smug look on her face, shuffled through some paperwork, and then looked up at Jack Clint and Al Gavin, brushing that beautiful blond hair out of her eyes, and said, "Sorry, the office has decided not to prosecute at this time," and she got up and left.

"How about we head over to Glacken's, Al, and one of those monster rum and cokes?"

"Sounds good to me," said Jack, and they left.

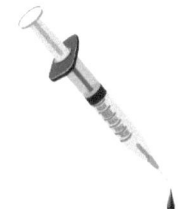

# Chapter 30

There came a time when most of the filming that was to take place at St. Bartholomew's in Elmhurst, Queens was finished, so the cast and crew of *These Bells Toll* packed up and headed to the Silver Cup Studios in Long Island City. It was easily the largest film and production facility in New York and the biggest, independent, full service film and production operation in the entire northeast. The locals knew it as the old Silvery Cup Bakery plant, and there was a time when the smell of fresh bread tantalized the neighborhood. But in 1983, the studio was established and, since then, no one had ever looked back. There were two lots on the premise, the Main and the East, and *These Bells Toll* would be utilizing the Main Lot. It was located on 22nd Avenue in Long Island City, and was comprised of thirteen, shooting stages, which worked out perfectly for director Fred Meunch and location coordinator Tom Rye. They were going to create the Catholic school classroom Meg was teaching in, and the on-site carpenters were going to construct a small pub Meg and her associates frequented. There was also a public school classroom to be created, because of an additional storyline in the plot that involved a New York public school that was a sister school to St. Bart's. They had decided to use the name of the school where so much of the filming took place in the movie.

There was no need for a technical advisor when it came to getting the details of the Catholic school classroom right; Meg had attended a parochial school. So she told the stage hands to: pack the room with some forty desks; get the cross up above the blackboard; have the American flag flying off the wall in front of the class; hang book reviews and science projects appropriate for her fictional fourth-grade class about; and pepper the walls with religious and patriotic sayings that reaffirmed God's love for them and the greatness of the United States.

In the fictional public school classroom, the workers placed eleven desks, all with personal computers. They also hung a sign on the wall describing the Heimlich Maneuver and a poster that read, "Christopher Columbus Didn't Discover America."

The additional plot involving the public school had all the trappings of the real New York City Public School System. One scene had the Teachers Union defending a crack head music teacher, and another had it backing an instructor who had been late for school virtually every day of her entire eight-year career. There was the usual nonsense about class size and the unfair disciplinary actions taken against minorities. And, of course, the Teachers Union officials saying, "It's all about the kids," and actually thinking people believed that. In fact, the union got wind of the plot line and occasionally had been picketing Monarch Studios. Trouble was, some investigative reporter from the *New York Post* discovered that the union was paying picketers less then minimum wage to be out there—and none of them were teachers. They tried to recruit some "bodies" that were spending time in the "Rubber Room," where teachers with disciplinary problems spent their time until the case was sorted out, but they were too busy taking care of their personal business on work time.

There was one scene in the movie that Meg especially loved.

Her fourth-grade class is being instructed by a Dominican nun, Sister Bernice, played in the movie by Karen Slater, who had starred in Meunch's previous film, *Magnum Lunch*, about a fat detective who investigates a string of homicides at a fast food chain. During instruction, a fifteen-year-old punk walks into the school, off the street, and tries to disrupt the class. Sister Bernice rolls up her sleeves and knocks the kid out.

The scene seemed like one of those feel good moments in cinema, but the "Black Lives Matter" movement took offense to the idea that a nun in a white habit would punch out a child of color, *even though* Karen Slater was as black as the ace of spades. Fred Meunch wasn't your typical Hollywood director. His father had run a hardware store in Detroit. When asked by a correspondent from *Extra* what he thought about the brouhaha, Fred responded, "Those assholes can go fuck themselves."

Now, on this day, they were filming the scene where Meg is able to coax an especially shy female student out of her shell. The plot has the girl as a Muslim refugee from Syria, who is having trouble with the language and adjusting to America. But Meg has an idea for some fun and some instruction.

What she does is play the scene from *The Sound of Music*, where Julie Andrews teaches the Von Trapp kids the *Do, Re, Mis*. Meg passes out the words to the song and plays it a few times, and don't you know, by the end of the action, there is the little girl singing in front of the class all by herself with the rest of the children singing along with her.

It was so moving there were teamsters on the set crying.

"That's a wrap," Meunch said, and then to the kids, "Great job, boys and girls. You made me proud."

"Absolutely," added Meg. "You guys were just wonderful." But here's the thing. Sure Meg was playing a teacher and the kids her students, but after weeks of filming, these kids looked at Meg lovingly as if they had that "classroom relationship," and so, when they broke for the day, many would come over to get a hug, the hand on the check, or the tussle of the hair.

Meunch could see it. "You know, Meg, you might have missed your calling. The kids *love* you."

"Don't tell anybody, Fred, but I would probably do this for free."

"Where are you heading now?"

"I'm having dinner with Artie, over in Greenpoint. Nice and close. You want to come?"

"No thanks. I'm meeting my daughter. You know, the one who never calls and rages against income inequality while I pay her tuition and rent. She needs some new designer wear from Saks."

\* \* \* \* \*

Artie had called Meg earlier in the day about dinner. She had certainly been busy recently—Artie, too—and they hadn't seen each other in a couple of weeks. Lots of phone tag and texting, but also an awful lot of voice mailing from Meg's direction. For some reason, that had her thinking of that guy, Jimmy McTigue, standing in the doorway of the pizzeria and pointing out the sauce on her mouth. And that line of his, "If you ever need a helping hand?" She had entered his number in her phone under "Jimmy McTigue, Cop?" because she still wondered, and, on those days on the set when one waited and waited, she thought of him.

\* \* \* \* \*

Meg drove over to Greenpoint, Brooklyn. She was meeting Artie at about six in Bamonte's on Withers Street, between Union and Lorimer. She parked the car in the lot next door and walked in, Artie standing at the bar in a suit, with the Yankees baseball hat crooked on his head. He looked to be on his second martini.

"Meg, honey, what are you doing?" He gave her a kiss, and was looking to prolong it. Meg wasn't cooperating.

"The hat, Artie. Give it a break. How long have you been waiting?"

"Not long," and then Artie checking his watch. "Let's eat. I'm fuckin' starving."

Meg now had a pained look on her face and glanced around to make sure no one was within earshot.

The wooden bar was on the left when you walked in, maybe twenty feet long, and then beyond that, the dining area opened up, straight back, with a definite Old World feel to it. There was a time, though, long ago, when late nights would find "made men" back there playing cards and relaxing.

They sat in the far corner, Artie ordering another martini, Meg just a club soda with a twist of lime, from the waiter, who looked an awful lot like Abe Vigoda.

"How's the filming going?" Artie checking his watch.

"Great, you got somewhere to go? Fred has been wonderful and I'm really getting a kick out of the children. None of them have had *any* acting experience. They haven't been corrupted and they are just lovely to be around. You've been busy lately."

"Working with a new guy to represent. Young ghetto rapper with his finger on the fuckin' pulse."

171

"And you think you'll sign him?"

"Did it already. Now have to sit down with the suits. Here comes the waiter. I'm fuckin' starving. Let's order."

Artie went with the Prosciutto and Melon to start, and then, Monk Fish *Livornese* with olives, onions, tomato, and white wine, for his main dish. Meg kept it simple and ordered the Broiled Shrimp *Scampi,* with a side of broccoli sautéed in garlic oil. The bread was wonderful, but the conversation wasn't. Artie spent most of his time texting and checking his watch. And then, it was over, and they were outside the restaurant.

"Got to go, Meg. Take care of a few things and got a busy day tomorrow. I'll call you," and Meg turned her cheek toward him and said, "Okay Artie, bye now."

Artie was already gone, Meg fishing for a couple of singles to give the guy who was getting her car, when she said to herself, "Maybe I'll satisfy my curiosity and give Jimmy McTigue a call

* * * * *

Artie got into his red Escalade and checked his watch—7:45 PM. Not too bad.

He was heading uptown to see Gladys Campos, scintillating little honey with a body you could write a book about. She was studying law at NYU, and lived in the George Washington Houses on Second Avenue and 103rd Street with her mother, who worked a four-to-twelve shift cleaning offices on Wall Street. He headed into Manhattan and took the FDR Drive north. Got off at 96th Street and drove up First. Artie was thinking about going north a little and then come south on Second Avenue, hoping for a spot in front of the building, but then he spotted a Toyota pulling out on First and 104th Street. *Why roll the dice?* He parked and walked over.

And Gladys was ready, all five feet eight, and a hundred ten pounds of light brown skin and dark black hair. She was standing in the entrance of the doorway when Artie got off the elevator, tight, white T-shirt, no bra, and a pair of painted-on, yellow shorts. Artie walked in, and she wrapped her arms around his neck and nibbled on his ear and whispered, "Oh Artie, how have you been, my little baby?" and then took his Yankees hat and threw it across the room.

They got right down to it, Artie with those sweet half-dollar nipples in his mouth, the music playing on the radio in the kitchen, and the cool breeze coming through the open window on the fifteenth floor. By the time Artie came up for air, it was a little after 11:00 PM.

Back in the red Escalade, his heart still pounding, Artie figured he could use a little weed and a nightcap. He pulled out of his spot and decided to head down to the Pioneer Bar on Chambers and Church for a nightcap.

Jake McNicholas

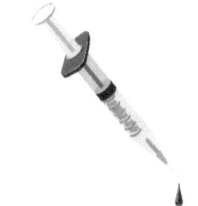

# Chapter 31

"**Where you going, Bobby?**" asked Sergeant Lewis.

"Going out to get some tang and I ain't talking about that shit the astronauts used to drink back in the day."

It was 11:00 PM, and Bobby Washington was headed over to the Woodrow Wilson Projects on First Avenue and 105th Street to see his little, sweet senorita, Maria. Mouth-watering sweet, twenty-five-years old, long dark hair, long legs and big tits—and all this girl wanted to do was fuck. Sometimes, Bobby could barely get his clothes off. A machine.

He was in his 2000 Nissan Maxima—shit, what else could he afford under the circumstances?—and listening to Barry White, Bobby being a little older and not really understanding the rap shit. Thinking about how good it was going to be, once he got up to the apartment, on the couch with a little cognac, the lights down low, and the music—a little bit of a warm-up before getting down to business. He sped up in traffic, and was heading south on Park Avenue just past 110th Street, when the phone rang.

"OOOOH, Bobby."

"Yeah, Maria."

"I'm waiting here for you, baby, waiting for you to COME over here. Got my sexy, French maid outfit from Victoria's Secret on, and my fuck-me pumps you got me from Bloomingdale's. And I'm waiting, Bobby, OOOOOOOOOH, God, I'm waiting." And she hung up.

Bobby got so excited, he dropped the phone, and it rolled under the passenger seat. He almost rear-ended a cab.

He headed east to First Avenue and, at 104th Street, said to himself, "Shit, it's my lucky day," when he spotted a car pulling out. He nestled up, right behind it, waiting for the driver to make the move, a white guy in a red Escalade—bright red. And then, Bobby remembered Jimmy McTigue telling Al Gavin and Jack Clint to keep an eyeball out for a red Escalade, just for the hell of it, when they were up at the Polo Ground Projects. Nowhere near the Polo Ground Projects now, and, besides, Jimmy said something about a Hillary bumper sticker. And then, the red Escalade pulled all the way out of the spot, and Bobby had a clear view and he saw it.

"Fuckin' Hillary!"

And then he said, out loud, in the car, "You fuckin' Irish prick, Jimmy McTigue, you owe me big time!"

Bobby's got no phone and a raging hard-on, and he can't read the plate, because it's covered in plastic to beat the red-light cameras that are all over the city. The Escalade heads north on First Avenue, and Bobby follows. He can hear his phone ringing.

The Escalade is in and out of traffic, driving fast, real fast, Bobby having a hard time keeping up, hoping a radio car shows up from somewhere and pulls the fucker over. Now he knows what the guys are talking about. This surveillance shit ain't easy.

At 116th Street, the car makes the right and heads for the FDR Drive.

Now, the Escalade goes south on the FDR in the left lane, flying through traffic. Bobby way back, but with his foot all the way down on the accelerator. He can just barely see him. But then some luck, because there is congestion by the exit for the 59th Street Bridge and Bobby is able to roll up to a spot no more than three, or four car lengths behind.

Heading south in the right lane, past the Midtown Tunnel exit and the heliport, past the old Con Ed exit at 14th Street. At South Street, the Escalade gets off without signaling. Speeding now, underneath the drive and past the New York Post Building, and then making the right and heading toward Police Headquarters; comes around onto Worth and then westbound, with Bobby still trailing behind. Goes down to Greenwich Street, makes the left, goes south and then east on Chambers Street. Bobby watches the Escalade park about a hundred feet short of Church Street. A male white, medium build, wearing a baseball hat sideways, exits the vehicle and enters The Pioneer, a bar on the south side of the street.

Bobby pulls in by a hydrant, because there is no other place to go. He reaches under the passenger seat and grabs his phone, and then up into the glove box for a pen and a piece of paper. He gets out of the car and goes to the registration sticker on the window and copies the plate, EX1246, NY. He heads back to the car and checks his voice mail: "I'm going to bed, Bobby. Don't bother coming over."

He calls Jimmy, and it goes to voice mail, and he tells him to call.

His hard-on has dissipated.

**Jake McNicholas**

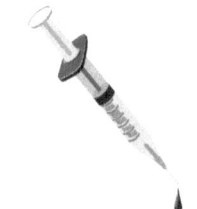

# Chapter 32

It was early morning and they were sitting around drinking coffee: Wally, Charlie, Tommy, Richie, Sgt. Lewis, Frank Martin, and Jimmy.

"Listen to this one," said Richie Whalen. "Just when you thought you had heard the craziest story around, here comes another one.

"Al Link tells me this. He's on the Two-Eight team. Those guys are crazy anyway. They got B and B, on the set, and sending out the undercover, when their boss, Underwood, gets a call from his wife. You need to know that this guy always refers to his young son as the Bambino. Anyway, he's on the phone and they're talking and he hangs up and he says to Link, 'That's it. We got to shut it down. The little Bambino won't put on his galoshes, and I have to go home.' Link looks at him and says, 'You got a great sense of humor, Boss, we're ready to get going.' Underwood says, 'No, I'm serious.' "

"What did they do then?" asked Jimmy.

"You know they're nuts. They take the hundred dollars of pre-recorded, buy money that they were going to use during B and B, and they head up to Glacken's for the afternoon."

"I got another one," said Frank Martin. "They have that guy on the team whose wife is the hand model, and he delivers bagels every night. Sometimes uses the P Van. I'm with him one time on a surveillance. All of a sudden, he's on the phone going, 'Three poppy, two onion, two sesame, four raisin.' I can barely hear the department radio. These are the bags he's ordering up for delivery. I don't have a clue what he's doing, but then he looks at me with this crazy smile and says, 'Got to do the bagels.' They had midnight enforcement, one time, and they had to borrow our P van, because he was out doing the deliveries with theirs."

"They also got that guy who has some mysterious connection to the club," said Tommy. "This was a couple of years ago. Me and Jimmy are coming up the stairs, smelling hot dogs. We get to the hallway and what do we see but a full-fledged, hot dog wagon, umbrella and all."

"If I remember correctly it was something special for pay day," added Jimmy.

"You're right," Tommy said. "The guy was out there selling dirty-water franks. We had Inspector Carney back then, a real gentleman. It doesn't faze him at all. He was going to step out for lunch, but he comes down from his office and buys two. The ICO went berserk, though, because Inspections was coming in an hour. Carney could think on his feet. He had me type out a voucher and attach it to the cart as if it was arrest evidence. Inspections didn't have a clue, and a half hour after they left, sales were back booming. The leftovers went to the homeless."

Al Gaven and Jack Clint came in with big smiles on their faces. They recounted the whole story regarding the surveillance up at the projects and the collar that wasn't to be. All Jimmy could say was, "Thanks boys. No worries and I owe you. Have to love those Bronx DAs. No wonder crime is off the hook up there. Just for the hell of it, give me a copy of Ordell's online and photo."

He spotted Bobby coming through the door. "Bobby Washington, my main man. Come over here, my little brother, and let me give you a hug."

"Jimmy, you owe me fuckin' big time. Don't got words to explain the pain you inflicted on me."

"I'm taking you out to dinner," Jimmy said. "I know you're used to dining on two dogs and a grape Nehi from Gray's Papaya King, but we're going for a nice sit-down—Frankie and Johnnie's Pine Tavern, if you like. Got a hankering for the veal cutlet Parmesan. Give me that plate again."

Bobby dug into his pocket and fished out a crumpled piece of paper and gave it to Jimmy, who went to his desk and brought up NYSPIN. He entered Plate EX1246 NY. And the results:

NAME: Arthur Levin
DOB: 4/12/1973
HEIGHT: 5'10
WEIGHT: 180
ADDRESS: 300 North End Avenue, Battery Park City, NY 10282

*Why would a guy named Slice have Arthur Levin of Battery Park City's vehicle at a Brooklyn mosque?* Jimmy reached down to the bottom drawer of his desk and pulled out a file folder, with a large question mark on the front in Magic Marker. Inside was the information on Slice and Rasheed Abdullah.

He figured he would Google Arthur Levin/Battery Park City. Wow! Lots of hits. *That's our Artie.* Big article in *New*

*York* magazine on the boy. Couple of pictures of him—all the time with a baseball hat.

"Yeah, that's the fuckah," said Bobby.

Artie was some sort of "super agent." Dexter Spencer, he knew. Tommy had him in a fantasy league. Howard Chance, he had heard of. Meg Cassidy?

"Anybody ever hear of Meg Cassidy?"

"You need to be released from your bubble, Jimmy," said Charlie. "Other things besides the *History Channel*, *FOX* and sports. Real beauty. Former model. She has already been in a couple of movies. I actually think she's a local girl—Long Beach or Rockaway."

Bobby Washington panted and said, "She fine."

He printed up the article and put it in the folder.

The Parking Violations Bureau for the City of New York provides a website that enabled the citizens to check for outstanding summonses. *What the hell? Let's see what comes up for Artie's vehicle.* He punched in the plate, and it indicated that there were three outstanding parking tickets for NY EX1246.

Those two make sense, Jimmy thought. Alternate Side in Battery Park City. But also a Late Night parking violation in front of 1520 Farmers Boulevard in Queens. He stuck the address in MapQuest.

And now, out loud, "Farmers Boulevard, out by the airport?"

"Yeah," Charlie Defranco, overhearing. "I know where that is. Drove a truck for the Post Office and delivered to the JFK Air Mail Facility at Building Two Fifty out there all the time."

"Let me get this straight, Defranco," said Bobby Washington. "All this time, me breaking your balls, and you worked for the fuckin' *Post Office*? I apologize and I want you to remember I said it when you get the automatic weapon and start shooting people."

Jimmy put all the paper in the Question Mark file.

"Let's take a ride, Tommy."

"Where to?"

"Out by Kennedy.  Lunch is on me."

\* \* \* \* \*

They took Jimmy's 2008 Jeep Liberty, with the sunroof and the leather seats, out to the airport, listening all the way to the Allman Brothers Band.  Tommy said, "You know, these guys are pretty good."  And Jimmy saying, "Southern Rock.  I really like them.  They come into the city every March.  I try to see them, if it doesn't interfere with Patty's Day."

They were on the Van Wyck, not too much traffic, riding under the monorail that shuttles airline passengers out to Kennedy from Jamaica, when Tommy got serious and said," You okay, Jimmy, aren't you?  Looks like you've been hurting.  Other guys wouldn't pick it up, but I can.  Something more that you just getting old."

"Still take you one-on-one, as long as it's caveman basketball—no blood, no foul.  No, pal, I'm fine.  Thanks for asking.  When's Michele back again?"

"Not for a week.  She and the girls are really enjoying themselves.  I retire, I'm definitely heading south and have a house built.  Have a back bedroom for you.  Even give you your own refrigerator for beers."

They got off the Van Wyck and hugged the outside of the airport where the cargo buildings and the parking lots were, and, the next thing they knew, GPS had them in front of 1520 Farmers Boulevard.

Two-story building. Huge sign with SUNRISE CARGO up on top. There were two, garage doors open to the street, and Tommy and Jimmy walked in. Inside, there was cargo stacked everywhere, and skids on hi-lows being moved through long rows of merchandise, the place a whirlwind of activity. There looked to be about fifteen or twenty workers, South American and Mexican, with a few guys from the Islands. There was an older gentleman with a full head of gray hair, off to the side, one hand holding a clipboard, his other arm draped around the shoulders of a young Mexican. He seemed to be explaining something, and looked up when he saw Tommy and Jimmy. The kid walked away.

"I didn't do anything, officers," he said, smiling.

Jimmy and Tommy looked at each other and laughed.

"What gave us up?" asked Jimmy.

"C'mon, boys. Salt and Pepper team, and your buddy there has his notebook hanging out of his pocket. I'm Chris Neil. Retired from The Job."

"Tommy Bell. I'm Jimmy McTigue. From where?"

"Street Crime."

"Man you must have some stories," said Tommy.

"Best job I ever had. Just being a cop. I don't envy you guys, the way things are now, though. I guess it's getting tougher and tougher to have some laughs. But stay strong. What can I do for you?"

"We're just looking into something, just for curiosity and shits and giggles, really," said Jimmy. "Trying to figure out why a particular vehicle would get a summons out here, late at night. On a Friday"

"Daytime, it's all this," said Neil, as he gestured to the activity in the warehouse. "Nighttime . . ." And he looked at Tommy.

Tommy picked up on it and said, "Brother, I'm all cop. Fire away."

"Put it this way. One Friday, I'm working a little late. It was like a perp graduation at the Pink Houses (Brooklyn's notorious projects, the Louis H. Pink Houses), you know what I mean. Gangbangers all over the place. The parking lot is full with late models, all tinted-out, and the music is blasting. Got some sort of bullshit studio upstairs, being used by some up-and-coming rapper. Thought I was going to get a 'contact high' with all the weed. No sense calling. Assholes burn my place down."

"That actually explains away a couple of things," said Jimmy. "Really appreciate you taking the time. Thanks again, Mister Neil."

"Chris."

"Okay, *Chris.*"

Tommy shook his hand, and Jimmy gave him a shoulder pat. They were both heading to the car when Neil yelled, "Remember, boys, we're the only ones out there fighting the good fight. It's a calling. God knows what we're doing. Be safe."

And they got into the car.

Jake McNicholas

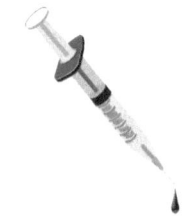

# Chapter 33

There is a plaque in the muster room of the 30th Precinct off all by itself, away from the wanted posters, crime maps, 10-13 flyers, and union announcements. If you didn't know it was there, you could miss it. Matt Quinn knew it was there. The plaque was testament to the everlasting impact of the Irish cop on law enforcement, and it reads:

"THERE IS A GRAVESTONE IN COUNTY CORK IRELAND THAT READS:

> *Maurice Healy*
> *Born: January 31, 1900*
> *Died: March 17, 1986*
> *Sons on the Police Force*
> *New York    Sidney*
> *Chicago   London*
> *Boston    Auckland*
> *Hong Kong"*

Every day Matt Quinn reported to work at the precinct, he took a moment to stand in front of that plaque and say a silent prayer.

His grandfather had sailed from Ireland and landed in New York with nothing. He joined the Army and served with the American Expeditionary Force in WWI, over in France, where he was gassed. On his way back to America, young and proud, and in uniform, he returned to the home of his mother, father, and siblings. It was the last time he would ever see them. He spent thirty years as a member of the NYPD and lived to see John F. Kennedy become president.

His dad continued the tradition and invested thirty-five years of good, hard, honest service in the old Two-Eight and, later, up in the One-Thirteen squad. Years later, God would call and beckon him home to walk the foot post at the Gates of Heaven.

Except for his initial training assignment after graduation from the police academy, Quinn spent his entire career in the Three-Oh. Prior to being promoted, he had been upstairs in the squad. Before that he walked a foot post, rode in a sector car, and did anti-crime. He was an honest, compassionate, and hard-working cop, and the corruption investigation and subsequent arrests in the Command during the mid-nineties darkened his very soul.

He caught a homicide right before he was promoted. It was an especially vicious murder, a young mother shot in the head in Trinity Church Cemetery on Broadway between West 153rd and West 155th Streets. It was an old burial ground that had been established in 1842, from the imagination of James Renwick Sr., who later went on to more famous works: St. Patrick's Cathedral in New York City, and the Smithsonian Institute in Washington, D.C.

Carmen Gonzalez was shot to death on an early November morning in the cemetery, right next to the grave of a Union officer from the Civil War. There was absolutely no apparent narcotics connection, nor were there any forensics, video in Trinity, or independent information. The squad worked tirelessly, canvassing, interviewing the registered owners of vehicles parked in the vicinity, passing out flyers on the street, using the media for assistance. Nothing.

And then one day, some months later, there was a phone call up to the squad, the female on the line stating that she had heard that Carmen Gonzalez had been out clubbing, the night of the murder, with someone called *Cicatriz*, Spanish for scar. There is a box for nicknames on the online booking sheet, filled out when making an arrest, and Quinn hoped "Scar" had been collared and that the arresting officer had taken the time to fill in the box. There was one individual who took a pinch for marijuana possession, and the A/O had indeed written in *Cicatriz*.

They pulled video from the Mobil Station on West 155th Street and Broadway, and, now armed with a photo, revisited the tape, and, sure enough, there was Scar, a.k.a. George Colon, walking eastbound on West 155th Street in the early morning hours of that November day, illuminated by the street lights and the lights emanating from the service station. The picture of George Colon was clear—ski hat and field jacket, dark jeans, and Timberlands.

A couple of guys from Anti-Crime brought George and his punk-ass brother, Hector, up to the squad on some other pretext. Matt Quinn and Eddie Lane were the only two up there when the brothers came through the door, laughing and giggling and talking to each other in Spanish. Lane was sitting at his desk, banging away at the computer, his reading glasses on the tip of his nose, when he yelled, in all seriousness, with that voice of his from the Deep South, "Stop talkin' that yang and speak fuckin' English."

The Colon brothers just laughed.

Quinn took George into the interview room and got absolutely nowhere. Old George knew the drill, and wasn't saying shit—playing with Quinn actually. He came out of the room and spoke Spanish to his brother, who was sitting at the desk as far away from Eddie Lane as he could get. They were back to laughing.

Then, Matt Quinn got an idea. He went downstairs, and a couple of minutes later came back up with the blondest, most blue-eyed uniformed cop anyone had ever seen. His name was Jon Oleson, and he'd actually been born in Bergen, Norway. The guys in the Command called him "Viking."

Quinn told Lane that they were needed downstairs at the desk. He told the Colon brothers, who were still laughing, to sit tight. He told Oleson to keep an eye on the boys, that they'd be back in a couple of minutes. Oleson grabbed a copy of the useless *New York Daily News*, went over to Lane's desk, put his feet up, and commenced to reading.

The Colon brothers engaged in a spirited conversation for a good ten minutes in Spanish. They talked about the female cop with the big tits by the desk downstairs when they walked in. They talked about the two asshole detectives they were dealing with. And they talked about the girl in the graveyard, *and* George got *real* specific.

Quinn and Lane came back upstairs and thanked "Viking."

Lane said, "I'll buy you a horn of mead at the next club meeting, as long as you wear your helmet."

Oleson said, "No problem, guys, anytime." Then, he walked over to George and Hector Colon, and, in his most impeccable Spanish, said, "I enjoyed listening to you guys. It was a real pleasure." Then he turned to Matt Quinn and, pointing at George Colon, said, "This guy's good to go. Mind if I put the cuffs on the asshole?"

George Colon, a.k.a. Cicatriz, had killed Carmen Gonzalez, because she was chatting with another man, when he came out of the bathroom the night they went clubbing.

Three weeks later, Matt Quinn was promoted to sergeant.

Eight months after that, he sat in front of an interview board, hoping to avoid Internal Affairs and get Narcotics.

He got lucky.

* * * * *

Clearview Golf Course is located at the base of the Throgs Neck Bridge, in the borough of Queens. It hugs the busy Clearview Expressway. Founded in 1925, it was formally known as the Clearview Golf and Yacht Club, and boasted long-time, New York Governor and the first Roman Catholic to run for President, Al Smith, as a member.

The Brooklyn North detectives were having their annual golf outing at the facility. It was a twelve-noon, shotgun start, foursomes going out on all the holes simultaneously. By eleven, the parking lot was filling up, guys unloading bags, toting coolers, and heading up to the BBQ for burgers, salads, dogs— *and* ice-cold beer from the keg.

Jimmy rolled in, along with Tommy. They headed up to the BBQ. Matt Quinn and Charlie Defranco were already up there, shooting the bull, in a circle with a few guys from Brooklyn North, and the guy running the outing, Mike

Amitrano, from the Eight-Three squad. Jimmy knew most everyone.

"What's up, boys? How's everyone? What's it look like, Mike?"

"Hey, Jimmy! Thanks for getting the foursome. I got your check. Should be a nice relaxed day. Seventy-two golfers, no one up your ass. Got a hole-in-one for five thousand bucks, longest drive, closest-to-the-pin, and low score."

"What do you think it will take to win low score?" asked Matt Quinn, who could golf.

"I figure five or six under," said Amitrano. "Unless, of course, there is a foursome of firemen out there. Then, we're talking twelve under."

They all had a laugh and headed for the carts, after the starter told everyone to keep it moving during the round, and throw the empties in the garbage.

"Tommy, you and Charlie go together. Charlie, you're driving 'Miss Daisy.' I got to talk to Matt."

"Let's go, 'Madam.' Your chariot awaits," laughed Defranco.

The shotgun start had Manhattan North starting at the Par 4, 5th Hole, a long 383 yards. Jimmy got right into it with Quinn.

"I've been meaning to talk to you about something. Remember that incident I had at The Terrorist a while back?"

"The one you've been trying to parlay into free beer for the rest of your career?" said Quinn.

"I wish. Make a long story short, one of the guys that was collared that day, from the Polo Grounds, is out, and got spotted by The Terrorist at a mosque in Brooklyn, hanging out with a radicalized ex-con, who Earl Hogan from JTTF says is all bad.

Throw in the agent for Dexter Spencer of the Lions, and it is a bit curious."

"Does sound *off*, doesn't it?"

"Here it is, Matt. I'm not asking to go full bore on it, I'm just thinking of looking into it a *little*. See where it pans out, do some poking. It won't interfere with the rest of the stuff we got on the table, and I'll keep you apprised. Al and Jack did me a favor, were up at the Projects, grabbed a guy with some serious hardware. Who knows? Tommy and me are heading up to check the location, when we get a chance. And I'm sitting down with Earl, shortly."

"You know, Jimmy, I don't have to tell you how it is with some bosses. Big cases, big problems. Little cases, little problems. *No* cases? *No* problems! I never subscribed to that theory, so I'm glad to have all you guys for my team. Go for it, but keep me posted. My cousin, Jimmy Berger, worked for Aon Insurance. Means 'oneness' in Gaelic. He was on the hundredth floor of Tower Two on September eleventh. Left a wife and two children. They never found his remains."

\* \* \* \* \*

It was all laughs, canned beer, and cheap cigars for the rest of the day. Tommy actually started getting the ball in the air.

"I think I might have to quit my job and join the tour."

"Take it easy, *Tiger*. Michele will be taking a six iron out on your ass. The only difference is the driveway will be in Queens Village, rather than Florida," said Charlie.

The last hole for them was the Par 3, 4th. It was 169 yards to the hole, and this was for the $5,000.

Mike Amitrano and his foursome were standing by the hole, drinking beer, and waiting for the show.

Charlie hit a worm-burner, a ground ball, that went past the ladies tee, so he didn't have to expose himself. Jimmy told him to run it out.

Tommy hit a ball that ricocheted off a tree, bounced back, and knocked a Bud Lite out of Charlie's hand.

"Take it easy, will you, Miss Daisy."

Matt Quinn hit a six iron to the front of the green.

Jimmy had his lucky Pinnacle, and was hitting a seven iron. Matt Quinn was behind him, when he launched his best shot of the day.

Matt said, "Hey buddy, that ball looks like it's going right toward the pin."

One bounce on the front of the green, a second, shortly thereafter, and then that lovely little Pinnacle went straight into the hole.

Amitrano and his guys were doing a weird version of the Macarena on the green.

Charlie said, "If that was me, I would be on the phone *immediately* with my wife, and let her know the good news. Honey, I just won a thousand dollars and I'm giving you half."

Tommy said, "I can see a lunch date in the future."

The "after party" was more laughs—a buffet dinner under the overhang by the first hole, everyone at the tables eating and waiting for the raffles to start.

Then Tommy. "Shit, I should have thought of this before, Jimmy. See the brother over there with the Knicks hat and the Miami Hurricanes tee shirt?"

"Yep, who is he?"

"Guy's name is Howard Amos. Works in Intel. Created himself a whole job. The hip hop, rap music expert, *slash*, liaison."

"That's got me thinking. You know him?"

"Say hello. First names. What do you think, I bullshit with the guy, maybe find out something about our music studio over by the airport?"

"Good, but be delicate. I don't want to raise anybody up. Who knows how close he is to the rappers anyway."

Tommy waited for Howard Amos to make a move to the bar for his "7 & 7."

"What's up, bro'? How's it going? Still doing the hip hop shit?"

"Yeah . . . Tommy, isn't it? Yep, found a home. It's good shit. I'm making sure the parties involved, the cops and the Hip Hop community, have an understanding."

"Must be some interesting shit going on, club dates and parties?"

"Man, you wouldn't believe it."

And then Tommy with the long shot.

"Got an old buddy of mine, works out by the airport, in a cargo place, on Farmers. Says they got a music studio upstairs, and those niggas takin care of business on the weekends."

"Oh yeah, an up-and-coming boy. Goes by the name of Sweet Pea Poon. Uptown brother from where you work. Terrance Byrd. Watch for him, if you're into the sound."

"Nice talking to you, bro'. Got to get the white boys some beer. Take care."

* * * * *

They paid Jimmy in cash. He kicked back five hundred dollars to the Brooklyn North Detectives.

"It's because I feel sorry for you guys," Jimmy said, getting the cash. "We Manhattan North guys get hungry and thirsty, we go a couple of minutes, we're south of Ninety Sixth Street. You poor guys got to chock out, just to get a burger."

They were in the car when Jimmy counted out sixteen hundred dollars. "I want you to give your dad a thousand for the soup kitchen, and the rest is for the girls, including Michele.

"God, Jimmy, you're too much. My dad will be *beyond* happy, and the girls will love you even more than they do now."

"The rest I invest in Super Bowl boxes. Let's head back to your house. You can make me a sandwich, and I'll put you to bed."

"What do you think about my golf game, anyway?"

"I think Bobby Washington is right," said Jimmy. "White men can't jump, and, except for Tiger, black men can't golf. And now even *he's* having a problem."

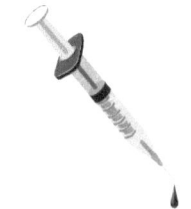

# Chapter 34

Santos Cruz was sitting at his desk banging out "post" search warrant paperwork. Kind of like a military "after action" report. A DD-5 that would describe the particulars of the execution of the warrant itself and the various pieces of paper that would be attached to it: search warrant application; tactical plan; online booking sheets for all the arrests; property vouchers; lab requests; pedigree sheets off the prisoner envelopes; lab results; apartment diagram; prisoner property receipts; any paperwork containing descriptions for Rosario; the DAR; and a whole lot more.

Sgt. Quinn was off to the side in the boss's cubicle doing a recap sheet that recapped all the other recap sheets that he had done recently. The paperwork was absurd.

Tommy Bell was organizing the surveillance tapes from *Dinero Mandar*, the store the undercovers were running up on West 158th Street. The videos had to be entered into evidence at the tape room at Special Narcotics.

Frank Martin was drinking a coffee, eating a pack of Devil Dogs, and nursing a hangover.

Bobby Washington was in the corner, by Rudy the Bullfrog, reading *Trick Baby* by Iceberg Slim.

Charlie Defranco walked into the cubicle carrying a stack of newspapers, the New York *Times*, nicely bundled and he put them on his desk.

"Hey Defranco what are you doing with those papers?" asked Bobby.

"Captain Sink reads the *Times*, daily. Says he always wants to know what the enemy is thinking. The *Times* is perfect for the bottom of my hamster, rabbit, and birdcages I got at home. I call it shit on top of shit."

Charlie asked Bobby, "Another *Slim* book?"

"That's right. Just finished *Alright Willie and Me*. This guy, Slim, is addicted to pussy more than Bill Clinton."

Jimmy rolled in and went right to his desk, entered his password for the NYPD data base and began to search for information on up-and-coming rapper, Sweet Pea Poon, a.k.a. Terrance Byrd, the name hip hop detective Howard Amos had given Tommy at golf.

Amos was right about Byrd. His last known address was the same building as Robert Bolt, good old Slice, and Ordell Mitchell. He had taken collars for narcotic sales on multiple occasions and had a couple of robbery arrests within the confines of the Nineteenth on the East Side. *And* he had been incarcerated.

"Tommy, where do you think our boy Sweet Pea Poon served time?"

"Only because you asked me the question like you did, I'm going to say the same place as our *imam*, Rasheed Abdullah."

"Right you are, pal of mine. Shawangunk Correctional. You know it might be worth our while, maybe see if we can find out some information about this program up in the jail, got these guys converting to Islam. Maybe speak to the warden quoted in the paper."

"Find out where he lives, make a day of it," said Tommy shaking his head.

Jimmy printed out all the information regarding Terrance Byrd. He accessed his photo. He took the paperwork and stuck it in the file with the question mark on the front.

And then Bobby Washington, from the corner, to Tommy Bell, "Forgot to ask you, Tommy. How was the golf shit?"

"Good, Bobby. Lots of laughs. Jimmy got a hole-in-one for five grand."

"Fuckin' money goes to money. They make the brother the caddy?"

"No, and I was into it. I'd do it again."

"World's gone crazy. Bell's golfing, and a fuckin' guy is the Woman of the Year. Next thing you tell me, McTigue stops drinking beer, and Martin stops smoking guys."

\* \* \* \* \*

The Paris Café was on South Street, within spitting distance of the East River and the South Street Seaport. It was established in 1873, and it had been serving the public continually until Hurricane Sandy walloped the Eastern Seaboard and New York. It took fifty-one, long, tortuous weeks to get the place up and running again. It was back in form.

Jimmy walked through the front door, the South Street entrance, a little before one. The place was all wood and glass, with a classic Victorian Bar in the back. Off to the left, inside the door, was a raised dining area. The tables were beginning to fill with the lunchtime crowd. Earl Hogan was sitting in the corner with the *Racing Form* spread out in front of him.

"Still into the ponies, aren't you, Earl?"

"Yeah, Jimmy. What can I say? OTB closing down in the City killed me. Had to open my own account, which can be dangerous. Take a seat. Great seeing you again the other night."

Jimmy's phone rang. "Yeah . . . okay . . . five minutes . . . I'll order for you. Tommy, he's a few minutes out."

"I can see he's a good man. You guys are comfortable together."

"Yeah, Earl, it's great. I don't have to tell you that you always need a running-around partner. I fell in love with his wife and daughters, too. You know, seeing you with the *Racing Form*, can't help but remind me of Haskell and Delgado."

"Shit, I almost forgot about those two guys. Never saw it coming. I knew Haskell liked to gamble, but God . . . and Delgado, what was *he* thinking?"

"How many years were they ripping off drug dealers?" asked Jimmy. "Just goes to show you that you never know. I worked with Delgado, and always thought he was a sharp piece of work. But fuck them both. I'm glad they're doing time. Made it hard for all of us."

Earl, changing the subject, "How about you, Jimmy? How are you feeling and how long has it—"

"Been?" Jimmy said. "Six years, four months, and nine days."

There was an awkward silence for a moment, and then, Jimmy said, "Let's order up. I'm starving."

The young waitress came over, and Earl ordered the herb-roasted, half chicken, and Jimmy, two Paris burgers for Tommy and himself. "I'll have a Guinness, too," Jimmy said to the girl.

Earl was already drinking some sort of craft beer. He started laughing.

"Do you still give up beer for Lent, Jimmy?"

"Yep, every year. But I get the special dispensation for Patty's Day."

Tommy walked in and said, "What's up guys?" and to the girl, "just a club soda in a pint glass."

Earl got down to business as soon as the waitress stepped off. "Here goes, guys. We, meaning the Feds, were looking at your boy, Abdullah, pretty frequently, but then some other shit came up, time sensitive, if you know what I mean. Plenty of 302s on him. That's the Fed version of a DD5. Up in the office, the five, now, for us is an ROI, report of investigation. Now remember we're talking about who's getting to the World Series, not anything two guys without a security clearance would be interested in."

Jimmy said, "Ten-Four."

"Rasheed Abdullah, I know you got his real name, did time upstate, I think it was Elmira."

"Shawangunk Correctional," said Jimmy.

"That's right. Got radicalized. Really took to it. Fluent in Arabic in five years—and a bad dude. We got him, even now, referring to the Jews as the descendants of pigs and apes. And right after Bin Laden got whacked, he was all over complaining the U.S. government killed the asshole. But the guy gets invited to lead a prayer service by the City Council, and the Democrats love him."

"He actually says the Jews come from pigs and apes?" asked Tommy.

"It's crazy, but true. And he tries to peddle himself off as a moderate."

"I've read articles detailing the same kind of stuff before," added Jimmy. "People don't want to believe it. I can't see how the Jews can still vote Democrat. It's just plain crazy. They're ready to cut ties right now with Israel. Jesus, that Iran deal. Wonder what Chuck Schumer is going to tell his constituents when the mushroom cloud is wafting over Jerusalem?"

"They got no scruples. They'd sell their souls to be politically correct and get into and remain in office. But back to our boy, Abdullah. We got him at the *Hajj* last year, took a Turkish Airline flight from JFK to Istanbul, and on to King Abdulaziz International. Checked into the Dar Al Ghufran Hotel in downtown Mecca. Satellite TV and a mini bar. People out in the dessert in tents. Go figure."

"I know I shouldn't, but I'm guessing some of this is from a CI?" said Jimmy.

"Don't ask. Besides the Feds don't use the term. It's a source."

The food came, and the boys took a couple of minutes to dig in. Jimmy ordered a Diet Pepsi with the meal, Tommy and Earl stayed with what they were drinking.

Earl, into it again, "He returns, like I said, we kind of backed off, because of other priorities. We know he's got dudes from the mosque heading to Poco Loco Paintball in Schwenksville, Pennsylvania to play army or something. Lots of mosques into the paintball. Don't know if he ever made the trip. We *do* know that he's an unindicted co-conspirator of Aboud Abani, the asshole that got convicted of conspiracy to blow up the Garden during the Westminster Dog Show. Only time I ever saw those PETA assholes on the side of the good guys. Its okay to butcher and blow up people, but don't fuck with Reginald and his terrier."

"Great, Earl. He was spotted with some gangbanger from the Polo Ground Projects. And just got some information on some up-and-coming rapper," said Jimmy.

"Raised us up a bit," said Tommy nodding.

"Here's the thing, too. Either of you guys know what the Handschu Guidelines are?"

Both of them shaking their heads, no.

"It goes all the way back to the seventies, the days of the Weather Underground and the Black Panthers, and it concerns monitoring political groups. Surveillance and shit. The rules got relaxed a bit after Nine-Eleven, but they are there, nonetheless. You can't be starting an investigation and running with it, unless you have reasonable evidence of a future crime. You want to see what you can dig up; I don't think it's a problem. We, meaning the Feds, already have an interest. We just took a break because of more serious shit. You can piggyback on our investigation."

"That's great, Earl," said Jimmy.

"I hear anything, I'll give you a call. You didn't hear any of this from me. They find out I'm giving you the heads-up, I'm back to patrol without a meal. Above all, be cautious. We're at war." And then, Earl was going for his wallet.

"No, thanks again, Earl. I got this." And Jimmy waved him off.

"Nope, you're always buying, Jimmy. Besides, I had "No One Told Me" in the fifth at Belmont, across the board, yesterday. Had to bet it. It was Hillary's answer, when she was asked why no one did shit regarding security for the Embassy in Benghazi. Need *anything*, let me know. We're at war, boys. Don't forget it. I'll finish the form."

"Okay, Earl, we'll see you," they both said.

And, as they went out the door, Jimmy said, "This question mark file is beginning to grow."

* * * * *

They headed out toward the back, past the Victorian Bar, and the televisions, and five or six guys drinking on the rail, and exited the Paris Café onto Peck Slip and the cobble stoned street that reached all the way up to Pearl.

"Where to?" Tommy asked.

"I got the car parked off Madison Street behind One PP. I knew a guy in the booth. Let's take a walk over to the Pioneer Bar, the place Bobby saw our boy, Artie, going into."

"You ever been in there? asked Tommy."

"Never even heard of it."

"Holy shit, a bar in New York that Jimmy McTigue hasn't been in, or heard of. Impossible."

"Keep it up, Tommy, and I'll make an EEO complaint on your ass."

They passed Water Street, going west. "Tommy, right down the block, the old Jeremy's. Quite a place, back in the day. Got hit in the eye by a flying bra one time. That kind of joint."

"Never was in there, Jimmy. The good old days, though, huh?"

"Yeah, and another reminder of how much the job has changed. Used to be, if you had to work the Barrier Detail for the day, you'd head down to the Twenty-Fifth Street Pier, get on a truck, and, after delivering one load to a parade route, or a demonstration location, you'd be in Jeremy's at ten thirty in the morning drinking a cold one. Bucket of nips for four dollars.

But that pier gave me the chills. *Eerie.* Way in the back, hardly any light, they had the radio cars that Eddie Byrne and Rainey and Scarangella were in, when they got ambushed. The cars were still considered evidence."

"Eddie Byrne I'm familiar with," said Tommy. "Assassinated by drug dealers in Jamaica, sitting out in front of a witness's house. I don't think I have ever heard of the other two."

They crossed Pearl Street and continued west to Park Row by Gracie Mansion.

"Nineteen eighty-one, Richard Rainey and John Scarangella are working in the One-Thirteen, and respond to a job in Saint Albans, Queens. They were behind a white van, when the back doors open up and two members of the Black Liberation Army start letting rounds go. Scarangella is killed, and Rainey gets hit fourteen times and survives. Just passed away, may God bless his soul. But here's the kicker. To this day there are many who believe that Joanne Chesimard was in the van, the same bitch that killed a Jersey Trooper in nineteen seventy three. And where is she now? In *Cuba.*"

"The same Cuba we're making nice with," said Tommy.

"Yeah, an absolute disgrace. The President, Kerry, they don't even have the balls to bring it up, the fact that Cuba is harboring a fugitive from American justice that has the blood of at least one cop on her hands. Absolutely pathetic."

Up on Broadway now, they headed north and at Barclays Street, Jimmy said, "Let's go over to Saint Peters. I want to say hello to God."

Tommy stayed outside, and Jimmy went in and knelt in the last pew, and asked God for forgiveness, and said, under his breath, "I miss you, Catherine. I miss you bad." He said a Hail

Mary and an Our Father. He made the sign of the cross and then he was out on the street, the corner of Barclay and Church, with Tommy, looking south at the Freedom Tower.

"I still can't believe it, Tommy," and there was a profound sadness in his voice.

"Neither can I."

It took a couple of minutes to get to the Pioneer, south side of Chambers, right off of Church. Real dive. Long wooden bar on the right as you walked in, with chairs and tables opposite. Johnny Cash singing *Drunken Ira Hayes* off the jukebox by the rest rooms. Three guys spread out at the bar, drinking beers right out of the can, two Pabst Blue Ribbons and a Bud. There was a young girl, in tight dungaree shorts and a pink bathing suit top, serving up the drinks. She had a body that demanded tips.

"What can I get you honeys?"

"Two Coors Lite in the can would be fine," said Jimmy.

They stood at the bar, the two of them, not saying anything, just thinking. Johnny Cash went off and now it was Jimmy Dean singing *Big Bad John*. The bartender was at the far end, now, bullshitting with a customer and fooling with the television. A white guy in his thirties, wearing a suit, walked in. Looked like a Wall Street guy, and he went right to the end of the bar.

Tommy and Jimmy were both looking down that way, when they saw the girl's closed, right hand make a move to the guy's open, left hand. He dropped a ten on the bar and said, "I can't stay. I'll see you later, baby."

"You see that?"

"Yeah, Jimmy. Little hand-to-hand."

"I'm guessing weed. Let's get out of here. I'll ring Manhattan South, just for the hell of it, and see if they got any kites on this place."

\* \* \* \* \*

They had signed out, and were in Jimmy's jeep and heading over the Triboro, when he turned to Tommy and said, "I'm thinking about what Earl was telling us. And I'm thinking of asking Basically Bill something."

"What's that?"

"How would he feel about converting to Islam?"

# Jake McNicholas

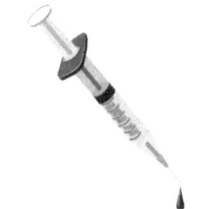

# Chapter 35

**The phone vibrated.** Jimmy noticed the unfamiliar number.

"McTigue."

"Yes," and then a long pause. "Jimmy McTigue?"

"That's right, Meg Wilson." He had been thinking of her. "What can I do for you, my dear?" He never said that and it surprised him.

Meg paused and then a nervous laugh. "You remembered! Listen, I must confess, my curiosity has gotten the better of me, so I'm coming right out and asking you. Jimmy McTigue, are you a cop?"

He gave it a moment for effect. "What makes you think that?"

"Well, when I turned to say goodbye that day at the pizzeria, I saw handcuffs hanging off the belt of the guy you were with, and I was just wondering."

"You realize that if I tell you I have to kill you. Let me ask you something before I answer. Are you still walking around with tomato sauce on the side of your mouth?"

"Aaah, Jimmy, give a girl a break."

"You got some great observation skills. Yep, I am."

"How come you didn't say anything?"

"No reason to."

There was an uncomfortable silence and Jimmy decided to come back at her.

"What about you, Meg? You still causing trouble in restaurants? What are *you* doing to put pizza on the table?"

She still wanted to keep the charade going so she went with, "I work in an administrative capacity in the movie industry. Very, very boring and certainly nothing glamorous. Long days, but it's interesting."

"Really, any movies that I might have seen? I'll be honest with you, I think the last flick I saw in the movies was Rocky Number Three. What are they up to now, Eleven?"

"Oh, you're funny, Jimmy. Probably nothing you would know, if you're not a movie buff."

"Oh, I didn't say that. I'm into the old stuff. What's the term? . . . I got it. Are you on location now?"

"Look at you. Got it down. No, I'm working over at the Silver Cup Studios."

"In Long Island City."

"Yes. It's a nice place, and I love the neighborhood."

"How long will you be working there?"

"Probably another couple of weeks," and Meg started getting a good feeling.

And then Jimmy surprising himself, because it came right out of the blue. "Do you like burgers?"

"Sure do!"

"Can you manage to sit down and eat one without leaving ketchup all over your mouth?"

Meg, giggling and having a hard time getting it out, "Wow Jimmy, you won't let a girl forget. I'll try."

"Tell me about all the recent movies I *haven't* seen."

"Sure, why not."

"Six, tonight?"

"Okay, where?"

"The best burgers in New York. Donovan's on Roosevelt Avenue. Should I pick you up, Meg?"

"No, that's okay, I've got my car." And then she asked, "Will you tell me about work?"

"I'll think about it."

\* \* \* \* \*

There was never, ever a time that Jimmy McTigue was over by Donovan's that he didn't go over to 57th Street and Woodside Avenue, by St. Sebastian's School, and stand in front of the memorial on the corner and say a prayer.

It was simple in its makeup, a formidable slab of granite with twenty-eight names listed on it—brave sons of this section of Queens, who were killed in Vietnam. The neighborhood zip code, 11377, lost more men in that war than any other in the United States. Above the memorial, etched in the stone, were the sentiments of a little girl from the school that read: "Our Finest, Our Bravest, Our Best, God Grant You all Eternal Rest." Below, just five simple words: "They Are Now With God."

He had gotten over by the restaurant early, parked his Jeep on Roosevelt Avenue in front of the McDonald's, and walked over. He stood in front of this sacred stone, with his hands behind his back, his head down, and lost in thought and prayer.

Meg pulled up shortly thereafter and found a spot in front of the school. She spotted Jimmy. At first she thought of just going into the pub and not disturbing him, but, then, she reconsidered, and quietly came up to him and stood at his side. She left it to Jimmy to break the silence.

"I always stop here, Meg. It just moves me. They were called upon and they served. That says it all."

"Kind of like cops, too. It seems unimaginable, so many young men. How their friends and families must have been affected."

He took a minute or two to explain the significance of that granite and the brutal sacrifice this old neighborhood had made during Vietnam.

"Think about it. See the name there?" Jimmy pointing to the monument. "Tommy Noonan, USMC, Medal of Honor winner, posthumously. There was another guy from right here, Robert O'Malley, who also won the Medal of Honor with the Marines. He survived. But what are the odds and what does it tell you about this special neighborhood. They were both in the same kindergarten class," and Jimmy's voice trailed off. And then, "You ready for a burger?"

"I certainly am."

"Let's do it."

They walked in and headed past the four old guys sitting on stools listening to Nat King Cole off the jukebox, and solving the world's problems. They made a right, past the bar, and hit the corner table in the small side room, Jimmy holding Meg's chair out and helping her sit. He sat with his back to the wall, facing the doorway.

"Have you been here before?"

"Not this one, Jimmy, the one over by Bell Boulevard."

"This one's the original, the one with the burger reputation."

The waitress came over and passed out the menus and asked about drinks. Meg was going with a club soda, Jimmy went with a pint of Guinness, when the girl looked at Meg and said,

"I *know* you, and I really do. I just can't figure out from where. Help me."

Meg, a little nervous said, "I have one of those faces." And then changing the subject, "Cheeseburger the way to go, right, Jimmy?"

"Oh yeah, the Woodside burger with mashed potatoes and a little gravy, instead of fries."

"Sounds good to me," said Meg. "Make it two."

They toasted with their water glasses and smiled at each other.

"All right, let's get to it," Meg laughed. "The interrogation begins, *Mister* McTigue. Let's have it. Are you a member of New York's Finest?"

Jimmy started laughing, but he was watching her all the time, the way the freckles danced on each side of her nose, and the light above the table played with her hair. Meg could see the way he was looking at her and smiled. "Let's go, my friend. Give it up. I want *all* the details."

"Nope. I'm the professional member of law enforcement, here. You first."

So Meg gave Jimmy everything: growing up in Breezy Point; the college years; travel; and work. Everything, that is, *except* the fact that she was a big-time movie star. He took it all in, but the biggest thing that registered with him was that she was single.

"Now your turn, my friend," and she started laughing again.

"Not much really, Meg. Marine Corps, a little college, and then the greatest job in the world, the NYPD—just like my dad, may God rest his soul. I'm a detective working in narcotics in the north of Manhattan. Doing God's work and having laughs.

Gets so, sometimes, you're afraid to take off and miss something."

"Have you ever shot anybody, Jimmy?"

"Meg, I'm like most of the guys that are cops. I've never fired my weapon except at the range. Hope to keep it that way. Hell, I don't even like shooting, and I'm not that good. My partner, Tommy, says if it hits the fan, I'd be better off throwing my gun at the bad guy."

The burgers came and they dug in, but not before the waitress again told Meg how familiar she looked.

Then Jimmy, joking, "Maybe she got you mixed up with a movie star."

Meg gave a nervous laugh and Jimmy a "Stop," when she surprised herself and said, "You're not married are you, Detective McTigue?"

Right away, she regretted it, because she could see something dark and melancholy come over him. He was looking at his plate, forking the mashed potatoes, and she just sat there in an awkward silence, listening to his breathing. She reached over to his forearm, put her hand on it, and squeezed, then said it, because she thought it *needed* to be said, "I'm sorry."

He took a sip of his pint and looked her straight in her beautiful, blue eyes, and said, "No need to be. I lost my wife over six years ago." And then, before she could feel sorry for asking, he said, "I can't believe it. I can't take you anywhere," and he made the gesture with the napkin indicating she had ketchup on the corner of her mouth—and they both started laughing again.

They spent the rest of the meal giggling together like two old classmates. Meg tried to pay the bill, but he took care of it and said, "You can buy some other time," and they walked out together onto Roosevelt Avenue, splashes of sun still shining through the overhead tracks of the Number 7 Train.

"Thanks, Jimmy, I really enjoyed that."

"Me, too. Can I walk you to your car?"

"No worries, it's just around the corner."

He went to give her a peck on the cheek, and she moved her head and kissed him full on the mouth.

"I have any ketchup on me?" he asked.

"Don't start," and she gave him a playful punch in the arm.

"I've got your number, is it okay?"

"Sure, Jimmy," she said. "Absolutely."

She was in her car and driving away, and he was pulling out and heading toward the city, when the waitress came out the front door, with the bartender, and said, "Now, I remember. *That* was Meg Cassidy."

Jake McNicholas

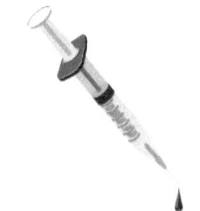

# Chapter 36

Jimmy and Tommy met Basically Bill in the park across the street from the Dyckman Houses. He was sitting on a bench, way in the back, the park pretty much empty, except for a young mother and her child. They weren't doing much. The days of kids having something to play on were over. Gone were the swing sets and monkey bars. Heaven forbid a kid fell and the parents didn't feel compelled to sue. Bill was reading *The Power Broker*, about Robert Moses, when they walked up.

Jimmy, out in front, "Billy Boy, how goes it?"

"It's all good, Jimmy. But basically, I'm just a little curious. Wondering what you got planned for me?"

"No worries, Bill," said Tommy.

"Something's come up and I want to run it by you. It's kind of involved, but the bottom line is we're hoping you can give us a hand on something completely removed from narcotics. It's out there."

"Well, I'll basically be happy to help you guys any way I can."

Jimmy got right to the point. "What are you, Bill, religious-wise?"

"Well, my Mother was Catholic and my Father was a Baptist, but I don't really attend either. Might pop into church on Easter Sunday, or Christmas. Why?"

"We need somebody to get into a mosque over in Brooklyn," Jimmy explained. "You could do it without raising anybody up. It's predominately a Black location, from here and Africa, with some Yemenis and 'Paki' cab drivers thrown in for good measure. The *imam* is a brother, goes by the name of Rasheed Abdullah—American-born, ex-con. Got religion in prison. We'd like you to get in there, give us a feel of what's going on. You're a smart guy. Read up on Islam. Anyone asks, you are just beginning to embrace it. Looking to convert. You know Brooklyn at all?"

"I basically do. Used to work at the Brooklyn Army Terminal."

"You know anything about Islam?" asked Jimmy.

"One thing I can basically tell you, something is messed up with a religion where people can justify cutting off heads and blowing up women and children. I know Muhammad is the prophet, Mecca, the Holy City, and you're supposed to make a pilgrimage there—they call it a *hajj*—at least once in your life. And all kinds of interpretations for different things in the Koran. Friday's the big day at the mosque. I work with a guy who is Muslim. That's about it."

"Listen Bill," Jimmy continued. "We give you a ride over there this Friday. In the meantime, you do some reading, get a *feel*, and, like I said, anyone challenges you, you're looking to come on board. Who knows, they might even have a program that assists newcomers. You're off Friday, Saturday, it could work out. We wouldn't even be interested in this, if someone hadn't said that the guy was talking shit. Apparently, hate crime stuff for everybody today *except* Muslims. You see what's up, especially if Abdullah is still yapping away. Stuff that's not . . . *appropriate*. If It Doesn't Sound Right If It Was Coming Out

Of The Mouth Of a Priest, a Minister or a Rabbi—*that's* what we're talking about. You think you can give it a try?"

"Basically I think I can do that. Let me do some studying."

\* \* \* \* \*

Basically Bill did some research, so he would feel a little comfortable inside the mosque. He peppered his buddy who was from the Ivory Coast, hit the Internet, and took a couple of books out of the library. But he wasn't the only one.

Jimmy knew virtually nothing about Islam, so he did the same. He learned that Muslim means "One who submits to God," and that they worshipped *God*, but *not* the prophet, Muhammad. *And* that there were well over a billion Muslims scattered throughout the world, which had him thinking. Even if only one percent were stone, cold crazies, who believed in murder and mayhem, that was an awful lot of people willing to blow themselves up for a ticket into Paradise and a *shitload* of virgins.

It turned out that the largest number of Muslim converts in the United States were Black. And they now made up twenty to thirty percent of all American Muslims. Awful lot of brothers. The prisons were rife with programs to make the switch easier, and there was plenty of information available that shed light on the classes, and the prison *imams* doing the teaching. It was documented, for instance, that some of those *imams* and their students were celebrating "The Towers" coming down on 9/11. But with political correctness corrupting all segments of society, raising a voice of concern regarding the prison programs, was tantamount to hate speech. The powers-that-be were just not having it.

Jimmy figured to send Basically Bill into the *Masjid* and see what Abdullah had to say right out in the open. Maybe he talks shit like the day Aiman Qantan was there. Maybe he doesn't. Also see who he's hanging with, keep an eyeball out for Slice. Show him that photo and the others from the Question Mark File. Give it a few visits, see what's up; nothing pans out, put it to bed. Go back to chasing the "Kilo Fairy" full-time.

Basically Bill was on board, and everything was set for Friday prayer in Brooklyn.

\* \* \* \* \*

You know, Tommy," Jimmy said, "we got some history with radical Black Muslims, the NYPD does."

They were in 582, Jimmy driving, with Tommy up front, and heading over to Broadway and Nagle to pick up Basically Bill for the trip to Brooklyn.

"I never knew this," he continued. "Nineteen seventy-two, up in the Two-Eight, a Ten-Thirteen comes over at the mosque on West Hundred Sixteenth Street. Only it's all bullshit, just a ruse to draw our guys in. The savages started yelling *Allahu Akbar,* and Philip Cardillo, first one on the scene with his partner, is shot. Dies six days later. Bunch of other guys are beaten senseless and the shit hits the fan. Rocks and bottles coming off of rooftops, the whole nine yards. But here's what's absolutely appalling. Our job surrendered, gave up, let the brothers that were in the mosque that day walk out the door without so much as a question. No one was ever brought to justice. The head of the mosque was Louis Farrakhan, and Ben Ward, the former PC, apologized to him. We had a spineless mayor then, too, John Lindsey, and he and the PC then, Pat Murphy, refused to go to the funeral. An absolute disgrace."

"God, I wonder how those poor bastards felt, like, back then," said Tommy, "to be abandoned like that."

"Kind of like the way we felt when the mayor treated us that way when he was running for office."

They spotted Bill on the corner, dressed in a pair of dungarees, black shoes, and a dress shirt, and he hopped into the car. Jimmy got on the phone then and told Richie Whalen and Charlie Defranco that they had the package and that they were heading over to Brooklyn, to the mosque. Those guys were going to meet them there, just in case something came up.

Bill was in the back seat getting comfortable when he said, "Basically, I read up on Islam. Used the Internet, but got most of my information from my buddy at work. He wouldn't hurt a fly. Born and raised and even made the trip to Mecca. He said the *Hajj* was both moving and scary. The crowds are unbelievable. There are people dying from stampeding most years."

Jimmy said, "I guess kind of like Black Friday shopping after Thanksgiving."

"He was more than happy to explain things. Like you guys said, I can basically always fall back to the fact that I'm just starting to get interested in it."

"That's great, Billy, now take a look at these," and Jimmy began to pass a series of photos to Bill one by one. "First guy here is the *imam*, Rasheed Abdullah; we're figuring he's going to be doing Friday's prayer, because that's the big one during the week."

"Yeah," said Basically Bill. "The *Jumu'ah*."

"Great, Billy Boy," said Jimmy. "You've been studying. Second guy is a brother he did time with," and then Jimmy showed him a photo of rapper Sweet Pea Poon. "Next guy he's been seen in the company of," and he passed the photo back of Slice, and then, just for the hell of it, Ordell Mitchell, the guy stopped by Frank White and Al Gavin up in the Bronx by Yankee Stadium.

"Just take a look, you never know. Again, what we're really interested in is if the guy is still talking smack. There's nothing going on, that's fine, too. We pack up and forget about it, leave it for the Feds."

"Basically, no problem, Jimmy."

\* \* \* \* \*

The Suleiman Mosque was located on Atlantic Avenue off Classon Avenue, north side of the street, in a heavy commercial area. Named after the famed Ottoman ruler, and the *masjid* built in 1557 by Islam's greatest Architect, Sinan, it had been a large auto parts store, which had been transformed some years back. It got its name years before Rasheed Abdullah had arrived on the scene.

They came over the Brooklyn Bridge and drove to Atlantic, then made the left, and Jimmy told Bill that the mosque would be up on the left, a bunch of blocks past the Barclays Center and the Atlantic Center Mall.

"Hunker down, Billy," said Jimmy, as they neared the location. "We're going to drive past, let you get a look-see, and then we're coming back around and dumping you off over on Underhill Avenue. You give me a call when you get out. You're on your own, as far as getting back up to the Heights. Here's thirty bucks for your trouble. Be careful, Bill, me and Tommy have taken a liking to you."

They made the drop over on Underhill and then Jimmy reached out to Charlie. He and Richie were already in the vicinity. Jimmy and Tommy took a slow ride on Atlantic Avenue east bound, and found a spot by Curesmart Storage and Logistics on the other side of the avenue from the mosque. They could see the front of the location, see the people heading inside for prayer, and taxis and other vehicles parking around the area. It was getting congested. They had the binoculars. Couple of minutes later, they had an eyeball on Basically Bill walking on the mosque side of the street. A little bit later, he was inside.

* * * * *

Basically Bill had no idea what the place had been before, because all evidence of that other life had been erased. The inside of the building had been completely gutted, and now it was wide open. He could see the prayer niche that he had read about, which faced Mecca, off at the far end, and, to the right of that, the *minbar*, or pulpit. No statues, nor stained glass, nor murals were present, but the walls were decorated in attractive tile. There was nothing to sit on, except some chairs in the back, which were beginning to fill up with the elderly and handicapped.

He followed the crowd, and, once in, removed his shoes and placed them on the floor to the left of the entrance. Off to the right was a room with eight spigots and basins, where the worshippers went to perform *wudu*, the purification ritual. Near the room there was a staircase leading downward, and on both sides stood two large Black males wearing windbreakers that said

Security on the back. They were there with their arms folded across their chests, and watched the crowd intently as it began to fill the room in preparation for prayer.

Bill then remembered the first photo that Jimmy had shown him, and now he watched as Rasheed Abdullah came up the stairs and walked into the room. He was dressed in dark pants and a long-sleeved tunic, and he wore the skullcap. The salt-and-pepper beard he sported was neatly trimmed. He made his way across the room and ascended the few stairs to the *minbar*.

And then the ritual began, and Basically Bill got right into it, remembering what he had read and heard and also following the others: raising his hands and bowing and saying three times to himself, "Glory to God Almighty"; standing and praying and then prostrating himself, his forehead touching the floor; then a medieval version of sitting; and the forehead once again to the floor. After some time, Abdullah addressed the worshippers.

"*Assalaamu 'Alaikum*, my brothers."

"We are united in a great struggle, the *kafir* being our sworn enemy whether it is here or in the lands across the seas. We see our brothers in the Zionist state continue their righteous *intifada*. Make no mistake, they are driven to protect our Jerusalem holy sites from the filthy feet of the Jew. And here in this impure land, we, in our own way, must continue the *Jihad*. Let no man or authority tell us what to do or how to live our lives. There is no law but Islamic law, *Sharia*, and we will not be happy or content until God and the Prophet Muhammad's law is spread throughout this corrupt and evil land in which we live. *Assalaamu 'Alaikum*, my brothers."

He stepped down from the pulpit, and then the two men in the security windbreakers appeared at the opening, by the staircase, arms still folded. Abdullah walked toward them and descended into the basement.

Bill grabbed his shoes, walked outside, and headed toward the Atlantic Avenue train station up by the mall. He gave Jimmy a call. "I'm out, and going toward Flatbush Avenue. Yeah, he was basically over the top. Talked about the *Jihad* and the filthy Jew. I'll get my thoughts together and write it all down. Have it for you later, Jimmy."

"Good man, Bill. See you tonight or tomorrow."

And then a call to Charlie Defranco. "We're going to hang for a while, see what's up. Yeah, he was dissing the Jews. You guys want to go back, no problem."

"You know what, Tommy, let's give it some time while we're out here. Charlie and Richie are in."

"Sure, Jimmy. Oh shit, take a look at the bumper sticker on the Chevy Traverse at the light. Tell me the world, as we know it, is not over."

The bumper sticker read: "My Son Was Inmate of the Month at Riker's Island Correctional Facility."

They sat there with the car running and listening to sports radio, the host trying to make the case that the catcher for the San Diego Padres, who had recently been arrested for gang assault on a Manhattan doorman, should be able to play his next game. They had their department radios on their seats, in between their legs, one on Division, and the other point-to-point, if they had to reach the other guys and weren't using the cell phones.

The crowd at the mosque had disappeared pretty quickly, and the taxis and double-parked cars were gone now, but not before Jimmy had used the binoculars and noted license plate numbers of some of the vehicles. Run them in the system, see what comes up. After a while Tommy said he was going to stretch his legs.

"I'll take a walk over there, get a closer look. See if anything is happening."

Jimmy sat back, closed his eyes for a couple of seconds, and thought of Meg—just the way she looked the other day, sitting across from him under the light, the way she smiled and giggled. Tommy's Michelle would definitely say that she was "a keeper." Yep, real nice gal, that Meg Wilson only . . . only. He was still having trouble moving on. Maybe call her some time over the weekend, see how she was doing.

Tommy came back, "All quiet on the western front."

"We'll give it an hour or two, and then head back to the base. We're out here anyway, and your company is so wonderful," Jimmy said.

"Easy, big guy. I think you're beginning to lose it."

Charlie called on the phone and told Jimmy they were heading over to the Sunset Deli for something to eat.

"I'm good, Charlie. Tommy, you hungry?"

"Let's wait, maybe go for a sit-down when we get back."

And then, not two minutes later, coming toward them on Atlantic Avenue traveling west, was Artie Levin's red Escalade. It pulled up in front of the mosque and out stepped a male Black in a blue baseball hat. Jimmy used the binoculars, handed them over to Tommy, and said, "That looks like our boy, Slice. What do you think Thomas?"

"Oh yeah. Look at him. Eyeballing everything, up on his toes. This guy spends every waking minute raised up."

"You know that. He doesn't relax. Exactly the way he was the other day when we verified his address, up at the Polo Grounds, and spotted him on the street."

"Would be a real bitch conducting surveillance on him. Definitely need a couple of cars."

Tommy tried reaching the boys on the radio and the cell phone. "Charlie and Richie must be on the Sunset line. It went right to voice mail."

They watched Slice walk into the mosque, and then watched, five minutes later, as the two security guys came out the front and stationed themselves some five feet from each side of the Escalade, facing the street. If they had been dressed in black suits with earpieces, you would think they were members of the President's Secret Service team. They were playing that game and surveying the area.

"Here comes our boy, Slice, holding the door," said Jimmy. "And look at *this*. It's the Jew hater, himself, Rasheed Abdullah."

Abdullah was dressed-down now, no long tunic, or skullcap. He wore a pair of dress pants and a sport's jacket, and he was carrying a package in his hand, about the size of a shoebox. He got into the front seat, next to Slice—the security brothers getting comfortable in the back.

Tommy tried Richie and Charlie with no luck, but left a message that they were on the move.

"We give them a loose tail. See how it goes."

"You want me to drive, Jimmy? You *are* getting old, you know."

"Have I told you to *stick it*, lately, Tommy? I don't know how Michele puts up with you?"

They went Atlantic Avenue to the BQE, and then to the Belt Parkway, Slice driving nice and slow and observing all the traffic regulations. He drove onto the Belt in the right lane, and Jimmy stayed a couple of cars back.

"He's probably the only guy in the car that has a valid driver's license—not revoked or suspended," said Jimmy.

"He *is* cautious, ain't he? But it works out as slow as *you* usually drive. You guys learn from the same instructor?"

"You are asking for it, Tommy, you certainly are."

They had gotten word to Charlie and Richie and they were lagging behind, but on the Belt, right around Coney Island.

Slice was still in the right lane when they passed the Pennsylvania Avenue Exit, and then Jimmy turned down the car radio and said, "Are you thinking what I'm thinking, Tommy?"

"If it's got something to do with the Airport and gangster rap on a Friday night, I'm right with you brother."

"Yeah, exactly what our Street Crime buddy, Chris, alluded to. Off the hook on a Friday. It's still a little early, but it's after business hours. Let's see where our boys go."

Slice was still cruising, no directional signal indicated, and he had been going to it from the moment they left the mosque. They passed the Erskine Street Exit, and then those for the Rockaways and Kennedy Airport.

"Farmers Boulevard should be coming up, Jimmy."

And then, off in the distance, Exit 21B, and, sure enough, the red Escalade with the directional on and staying right. Jimmy eased back, gave them some more room, and said, "No use blowing it now. Let's give them plenty of play. We'll pause a bit and give them time to get settled."

Tommy was on the phone with Charlie and Richie.

They pulled off the exit and grabbed a coffee on the corner, and gave Slice and the boys ten minutes. Then they headed over to Sunrise Cargo. The two garage doors that had been open, when they had visited before, were closed, and there was absolutely no activity in the front of the building. The street out front was virtually empty and there was no sign of the Escalade.

"Pull down the block, Jimmy. I'll take a stroll and peek into the parking lot."

Tommy took a slow walk over to the spot to the right of Sunrise Cargo and behind the high wooden fence. Only a few vehicles parked in the back, but right up against the wall and the entrance, Artie Levin's Escalade.

"Our boys are there, Jimmy," as Tommy sat back in the car.

"Good stuff. Let's see what's up. Charlie and Richie are five minutes out. And they wound up getting us a couple of sandwiches anyway."

Jake McNicholas

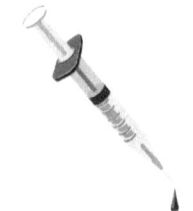

# Chapter 37

**One thing was for certain.**  Half the time, Artie Levin couldn't figure out where the brother was living.  One day, Artie would get him uptown, the next day, somewhere in Brooklyn. This Friday, he headed out to South Jamaica, by Archer Avenue and got Poon at, what he said was his auntie's house—actually used the word, "auntie."

By now, he was calling his rapper, Terrence Byrd, Poon, all the time.  He didn't want to be called anything else, which made it a little bit uncomfortable when he was introducing him to the movers and shakers of the music industry.  "Yes sir, Mr. Blanc, this is Mr. Poon."  But that's the way Poon wanted it.

The two of them had headed into Manhattan to take care of some business.  Poon was in full uniform: the white T-shirt; oversized dungarees; blue baseball hat, this time with no team affiliation; massive gold around his neck.  He spent half the time with his right hand—playing with himself.  If he was rapping, it would have been full time.

They took a ride over to Chelsea, over on the West Side. Artie had scoped out a professional music studio to use, once they got into full production mode.  The days of using that shit hole over by the airport would be over.  That and you couldn't keep having the wannabes, the hangers on, and the gangbangers all over the place. Artie was sure he was going to miss the weed and Tabisha's lips.

They finished up, and, in the Escalade, Poon said, "Yo, my nigga, out to the airport."

Artie still got a real kick out of being everybody's "nigga."

"Sure thing, Poon, but you got to realize that when we start the real shit, over in the new studio, we have to be careful, keep it weed-free, and the visitors to a minimum. These people don't play that shit."

"Yo, don't worry, homey, everything cool, and everything going to *be* cool. For the time being, we get out to Farmers Boulevard, got some stuff I want to do tonight. Got some good weed, and been hearing that Tabisha lookin' to get a taste of you."

Just thinking of Tabisha smoking his pipe nearly sent Artie into the Heliport on West 30th Street and the West Side Highway.

They listened to rap shit all the way out to Farmers—on so loud, Artie could feel the music vibrating in his chest. Sunrise Cargo was still open for business when they got there, the forklifts tooling around between the open garage doors, and the trucks and vans parked on the street in front. Wouldn't be long before the operation would be put to bed for the weekend. Artie pulled into the lot behind the high wooden fence. There were three other vehicles parked, all late models with tinted windows. Artie knew there were people already inside.

Poon led the way upstairs. There were maybe ten brothers hanging around, and everyone went through the six-step handshake with Poon. Slice came up and gave Artie a "my nigga" and handed him a blunt. He then gave Artie a wink, and then a nod, at Tabisha coming out of the room with the long table and chairs. Tabisha, dressed in short mini-skirt and FM high heels, and coming up to Artie and saying, "Hi baby," and reaching down between his legs and cooing, "Oh baby, you happy to see me."

She had Artie by the hand, walking with him, when Slice came up and asked, "My nigga, how 'bout letting me hold the keys? Picking somebody up, and then coming right back." Artie was about to give the request careful consideration, when Tabisha stuck her tongue in his ear, and he surrendered.

The place was pretty much the way it was left on previous occasions. All the music equipment was still set up in the same area, the tables with the computers and the digital audio workstations, and all the cable laid out on the floor, as it was before. The room off to the side had been cleaned up, the KFC cartons, pizza boxes, potato chip bags, empties, and the lot, thrown away. The place had been scrubbed down, but there was still no way to get rid of the smell of marijuana; it was in the walls and furniture. There were two guys in there, drinking Remy from a half-empty bottle on the table.

"Let's smoke a blunt, Artie baby, and then, after we're finished, I'll smoke *your* blunt."

Artie couldn't light it up fast enough.

\* \* \* \* \*

Slice was in Brooklyn in no time. He was getting Rasheed, the *imam,* and two of the security dudes, Abdul and Anwar. They liked to call themselves the A Team. Rasheed had done time with Poon up at Shawangunk. That was hard time, something that Slice had managed to avoid.

He entered the mosque and walked past a security guy by the inside of the door, and then down the stairs. Rasheed was in the basement, in his office, with the A Team, watching news reports concerning events in the Middle East. Most of the coverage was about the crazies in Israel, running down and stabbing Jews. The *imam* was railing at the television, when Slice came through the door.

"The Jew is the devil, and he has no right to exist. Until he realizes this, he will suffer from the vengeance of our Brothers." Abdul and Anwar were nodding in unison, and then Rasheed spotted Slice and gave him an *Assalaamu 'Alaikum.*

Slice was still a Baptist, on paper, and wasn't really looking to trade in, and just said, "Good afternoon, Rasheed."

He knew enough to turn the rap off the radio *before* they got into the car. He knew enough to keep a low profile up in the front seat with him. Rasheed got in with the box, and placed it on the floor between his legs. He didn't say a lot during the trip over.

There wasn't much traffic, once they got onto the Belt, just the usual delay when they got close to the expanse where the kite flyers hung out. Always backed-up, the traffic, drivers slowing down to watch the show. Twenty minutes out, Slice called Poon and told him they were getting close. That gave Poon time to get the brothers to stash the booze, finish the blunts, and get Tabisha on her way. Imam Rasheed didn't play that shit.

Slice took it nice and slow, kept checking his rear view mirror. Nothing.

* * * * *

Poon told everyone that Imam Rasheed was on the way. That was one of the reasons why there weren't too many people up in the studio. If it had been a regular Friday night, the place would be teeming with brothers. But now, the only guys up there were true believers—and dudes really close to Poon—who were music tech guys.

He walked into the room off to the side, and gave a nod to the two guys drinking the Remy, and one dumped the bottle under the table, and they got up and walked out. Artie had been looking at Tabisha, so he didn't see the nod, but she had picked up on it and knew it was time to leave. She said to Artie, as she squeezed his crotch, "Save that for me, baby. I got to go."

"Not now, honey. We're just getting started"

"Something's up. I'll treat you better the next time," as she put out his blunt, led him by the hand, and walked outside the room to where Poon was standing.

"See you, Poon. Take care of my baby," and she went down the stairs.

"What's going on?" asked Artie.

"Got my religious advisor coming up. A righteous brother. Don't go for the pussy and the booze and the weed. Slice picked him up. You meet him, Artie, but then you gots to go. Old school motherfuckah. Don't think he'll take to you. We're going to hang here a little while, do a little musical fuckin' around."

"Okay, Poon, you the man."

"You *know* that shit."

Slice rolled up outside, now, and put the Escalade right by the entrance and the wall. Everyone exited the vehicle, Rasheed

235

out front, up the stairs with the A Team, and Slice bringing up the rear. Poon was standing there with Artie, the only reason he was still around being the fact that Slice was using the vehicle. Rasheed hit the top of the stairs and stood there for a moment, taking it all in, and then, Poon came up, and Rasheed said, "*Assalaamu 'Alaikum*, Terrance."

"*Assalaamu 'Alaikum,* teacher." And then, the introduction, so he could get Artie on his way, "This is my agent, Artie."

Artie stuck out his hand, but Rasheed kept his together, behind his back. The *imam* was looking straight through him, and Artie could see real hatred in his eyes. Just then, Slice came over and said, "Thanks for letting me hold the keys." He walked Artie down the stairs to the car.

"Brother has his ways. Don't mean shit. See you."

Upstairs, Rasheed said, to no one in particular, "That filthy Jew Sodomite." Then, he walked over to one of the music tech guys and handed him the box. Poon and Slice were together when the guy was examining it.

"Really only seen one of these, once before. This is top-of-the-line shit. Call it a voice transformer. It not only plays with the pitch, but also the format element of your voice. What's the *format?* Non, pitch-sensitive, fixed harmonics that change . . . oh, just forget it. Make it simple. Usually hooked up to a phone, but we got a device that makes it adaptable. We hook this up to the mike, Poon here starts rapping, we can give him a whole new voice. His *Mama* wouldn't know it's him."

"Beautiful, just beautiful," said Rasheed.

The guy had it attached and ready to go in minutes, and, then, Poon started getting into it, rapping a couple of non-vile ditties, the music guy playing with the settings to get the right octave. Pretty soon Poon's voice was unidentifiable.

Artie was still downstairs with the front door open, making a couple of phone calls, when he heard the noise and said to himself, "Who the *fuck* is that?"

\* \* \* \* \*

Rasheed had his eyes closed, listening to Poon warming up. He really couldn't believe it. He sounded like a whole different brother. After a while, the two recording experts were ready to go. Rasheed gave Poon two sheets of music, one with the rap in English, the other, the same song written phonetically for Arabic. A tribute to the Jihad brothers here and overseas:

> *The Jihad warrior*
>  *The heroic few*
> *Armed in struggle*
>  *To fight the Jew*
> *Whatever it takes*
>  *We make a stand*
> *Here where we live*
>  *Or the other land*

"Couldn't *be* any more righteous," Rasheed said to himself. It was appropriate for living here and thinking about the Middle East, or being in Pakistan, or Yemen, or any other holy country, and thinking about the United States. Wherever it was playing, the brothers would get the message.

\* \* \* \* \*

Tommy spotted the car first.

"Escalade on the move, Jimmy. Looks like a white guy, driving all by himself."

"Must be our boy, Artie. Charlie, Richie, you on?"

"Yeah, Jimmy. We got an eyeball on it," said Charlie. "You want us to take it."

"Ten-Four, Charlie—*if* you could. Don't kill yourself. He parks, give me a call. We're not hanging out all night—and thanks again for lunch."

"Anytime. We'll keep you posted."

Then, Jimmy to Tommy, "I know Michele and the girls have returned, and you're back to being sleep-deprived. You want to close your eyes, be my guest."

"Thanks, 'bro, I could use it."

Jimmy watched for an hour, maybe hour and a half. He could hear music in the background, distant and unintelligible, but there was no other activity, no sign of the gang bangers and late model cars described by Chris, the owner of Sunrise Cargo. Then, some time later, Charlie on the phone. "We're over here in Long Island City after a couple of stops. Guy just rolled into the parking lot at the Silver Cup Studios."

"The *what?*"

"Silver Cup. Where they make the movies."

"Geez. Yeah, I know," Jimmy really thinking, *what do you guys want to do?*

"I guess you haven't heard from the boss?" asked Charlie.

"No."

"He's probably getting ready to call you. All hands on deck for tomorrow. Going to be a long one. Operation Chariot will be in effect."

"Good, Charlie, thanks. Call it a night. You'll beat us back in. See you tomorrow."

"That's a wrap, Tommy. Chariot, tomorrow."

And then, Jimmy pulled away, thinking of the movies, coincidences—*and* Meg Wilson.

# Jake McNicholas

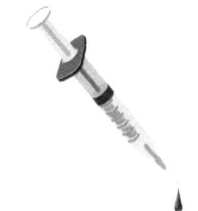

# Chapter 38

"Something, though," Jimmy said. "He went straight over to Silver Cup, huh?"

"Yeah, looked like they were still working over there, filming something," said Richie. "Place was lit up like a Christmas tree."

The whole team was sitting around, waiting for the fun to start. Jimmy decided to give everyone the latest on what was happening, regarding the Question Mark File. Some guys had known bits and pieces, but now everything was out in the open.

"What the fuck?" asked Bobby Washington. "I can't get in on the fun?"

"Bobby, I'd *love* to get you involved, but I'm not quite sure how," said Jimmy. "We got someone in the mosque right now. You got any ideas, I'd be happy to hear them. That goes for everybody."

"Be nice to be able to get into the music studio," said Santos.

"Well now," said Charlie. "With all that Iceberg Slim shit he's reading, Bobby here would really fit in."

"Relax, Defranco, and have some linguini," said Bobby.

Jimmy, with his hands together on top of his head, was leaning back in his chair. "Let's think on it, boys. Someone is sure to come up with an idea."

Lt. Bilge came over and said, "We're out the door in an hour. Be prepared, it's going to be a long night. You guys, Sergeant Lewis's teams, and those maniacs from the Two-Eight."

At least twice a year, Manhattan North Narcotics conducted an exercise that concentrated on individuals who drove to locations in the North to purchase narcotics. It was called Operation Chariot, and it was an all-out effort by every team in the building to take the vehicles of drivers who were buying weed, crack, heroin, coke, Khat, or any other illegal substance, and using their cars to do it.

Which pretty much meant that everybody would be looking for male whites, driving vehicles with Jersey plates, who had just come over the George Washington Bridge from Fort Lee, Edgewater, Leonia, Ridgefield Park, or any other locale in the Garden State.

The politically correct mob wouldn't want to hear it, because it didn't fit "their take" on law enforcement, but what the white, Black, Hispanic, and Asian members of Manhattan North were doing, according to the left's definition, was *this*— racial profiling. Everybody was looking for white boys.

It was an all-day, and into-the-early-night affair. The base of operations was "The Speedway," the long, wide transverse located off West 155th Street.

There were two city buses there that had been secured for arrest processing; police vans; a couple of ambulances; a vehicle from road repair; a couple of tow trucks; and ESU with floodlights for when the sun went down. There were a bunch of people assigned as arresting officers. Manhattan North was split up geographically among the teams, with very special attention paid to the Three-Four and Three-Oh precincts, the commands

242

most affected by assholes driving in from New Jersey for the sole purpose of buying drugs.

All the undercovers would be out in the "unmarks" with the tinted windows. Guys would be up on rooftops, and in cars, with the binoculars. It really didn't take long for the radio to start humming, jumbled syntax in "law enforcement speak," bound to keep you laughing, and coming in, minutes apart.

Richie Whalen, up on a roof on Amsterdam Avenue: "Oh God guys, you ain't going to believe this. White dude just rolled up in a green, Ford Edge. One-Six-Five and Amst', facing south. Looks like a couple of kids in the back seat, one definitely in a child seat. Okay, yeah, he just got done. Stuck it in his right pants pocket. On the move."

Bobby Washington: "You white boys are crazy. Dude just stepped out in a clown costume. Looks like Crusty, got the big shoes and all. He's all happy, back in a black Omni. North from One-Seven-Three and Wadsworth. Jersey plates, what else."

Wally Wong: "Red, Ford Focus with Jersey plates. White boy in a security guard uniform. Just got hit off. Stuck in the backpack he's carrying. West on One-Five-Five from B-way."

Inspector Lucas was up by the Speedway, and this was his first operation, so he didn't really know what to expect. The vehicles were coming in bunches, a good dozen now, and then a lull, and then Al Gavin came in driving a tractor trailer with Pennsylvania plates. The guy had been heading to the Stop & Shop, over by the Outback, in College Point, when he got bagged buying coke.

Al Link came flying onto the Speedway riding a 1997 Harley Davidson Heritage Springer, with Cal Bunion in the custom, matching sidecar. Where they got the goggles and scarves, no one could say. Even the Vicious Jim Carrey couldn't help himself, and screamed, "Please, in the future, would you sign out a couple of helmets from the equipment room *before* you start enforcement."

Bystanders were shocked; no one knew he had a sense of humor.

Jack Clint came in with a Chevy Tahoe with the standard Jersey plates. There was some legitimate medicine in the vehicle for the driver's wife, so Jack made the call, and told the missus, in Little Ferry, to come and get it. She drove over the GWB, and was headed to the Three-Four, when she decided to stop and buy some coke. She took a collar, and her brand new Saab was confiscated. Two cars, one family—you can't make the shit up.

The operation was going along quite smoothly. It was getting dark, but there were subtle signs that things might be quieting down. They had contacted the mother of the kids from the car, and sent the tykes back home, after some ice cream, and, so, had avoided Children's Services and one monster headache. No one had gotten hurt so far; everyone was making money; and the Vicious Jim Carrey was in good spirits. All was good in the world.

They ran Chariot for another couple of hours, until both sides of the Speedway were filled with vehicles. Most of the prisoners had been processed, and one of the city buses had already left. The tow truck was getting ready to make a move, and, pretty soon thereafter, Lucas decided that enough was enough. He shut the operation down, and everyone who wasn't involved with driving the vehicles to the College Point Tow Pound, or transporting the prisoners downtown, came back to the Armory to voucher property and arrest evidence.

And even though Chariot was problem free, anytime you dealt with narcotics and suspects in moving vehicles the stress level was rather high. So the mere fact that everything went off without a hitch was reason for celebration. It was a party atmosphere, once the teams got back to the base.

They were carrying property, for sure, but were also toting hero sandwiches, Brother Jimmy's wings, Chinese food, large bottles of soda, cans of Red Bull, and plastic cups for the ice-cold beer they smuggled in. The television was on, and the music was kicking. Charlie Defranco was in such a good mood, he gave half of his Chicken Parmesan hero to Rudy The Bullfrog.

The typewriters and keyboards were humming.

Off somewhere, out of sight, the office could hear Captain Sink screaming, "Fuckin' Arnold, are you *nuts*? You can't voucher gasoline cans with gas in them."

That got a laugh out of everybody, because Arnold could pretty much fuck up a wet dream.

"A good day, boys. That really went well," said Sgt. Quinn.

"Nice seeing a bunch of white boys collared, for a change," said Bobby Washington. "Does the heart good."

"I hate it when you engage in such *racial insensitivity*, Bobby," said Richie. "It's *so* beneath you."

"I hadn't seen Bobby that focused since Alba was up on the roof at the barbecue," said Santos.

"I haven't told a Puerto Rican to fuck off in some time . . . hey, Santos, fuck off!"

Charlie said, "Homey, take it easy on Santos. He can't help it if he's Puerto Rican."

"Why, thanks, Charlie," said Santos, laughing, "I didn't know you cared."

Bobby turned to Charlie. "Listen, Carmine, here's hoping a Zika-infested mosquito bites the lower lip of your marinara-encrusted mouth."

"Fuckin' Bobby, touché, and I like the Carmine addition."

Wally asked, "You *do* know who's responsible for the Zika virus, don't you?"

"Shit, yeah," said Richie Whalen. "George W. Bush. According to the Dems, *everything* is Bush's fault. Asshole, Harry Reid, can't take a dump, he blames it on George W."

And then Frank Martin. "I think I got it."

"What's that, Frank?" asked Jimmy.

"How we are going to get our boy, Bobby, involved with the mosque assholes."

\* \* \* \* \*

Frank's idea was this: Tommy and Jimmy had been up at the Polo Grounds a few times and had, on more than one occasion, spotted Slice coming out of his building around 11 AM, and heading over to the corner *bodega*, a few blocks away.

"Say we're up there," Frank went on. "Say Slice makes his move, and say we get Bobby out on the street at the same time. We wait for them to get near each other and—"

"And we stop both of them together?" asked Jimmy. "Is that what you're thinking, Frank?"

"Yeah. We stop them both, and really give Bobby a hard time. Rough him up a bit, and, all the while, Slice is watching. We're practically *introducing* them to each other."

"You white boys are going to enjoy this," and Bobby was laughing. "I see where this is going. I like it. Could work. Jimmy, you, Charlie, Richie and Frank. Four racist crackers looking to thump a brother. Slice sees me as your target, and me giving you shit right back, might be impressed enough to make an introduction. Which one of you guys wants to do the manhandling?"

All four of them raised their hands.

"I have to say, you are some *funny motherfuckahs.*"

"I think this might work," said Jimmy. "Everybody in for tomorrow? Good, then we'll take a shot. Okay, Sarge?"

"I'm going out with you."

"Great. I think I got one more ingredient that I might add to the mix. I'll sleep on it."

Jake McNicholas

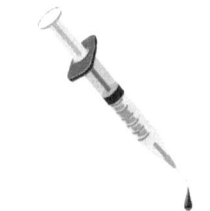

# Chapter 39

It wasn't like Slice was getting up and going to work, so the boys headed up to the Projects at around 8:00 AM. Team One was Sergeant Quinn, Tommy Bell, and Santos Cruz. Team Two was Jack Clint and Al Gavin. Team Three was what Bobby was calling the "Klan Car"—Jimmy McTigue, Charlie Defranco, Frank Martin, and Richie Whalen. Wally Wong and Bobby Washington were in the UC car.

Right before they went out, Jimmy asked Bobby who he preferred to do the shit-kicking. He looked around and pondered the question for a moment, and then said, "Defranco's Italian, mobbed up. He's out. Frank's looking for number four and he might cap my ass. *He's* out. Fuckin' Whalen, he'd be having too much fun. It will be you, Jimmy, we been together a long time, and, deep down, I know you love me."

Jimmy took both his hands and laid one each on Bobby Washington's cheeks and said, "I *do*, Bobby." Then he ran out his last idea. "How about this? Leave your walk-around, back here. Take my five-shot, .38. When we make the stop, we'll miss it during the search."

"Yeah, I got you. Solidify my street cred. And never know what kind of reaction from Slice. Yeah, good shit."

Sgt. Quinn, Tommy, and Santos had set themselves up in a perfect spot to watch the front entrance. They weren't that far off, but they had the binoculars just in case. Wally and Bobby were tucked away, down on Bradhurst, Clint and Gavin not too far away. The Klan Car was south on Fredrick Douglas Boulevard. It was a little overcast.

Sure enough, at around 11:00 AM, Slice came walking out the front door, pants around his ass, rubbing the sleep out of his eyes, and heading south. He was doing his usual look-around, as he shuffled away from the front door.

"Our boy just made an appearance," said Tommy. "Blue jeans, his KC lid, and a dark T-shirt with Tupac on the front. South on Douglas, you getting this, Wally and Bobby?"

"We got it," said Wally. "My boy, Bobby, here—I mean *Shabazz*—thinks he's Denzel. Keeps saying, "What's my motivation?" like he's getting ready to play a scene"

"Take it easy, Bruce Lee. Send your ass back to the dry cleaner."

Jimmy got on and said, "We're all ready. Just give us the word."

"We read," said Jack Clint.

Wally, driving, made his way south, and Bobby got out of the car at 150th Street and Fredrick Douglas, Jimmy's five-shot in his waistband, and tucked away nicely. He started heading north bound. The Klan Car was behind him, just far enough away as to not raise up Slice, coming south. Sgt. Quinn was giving the play-by-play.

"Slice just crossed over a Hundred Fifty Fourth. Just doing a slow amble. Not many people out, either—looking like rain. How about we try to do this between a Hundred Fifty Second and a Hundred Fifty First Streets?"

"Yeah, we're ready." Jimmy said.

Closer and closer they got, until Slice and Bobby were ten feet apart, and alone on the sidewalk. Then the Klan Car rolled up, and the boys exited and started the show.

Jimmy and Charlie grabbed Bobby; Frank and Richie, Slice; and they pulled the two to the side of a building, and threw them up against the wall.

"What the fuck you doing, you white motherfuckahs?" yelled Bobby. "Get your fuckin' hands off me."

Jimmy smacked Bobby across the side of the head and said, "Shut the fuck up, hamster," and he began kicking his legs out and rabbit punching him up on the wall. Slice didn't say anything, but he was real close and staring straight ahead.

"You fuckin' pigs!" and then, *bang*, Jimmy hit Bobby one more time for good measure, and then Charlie Defranco, with the radio up to his ear, made like he had heard something come over, and said, "We got a man with a gun on Five-Five and Saint Nick," and everyone raced to the car and got in. The bubble was already on the dashboard. They lit it up and were gone. It was just enough to make an impression.

"I hate those motherfuckin' pigs," Bobby was saying. "Shoot them all, every last fuckin' one of them." He was looking at Slice, a couple of feet away, for effect. Slice was still watching.

Bobby, then, with a big smile on, face-to-face with Slice, raised his shirt a bit and tapped the grip of Jimmy's .38, and said, "Dumb fuckahs, ain't they, brother?"

Slice said, "You are one crazy nigga and you *right*. Every last one of these pigs should die. Especially the brothers working. Oreo motherfuckahs. I'm Slice. You live up here?"

"Shabaaz, bro. No. Visiting people. Shit, rather be in Brooklyn or Queens."

"Where did you get *that* little fucker," asked Slice, meaning the piece.

"Dude owed me some money. Never used to go out strapped, but the pigs ain't stopping niggas that much anymore. I'm always looking for extra firepower, though."

"I got you," said Slice. "You got a number, Shabaaz? I might be able to provide you with a little *improvement*. Crazy nigga like you would need it."

Bobby, smiling like he had just gotten laid, saying, "Oh yeah, I be interested," and he gave over his number, leaving it like that, not pushing it. Let Slice take the bait.

"Talk to you, maybe," and they did a handshake.

\* \* \* \* \*

Back in the office and sitting around, Bobby said, "I really was happy it was you, Jimmy. Defranco looked like he was itching to go."

"Oh, yeah," Charlie said, "I always love the opportunity to kick the shit out of one of you brothers."

"That went well," said Sgt. Quinn. "Let's hope the City Council doesn't find out that we performed a stop-and-frisk and didn't hand out a receipt. Have you ever heard of such insanity?"

"I gave him a receipt, Sarge," Jimmy said. "I'm also required to buy him lunch. Keep our fingers crossed. See if our boy, Slice, has taken a liking to our boy, Shabaaz, here, and gives him a call."

"Let's hope so, Jimmy. Nigga got no problem wanting to see cops dead," said Bobby.

And then everybody was quiet.

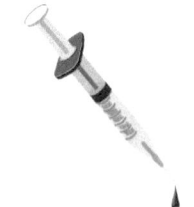

# Chapter 40

"You know, Tommy, we really should take a ride out and see the warden."

"The guy from Shawangunk?"

"Yeah."

"You mean, take a trip to Wallkill?"

"No, I did a little research. Warden Servino is retired and living the good life, I hope, in Toms River," said Jimmy. "The boss said no problem, just don't get into trouble. I called Servino, and he said he was good with a visit. We take a ride out now."

"Let's do it."

They took Jimmy's Jeep, but not before Tommy called the Chief of Detectives' office, and chocked out, notifying the desk that Detectives McTigue and Bell of Manhattan North Narcotics would be leaving the confines of New York and the Five Boroughs, and heading to Toms River—using Buy Operation Number 1506 as the case number. They headed to the Lincoln Tunnel and into Jersey, I-95 to the Jersey Turnpike and then the Garden State. There was absolutely no traffic, a beautiful day, the boys riding with the windows open, and the wind in their hair.

"Could you get used to this?" asked Tommy.

"Yeah, if you mean driving with the music on, the sun shining and no stress, oh yeah, Tommy. I could, but you know what?"

"I know what you're going to say. You'd miss it."

"Yeah, and so would you. We're cops."

They got off at Exit 82, and a few rights and lefts and a couple of side streets later, they were driving with the Toms River Country Club on their right. Mike Servino's house was on Madison Street, on the corner, with a beautiful patch of green grass all the way from the edge of the home to the sidewalk. They got out of the Jeep, walked to the front door, and rang the bell. Moments later, they heard a loud, booming voice that said, "I'm in the back. Come through the fence on the side."

The backyard was spacious, with an in-ground pool, under shade trees, surrounded by more grass and a ring of concrete. There was a deck up at the house, with patio furniture, a picnic table, assorted coolers, and a top-of-the-line grill. A rowboat that had seen better days was off to the right. Mike Servino was sitting on a chair, with his feet on a cooler, smoking a cigar, and nursing a beer. He looked every bit a corrections officer.

He was probably 65, with a full head of black hair—short and stocky, wearing a tank top and shorts. His forearms were massive. He got off the chair, as Jimmy and Tommy came up the deck, put out his hand and said, "Pleasure, my friends, to have the NYPD to my humble abode."

They made the introductions, and then, the Warden asked, "What can I get you guys? And I won't take no for an answer."

Jimmy shrugged and said, "I'll have what you're having," and Tommy said, "Me, too," and they went over to the picnic table and sat down.

"You know, Jimmy, you really had me thinking about those guys," said the Warden.

If you closed your eyes and listened to Mike Servino speak, you would never be able to match up the sound of his voice to the man himself. He sounded like he should be teaching English at an Ivy League University, every word annunciated, every phrase perfectly formed. He was a pleasure to listen to.

"I just want to thank you again for seeing us," said Jimmy. "We appreciate it. I see you are enjoying retired life. How long were you with Corrections, and what got you there?"

"Seems like an eternity, but thirty years." And then, Servino reached over and grabbed his cigar. "My dad was a corrections officer. He was stationed at Attica, in nineteen seventy-one, during the riots. I guess you guys weren't even born yet. It was bad—very, *very* bad. There were over two thousand inmates involved. They took control of the facility and grabbed hostages. One guard, Bill Quinn, a very good friend of my dad's, was beaten severely and thrown out a window. He died two days later."

"My God," said Tommy. "Your Dad was okay?"

"Yes, but what happened was this: The authorities were forced to storm the prison. During the attack, twenty-five inmates and ten hostages were killed. My dad was shot in both legs. Never worked again."

"But your dad was in Corrections, and it made *you* want to be in Corrections?"

"Yes, Jimmy, probably much like you, though I'd guess Tommy, here, may be the first cop in his family. My dad had a profound influence on me. I went out and got my Bachelor of Science Degree in Criminal Justice at Post in Waterbury, and then I received my Masters, online, in Correctional

Administration from Kaplan University. Also took plenty of behavioral science and sociology courses on the side. All the while working the cellblocks. Maximum Security at Clinton in Dannemora; at Southport in Pine City; and a stint at a Minimum facility at Ulster in Napanoch. Even did a tour at Taconic in Bedford Hills—women's prison, a thousand times worse than the guys."

"I can see that," Tommy deadpanned. "I have a wife and two daughters."

Servino was laughing, and got up and fetched three more cold ones from the cooler.

"You gentlemen definitely know what I'm talking about, though, when I say this. At the end of the day, you have to have a sense of humor and treat people properly. I read this book, years ago, called *The Fatal Shore*, about the penal colony that was Australia, and there were descriptions about rules and regulations and correctional theory in it that are still relevant today. Certainly, during my time working in the prison system, I recognized that people deserved to be treated with respect and dignity."

"Everyone gets treated like you would want someone in your family to be treated—*initially*," said Jimmy.

"Absolutely correct. But once the contract is broken, whether you're a cop or a prison guard, all bets are off. But I'm drifting here. You guys want to know about the Islam program at Shawangunk?"

"Yes sir," Jimmy said. "We Googled the program and came across an article that quoted you. You spoke highly of it."

"Jim, my friend, that was all bullshit. I never said that, and it was one of the reasons that I decided to pack it in, come out here, drink beer, and fish. The quote was a talking point that was being pushed by the Bureau of Prisons. How great was the program? I was working on Nine Eleven. I saw, with my own eyes, plenty of these inmates that had turned to Islam celebrating as The Towers fell—*especially* your boy, Rasheed. I tried to point out that inconvenient truth, but no one wanted to hear it."

"You couldn't take it anymore, the nonsense?" said Tommy.

"You are right, Tommy. I couldn't take it anymore." His voice trailed off; he got up again from the table, grabbed three more beers, and then ground out his cigar. "But you are in luck, boys. It could not have worked out any better. For my own peace of mind, I kept a list of all the inmates that went through the program when I was there, just to see if any of those guys popped up later on. I pared it down a bit for you gentlemen, included everyone that was there while Rasheed Abdullah was incarcerated. Let me get it."

He went through the sliding-glass doorway, and was back out in a couple of minutes with a white envelope.

"I hope it helps you guys out. You're welcome to stay. I'm getting ready to put on the steaks."

"Thanks Mike," said Jimmy. "We got to make a move."

They left Mike Servino sitting in a chair, drinking a cold beer, and lighting up another cigar.

\* \* \* \* \*

The top of the first page, of the five from the envelope provided by Warden Servino, was titled "Prisoners who attended Muslim Conversion Class with Melvin Barnes." Underneath were listed the names and pertinent information of some thirty inmates. Next to each name were: a DOB; NYSID number, if appropriate; Social Security Number; length of sentence;

conviction for incarceration; date of release; address upon release; and a number of addresses that were indicated on outgoing mail.

Jimmy was going to run every one of the individuals eventually, but, for the time being, he took a yellow highlighter from his desk, and marked those names with New York roots. All those individuals had NYSID numbers, which made it very easy to run their criminal history, and bring up a photo. Servino had provided small prison pictures of each, with their names and dates of birth on the back. Jimmy opted to add the larger photos on file.

By now, with the information and paperwork increasing with regard to the investigation, he had gotten himself a blue binder from Staples. He bought a package of three-hole, transparent sleeves, and, in each one, he placed the individual's 8-1/2" x 11" picture, with all his criminal history and related information behind it. When he had finished with all the entries, the collection resembled a narcotics, set book. Now, he had everything at the tip of his fingers, including the DD-5s he was doing, which made it easy to carry around and show.

It didn't take long at his desk to get the stuff done. Jimmy did the criminal history and Tommy did the photos. The cubicle was quiet. Bobby and Wally were at training. Charlie was getting "doled," urinating in a bottle down at Lefrak City, to make sure he wasn't using drugs. Bobby Washington had told him he'd probably piss tomato sauce. Frank Martin and Richie Whalen were down at IAB on Houston Street regarding an allegation that they stole money from a dealer. They had vouchered the eighty-eight dollars, and had the paperwork to prove it. Santos Cruz was in uniform in Midtown, fighting the good fight in Times Square. Seems Justin Bieber was appearing, and thousands of pubescent girls were beside themselves. "The trials and tribulations of a narcotic's detective," Santos had said, as he headed out the door.

"I got them all, Jimmy," said Tommy, and placed the pictures on the desk.

"Do me a favor. Start throwing them in the book. Then, one-by-one, give me their names, and I'll hand you their prison photos and the paperwork, and you can stick it in."

Tommy had looked at all the photos. He and Jimmy had never been that close to the mosque, and, though they were often using the binoculars, it was still tough to get a good look. Jimmy finished handing over the paperwork, and then he clapped and said to Tommy, "Let's have a look."

"Nothing from me. Any of these guys look familiar?"

"No," Tommy said. "You want to take a walk over to The Terrorist?"

"Yeah, I just thought the same thing. Hit The Terrorist and then see Basically Bill—kill two birds with one stone."

Aiman Qantan was where he usually was, behind the counter. Juan was where he usually was, by the grill, and firing up something he claimed was a Philly Cheese Steak sandwich for Jack Clint standing off to the side, head down and reading the sports pages in the *New York Post*.

"Mr. Jim, nice to see you. Would you like something to eat?"

Jack Clint looked up and saw Jimmy with the binder, and Tommy by the door, and said, "I was in the office. Where *is* everybody? I get lonely, I got to eat." He was laughing.

Jimmy said, "Aiman, get that sandwich, on me, and throw in a package of Tums."

"C'mon, Jimmy," said Jack, "nothing like a little grease and fat to keep the heart pumping. Thanks for the sandwich. I'll leave the Tums," and he headed out door.

Jimmy gave Aiman a head nod, and they both walked to the back room of the store. Tommy stayed by the front door, and Juan cleaned the grill, which consisted of moving the grease from one side to the other.

"Just take a seat and look at the photos here. Anyone you recognize, let me know."

Aiman was slow and deliberate. He spotted Slice, right off the bat, and then, Rasheed. Fifth photo, he looked up at Jimmy and said, "This one wore a security jacket at the mosque." Jimmy took a yellow sticky, and placed in on the plastic sleeve. He examined a couple of more pictures, and then, said the same about another individual: the guy was at the Mosque in a security jacket.

"No names, though?"

"No, Mister Jim. I do not know either of their names. I am sorry"

"That's fine, Aiman. How is your family? Kids getting big?"

"Yes, Mister Jim. Everyone is good, and the children grow. I am very proud."

"Okay, my friend, thanks. I will see you."

Outside the store, Jimmy said to Tommy, "Yeah he ID'ed two guys from the mosque. Let's see if Basically Bill is around, and we'll try him."

They walked back to the Armory and the Jeep, and Jimmy got Basically Bill on the phone and told him to be up on the corner of Seaman and Cummings in a half hour. He was standing there when they rolled up. He hopped in, and they headed west on Dyckman, all the way to the Hudson River.

Jimmy handed Basically Bill the set book, the yellow stickers all removed from the photos, and told him to take a look.

"I saw the *imam* and, basically, this guy," said Bill, pointing to the first picture picked out by Aiman. "And, basically, this one," pointing to the second. "They're the security guys."

"You didn't pick up any *names*, did you? Something foreign-sounding, maybe."

"No, sorry, Jimmy. I basically didn't."

You're heading over again, Friday, aren't you?"

"Sure. You *want* me to, don't you?"

"Yeah, I *do*, please. Where do you want to go now?"

"Actually, this is fine, right here," said Bill.

They headed back to the Armory.

\* \* \* \* \*

At their desks, with their feet up, Jimmy with the set book in his lap thumbing through it. "First guy, Paul McBean, Brooklyn Address, did time for weapons possession and assault. Second guy, Chris Hinton, Brooklyn address, did time for rape. Two, really holy brothers."

"I sense a touch of *cynicism*?" said Tommy.

"Hold it right there. Where did you get *that* from, a touch of cynicism? You use that on Michele yet?"

"Yeah, the other day. She almost blew a blood vessel laughing so hard."

Jimmy's phone vibrated, and it was Bobby Washington.

"How's training?"

"Fuck training. Guess who called me?"

"Nicki Minaj."
"I wish."
"Slice."
"Fuckin' eh."

\* \* \* \* \*

Bobby was in training, saw the unfamiliar phone number, and let it go to voicemail. First break the class got, after watching the Chris Rock video "How Not to Get Your Ass Kicked by the Police," the shit having everybody screaming with laughter, he went outside and checked. Slice had left a message on the phone: "Shabaaz, what's up? Slice."

He called back, and, after three rings, Slice was on.

"Yo, brother, what you doing?" asked Slice.

"Chillin', nigga."

"You still looking for something more sophisticated?"

Bobby, knowing he was talking about a firearm, "Fuck yeah, you know it."

"Let me ask you something. You got access to wheels?"

Bobby, thinking fast, "I gots wheels, and, ain't like the rest of the homeboys, I got me a license."

Slice asked, "You care much about the degree of sophistication, or you just looking to upgrade?"

"I need an upgrade," Bobby raising his voice.

"Relax. I got me something I think you'll like. Might work, you got a ride, help me out with a little business in the future. I'll be in touch. Later."

"I hear you," and Bobby left it like that.

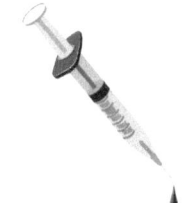

# Chapter 41

**Rasheed was the one who decided** that the safest place to stash the weaponry was in the mosque itself.

It was a brilliant idea, and all the brothers Rasheed trusted unconditionally thought so—Poon, the A Team, Slice, Floyd Batten, Junior Bishop, and a couple of others. They were *all* in his office when he made the announcement.

How could it be any better? According to Rasheed, the infidels were already growing weak at the knees, politicians calling on law enforcement to leave the Muslims alone—praise be to Allah for that. NYPD was forced to shut down operations initiated by the Intelligence Division. No one told them to do that when they were investigating any other group, but that's the way it was now. Had to laugh, too, according to Rasheed. "The Jew papers and the Jew media is our greatest ally," he said. "We brothers don't have to do a thing. Just say we being harassed, and the pigs get called off."

It was actually Poon, who hooked up Rasheed with the carpenter who built the hidden spot behind the back wall of Rasheed's walk-in closet in the office. Didn't take long, either, to start storing shit in the "Armory." That's what Slice called it. Brothers were coming up from Virginia, or South Carolina, with hardware, and it was up to Slice to make sure everything was put away safe and secure.

The collection was growing: a couple of Sig Sauer automatics; the Ultimate Tactical Shotgun, the fifteen-rounder; three, M1As, with the precision, adjustable stock; M4s; three, Vepr-12 shotguns; five, Les Baer, 191 Boss .45s; and a Sig Sauer, MPX, 9mm submachine gun. A whole *shitload* of automatic handguns. Even had a Mission Craze crossbow, prompting Junior Bishop to always be picking it up and *always be saying*, "I'm fuckin' Robin Hood from the fuckin' Hood."

There was also a Glock, 9mm Luger with the black, textured, polymer frame that Slice was going to sell to Shabaaz. It went for six hundred dollars. But after seeing him in action and learning the brother had wheels and hated the pigs, Slice figured he might just dump it for face value. Friendly gesture to Shabaaz and his wheels.

The plan was this for Slice: Grab the piece this Friday from the mosque, walk over to the Atlantic Mall and meet Shabaaz, over by the Chucky Cheese, or the Pathmark, or something—see if old Shabaaz was interested in playing.

And that's the way it went down.

* * * * *

They were heading to Brooklyn in two cars: Sgt. Quinn, Jimmy, and Tommy in one; Richie, Santos, Frank, and Charlie in the other. There were a couple of flash cars assigned to the office, vehicles used by the undercovers to play the role, and Bobby was going to take the older of the two, the black Beemer.

Slice said he'd be there around 1:00 PM. He also told Bobby it was a Glock 9 mm, and he was asking six beans. It'd be in a Dunkin Donut bag. Frank Martin knew guns and said, "Unbelievable, that's what it costs. He *likes* you, Bobby. We're not overpaying, like we usually do, just so we can get a gun off the street."

They were in the V/O early, with plenty of time to kill. Bobby parked the car by Sterling, off Fifth Avenue, and took a walk over to the Victoria's Secret on Flatbush to do some window-shopping.

Everyone else went into the mall. Tommy and Santos were going to be the primary ghosts, and Frank, Charlie, Richie, and the Boss would be nearby. Since he and Slice had history, Jimmy went over to the Buffalo Wild Wings Bar & Grill. He'd be out of sight, but able to get the final location from Bobby, and text the information to the field team.

There were four or five people at the bar, half the tables occupied with the growing lunch crowd. The young girl behind the stick came over with a napkin and asked Jimmy what he wanted. He opted for a Coors Lite and then opened the paper and started on the crossword. His cell phone was on the bar, in front of him.

The television was up high in the corner of the bar, and it was set on a channel that was airing one of those cable shows that spend an hour or so chronicling the life of useless movie stars and celebrities. Jimmy had his head down, when the correspondent, Chick Whitehead, began his spiel.

"We're here on the set of *These Bells Toll*, the new movie being directed by Fred Meunch. Filming is close to wrapping up, and there is already Oscar buzz from the people who have seen the dailies and Meg Cassidy's performance. And we're lucky to have Meg with us now. How are you, Meg?"

"Wonderful, Chick. Thanks for asking."

Jimmy was stuck on 35 down, five-letter word for "fresco."

"You were required to gain some weight for this role, Meg. How'd you do it, and are you worried at all about taking it off?"

"I drank a lot of Guinness and ate a lot of pasta," said Meg, and she started to really laugh.

Jimmy got "mural," and was checking 33 across, a seven-letter word for "paper-folding art," when he started to tune into the laugh coming off the TV, and he raised his head and saw Meg Wilson, a.k.a. Meg Cassidy.

Just then, his cell vibrated.

Bobby, in character, "Home Slice, Chucky Cheese out, frozen food aisle in the Pathmark. In a Dunkin' Donuts bag. Five minutes."

"Be careful, Shabaaz."

Jimmy did a group text: Frozen food, Pathmark, five minutes.

The Meg Cassidy interview was over.

Tommy grabbed a cart and threw in an eight-pack of paper towels, a couple of boxes of Bubba Burgers, and a case of water. Santos had one of those carry-around baskets, and had a bottle of Lysol and a rotisserie chicken in it. The rest of the boys were out in the mall, close enough to the Pathmark entrance, but not *too* close. They were all playing mall shopper, and waiting for things to get started

\* \* \* \* \*

Slice on the phone. "You gonna like this shit, Shabaaz. And I'm hoping you don't forget I'm hooking you up big time."

"Fuckin' etched in my brain."

Charlie Defranco was the first one to spot Slice walking toward the Pathmark with the Dunkin' Donuts bag. He texted, "Slice is 84," to the field team.

Jimmy was by the entrance to the Buffalo Wild Wings.

Santos was over by the deli counter.

Tommy was squeezing melons.

The rest of the boys continued to play "mall inhabitant."

Shabaaz gave Slice a "What's up, my man?" and then a handshake with six, one hundred dollar bills of pre-recorded buy money in a white envelope, right in front of the frozen vegetables.

Slice gave Shabaaz the double, Dunkin' Donuts bag, and then said, "I'll give you a holler later."

And it was over.

Slice hardly even paused; he was out the front of the Pathmark and gone.

Tommy and Santos gave Bobby plenty of room while they followed him back to the car, and waited till he drove off. Jimmy got the call. "You know, Jimmy, I don't know shit about guns, but this looks like the real deal to me. Let Martin, that gun nut, take a look."

"Good work, Shabaaz. See you uptown."

Jimmy was back in the car with the Boss and Tommy, and he called Charlie.

"You guys in your car?"

"Yeah, Jimmy."

"Everything went great. Meet me up at Patsy's for some pies, on me."

"Good stuff. We'll see you up there," said Charlie. "Oh yeah, Frank can't wait to get a look."

And then Jimmy said to Tommy. "I just saw the girl from the pizzeria."

"She was in the *mall*?"

"Not really. She was on TV."

\* \* \* \* \*

They found two spots right in front of Patsy's. The place had been around since 1933, and was on the corner of First Avenue and 118th Street. Jimmy went in and ordered three pies, gave Tommy some money for the food and drinks, and then walked outside to the corner and dialed Meg's phone number.

"Hi, Jimmy."

"Hi, Meg. How's work?"

"Oh, the same drag as always. Nothing new. You working?"

"Yep, out with the boys fighting crime. Just stopped for pizza. I'm going to be in Queens tomorrow, on Woodhaven Boulevard, not that crazy of a ride from Breezy. You want to meet me for lunch?"

"Yeah, I'd like that."

"You know the Woodhaven House, the old Kate Cassidy's."

"I do."

"Then okay Miss . . . Wilson,"—and Meg thought it was almost a question—"One o'clock."

"See you then."

The pizza eating area of Patsy's was tiny, so Tommy came out to the street with the pies and laid them on the hood of the car. The boys ate from there. The department radio was turned up and lying on the windshield.

"Bobby said the piece looked good to him," said Jimmy.

"Can't wait to take a look," said Frank Martin. "I still think Slice must have taken a shine to our Shabaaz—been impressed with his *righteous* anger during the stop. If that turns out to be a Glock 9 Luger, and, we paid six hundred dollars, we really made out."

"Yeah," said Sgt. Quinn. "And we got another gun off the street."

And then the department radio exploded with "Ten Thirteen, Ten Thirteen, Shots Fired, Officer Down, Wagner Houses, Two Three Nine Six, First Avenue."

There was pizza all over the street in front of Patsy's.

Jake McNicholas

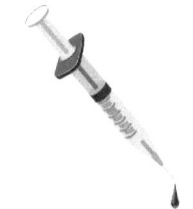

# Chapter 42

The first shot hit Alba Castro square in the chest, a little blunt force trauma to her breasts, but she remained on her feet, with her back up against the wall of the stairwell.

The second shot hit right below her bulletproof vest, and ripped through the mesentery of the intestines, the cover that holds them together. It was vascular, big time, and the .380 slug from the Taurus International went right through, and also penetrated the bowel. Alba was on the floor now, a bloody, stinking mess.

What had happened was this: Alba and her team had been doing Buy and Bust over at the Robert Wagner Houses that spanned from 120th to 124th Streets, the FDR to Second Avenue. They were conducting operations on First Avenue and the corner of 120th Street. The weed and crack sales were off the hook. She was in the car with Eric Boltz, when the undercover got done by a male Hispanic wearing a red shirt and cargo shorts. Bought ten, green-top vials of crack.

Alba and Eric could see the guy in the courtyard. He didn't seem raised up at all, and the UC was long off the set. He started heading for the corner building. They followed him in, and got a fleeting glance of "Cargo Pants" riding up in the elevator. It stopped at nine.

They took the other elevator up to ten, got off and went to the stairwell and were planning on coming down one flight. It was really no big deal. The UC could easily identify him, so, if they didn't grab him today, he became a lost subject, and they would snatch him up sometime in the future.

No one would ever be able to figure out why he did it, but when Castro and Boltz were just about to come down from ten, Cargo Pants opened up the door on nine and fired twice, striking Alba. Eric returned fire, called a 10-13, and then picked up Alba, walked back into the hallway, and took the elevator down to the lobby of the building.

Jimmy, Charlie, Frank, Tommy, Richie, Sgt. Quinn, and Santos, with a ram, were just coming in through the front door.

"It's Alba," Boltz screamed. "Male Hispanic, red shirt, cargo pants. He opened up from the ninth-floor, stairwell door. We were coming down from ten. I let one go. Might have hit him. I see my guys. I'm heading to the courtyard. Get the motherfucker."

Jimmy, Tommy, and Charlie took the elevator to ten. They came through the stairwell door, and could hear the footsteps from Frank, Richie, Santos, and Sgt. Quinn on the stairs, drawing nearer from below. The tenth floor landing was full of Alba's blood, sneaker footprints in the pool from Boltz. They walked around it and came down slow to nine, when Jimmy spotted it. By this time, the whole team was together, including Santos with the ram. Jimmy snapped his fingers, pointed to his eye, and then pointed to the floor. A small pool of blood. And then more drops heading down to the lower floor. He looked at everyone and whispered, "Blood trail." The guys were so quick to get up to ten, they had missed it.

As it happened, the Vicious Jim Carrey had been at the Armory reviewing overtime figures, kites, and search warrant applications, when word came over that Alba had been hit. The office had been unusually full—it was an up day for just about everyone—and now the members of Manhattan North were getting ready to rush out the door and head to the scene. No one figured that the Inspector would say anything, but, all of a sudden, he got up on a desk, right by the exit door.

"I regret to inform you that Detective Castro . . ." And then his voice trailed off. He stood there for a moment and he traveled back in time, and remembered what it was like to be a cop, and why he became one, and why you risk your life for something greater. For one shining moment, he forgot all the bullshit and the nonsense and the insanity The Job often created, and he got right to it.

"Fuck it. Some shithead just shot our Alba—a great cop, and a wonderful gal. That crew up there in the Wagner Houses just signed their own fucking death warrant, I promise you. We're going over there and we are going to be careful, but we are going to take care of business. I got your back. God Bless you all."

It was a stampede that headed out the door.

Back in the stairwell, the boys were coming down in two rows, quiet like, radios down, phones on vibrate, and Jimmy crouched over, out in front, following the trail. The drops were pretty frequent, a definite pattern favoring the left side of the staircase *until* they got to five. The blood led to the door, and there was some streaked on the knob. Jimmy looked through the glass, and then gently opened the door and glanced right and left. The blood trailed left, and, now, the sergeant and six detectives were spread out equally on either side of the hall, their firearms at the ready, walking softly behind Jimmy, who was still crouched over. He put his right hand up before 5C and made a fist. The trail had ended.

He stuck his ear to the door and heard nothing. He tiptoed back to Sgt. Quinn, and whispered in his ear, "The blood ends right there. Even some on the knob. What do you think?"

Sgt. Quinn whispered back, "Okay, boys." Then he looked into the eyes of everyone on the team, and said, "Let's take care of some business."

Jimmy gave everyone the thumbs-up, and then no one said a word. It was muscle memory. Santos had the ram, and crawled to the other side of the door to avoid the peephole, followed by Frank and Charlie. Jimmy raised his right hand and counted on his fingers to five.

Santos banged the door, just below the knob, the first time, came back with a shot just above, and the door flew open. He tossed the ram. Sgt. Quinn entered first and went right, into the kitchen, searched and yelled, "Clear!"; Jimmy to the bedroom on the left and "Clear!"; Richie to the bedroom on the right and "Clear!" Everyone was together, but spread out, if that makes any sense, by the time they got to the living room in the rear.

They saw the guy, with the red shirt and the cargo pants, in the corner. There was blood dripping from a wound to his left shoulder. He had his hand over the mouth of what looked to be a ten-year-old girl. She was shaking. The barrel of the Taurus International was up against her temple.

"You motherfuckahs just lower your shit and back the fuck up out of the apartment. You got about—"

Frank Martin put one right between his eyes.

The girl came running to Jimmy, and leaped into his arms crying, squeezing like she never wanted to let go, and he walked her out into the hall and down away from the apartment, all the while saying, "It's all over now. Shhhhhhh. It's okay. No one is going to hurt you." He ran his fingers through her hair, and rocked.

Sgt. Quinn got on the radio and advised Central that there was no need for further units. Then he couldn't help himself. "Central, be advised that we are *not* going to need a bus for the perp. Have the M.E. respond." And there was a colossal roar of approval from every cop that heard it on the radio—*and* from the guys who were told about it. There were still uniforms responding, and the hallway began to get packed.

Inspector Lucas got to five, and he could see the seven of them down the hallway—Charlie, Richie, and Santos crouched over with their hands on their knees, Sgt. Quinn and Tommy leaning up on the wall, and Jimmy still with the little girl in his arms. Frank had his arms folded and was off to the side.

All Inspector Lucas could think of doing was to give them a salute.

And then, Frank Martin walked over to Sgt. Quinn and said, "I'm still not going to the outdoor range."

\* \* \* \* \*

Boltz didn't wait for the bus. He threw Alba in the back of an RMP, used it as the ambulance, and they got her down to Mount Sinai on Madison and 101st Street in minutes. They knew she was coming.

They got Alba upstairs, and it looked okay. The colon, the stomach, the kidney were all untouched. The .380 had damaged the mesentery, but went below the colon and stomach, just above the pancreas, and came up short of the splenic artery. The gunshot was not life threatening. Painful, of course, but she would make it.

But here's the thing. The doctors got in there to clean the wound and check the organs in the vicinity of the blast and what they found was a monstrous, cancerous tumor, bigger than most of them had ever seen and it had wrapped itself around the liver and had seeped into the nearby arties and veins and spread to the pancreas.

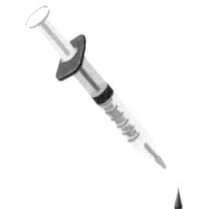

# Chapter 43

"**Turn it off, Tommy.** I can't listen to it anymore."

"The news, or the radio itself, Jimmy?"

"The radio. A little quiet. We could use it."

They were coming over the Triboro in the Jeep, and it was well past three in the morning. It had been a brutally long day: Alba getting hit; the shooting and trip to the hospital for trauma; and then, hour upon hour at the Two-Five. Now, they were driving in the right lane, slow and easy, with the windows open and the air almost sweet, heading to Tommy's house for the drop-off.

"I didn't get a chance to tell you," said Jimmy. "Basically Bill called, said he heard it on *WINS*. Wanted to make sure we were okay. Something, huh?"

"Yeah," said Tommy, "they broke the CI mold with him. Anything else?"

"Yeah, and you are not going to believe it either. He tells me he was in the mosque, no Rasheed, but he spots a guy from the set book, coming up the stairs carrying a Dunkin' Donuts bag and heading out the door."

"My God, Jimmy. Slice must have got the piece from the mosque itself."

"That's what I'm thinking. Makes sense. Those places are *almost* off limits to investigations. Come Monday, I'm calling

Earl. See if the Feds know about this. I got to be honest with you, I figured we would have been done with all this by now. But this gun angle and Alba getting shot, kind of changes everything."

"Good idea, Jimmy. The Feds got the resources and can work it full-time. They don't have to worry about B and B. Oh yeah, I know what I wanted to ask you. Before the shit hit the fan, you mentioned the girl from the pizzeria."

"Still trying to figure this out. I'm up at the Buffalo Wild Wings before the buy and hear this voice and a laugh off the television and it's her. Only her name isn't Meg Wilson it's Meg Cassidy."

"That's right," said Tommy. "You remember I said she looked familiar. You stepping out with a *movie star?*"

"I guess I am," and Jimmy's voice went low.

"Wait a minute, Jimmy. You got that funny feeling in your stomach when you're with her, don't you? She's doing stuff to your insides."

"Yeah, buddy, I think so."

"Here's something you're probably not gonna remember. We figured out that the Escalade belonged to that agent, Artie Levin. We Googled 'Artie' and found out that he had three clients, remember? Dexter Spencer from the Lions, the guy from *The Transgendered Butler* and—"

"Jesus Christ, Meg Cassidy!" said Jimmy.

"You can't make this shit up," said Tommy, shaking his head.

They were quiet again, and well past LaGuardia on the Grand Central Parkway. They both yawned at the same time and had to laugh about it. Jimmy got on the Cross Island, took it to Braddock Avenue, and exited. A couple of minutes later, he was pulling into the driveway.

"Come on in for a nightcap, 'bro. We could use it."

"Sure, Tommy."

They came through the back door and took their shoes off and went into the kitchen. Tommy went into the fridge and grabbed two Buds, and they sat at the table and toasted Alba.

"I only pray that cancer stuff is just bullshit. It breaks my heart just thinking about it, Tommy."

They heard some stirring in the living room, and Michele came to the entrance dressed in a Notre Dame sweatshirt that went to mid-thigh, and a pair of flip-flops. She came behind Tommy, wrapped her hands under his chin, and kissed him on the top of his head, and, then, she came around to Jimmy and did the same thing. She said to both of them, "How's my boys?"

"We're okay, honey," said Tommy. "You tell the girls?"

"No, I didn't. No use worrying them. You guys must be exhausted. You want anything to eat? Jimmy, what are you looking at?"

"I'm just admiring your bedtime attire," and he smiled.

"Yeah, Jimmy, it's yours. Finder's keepers. But it's *so* comfortable."

She went over to the sink and reached above to one of the cabinets, and brought out a bottle of twelve-year-old Jameson's and placed it on the table. She got two coffee cups from the sink, rinsed them out, and placed them alongside it.

"The sofa bed is made, Jimmy. You're staying the night. The girls will get a kick out of seeing you in the morning. Sit here and take the edge off. I'm proud of you guys."

She went over to Tommy, who stood up, and she wrapped her arms around him and kissed him on the lips. She went over to Jimmy, who also stood, and reached up, on her tiptoes, to wrap her arms around him and kiss him on the cheek.

And then she began to cry as she left the kitchen.

Tommy poured whiskey into both cups.

"This isn't the bottle I bought you four years ago, is it?"

"Yeah, Jimmy. The stuff's a little hard for me. But it's good to have around—just in case my car runs out of gas."

For five minutes, they sat there, sipping their whiskey and drinking their beer—and thinking. The only sound was the minute hand off the clock above the doorway.

"You know, Tommy, all these years I was never really afraid of getting shot and dying. Actually, never really thought of it. I accepted the fact that it was part of the job description. But I mean this, when I say it. This Nine Eleven shit scares me a little. It's like it's percolating in people. Seems like they're putting a name on the wall at the Police Memorial at Battery Park every week. And now, Alba. I don't know if there is a sweeter person in the building."

"I know what you're saying, Jimmy. I look at the girls, sometimes, and it scares me, too. Ground Zero is going to wind up sending hundreds of us to our graves."

"Funny, Tommy, but as surreal as The Pile was, *especially* the days after the attack, when all the fires were still burning, I still say the Landfill was even worse. The smell. The ground, bumbling. Standing on that conveyor belt in the morning, with the sun barely up, trying to pick out bones or anything meaningful that survived the attack, *that* was sobering.

"Let's just pray that what we heard about Alba was just misinformation," Jimmy continued. "Jesus, to survive the shooting and then to die from Nine Eleven, all these years later, it's just . . . I know life's not fair, but, God, please help her."

Tommy got up and grabbed two more beers from the fridge, poured a couple more generous shots of the Jameson's, and looked Jimmy in the eye, asking, "When are you going to see her?"

"Tomorrow."

"You feeling . . . *disrespected* . . . she lied to you?"

"No, not at all. I'm sure she has her reasons."

"That's good. I like that. Remember, partner, you deserve to be happy. You know, on second thought, that's it for me. I'm heading in. Will you be here when I get up?"

"What? Three o'clock in the afternoon?"

"You are funny. I guess you'll be doing one of those Irish goodbyes. Just make sure you get a little sleep."

"Will do, Tommy. I love you, man."

"I love you, too, Jimmy."

Tommy went off to bed.

* * * * *

Jimmy was already sitting at the table, in the dark, hunched over a cup of tea, when he heard Michele in the living room telling the girls that there may be a surprise in the kitchen. Bonnie and Britney were coming in, cautious, when they spotted him and started screaming, "Uncle Jimmy! Uncle Jimmy!" Michele told them to keep it down or they'd wake up their father.

The girls sat on either side of Jimmy and chatted away. Michele took the frying pan off the nail, behind the sink, and started the bacon. She began laying out the slices that were finished on a paper towel, and then she asked her diners how they wanted their eggs.

"Sunnyside up, Michele, please," said Jimmy.

"We want them like Uncle Jimmy's," screamed the girls.

"Tommy is out cold, Jimmy. You must still be exhausted. He was telling me, though, before he went out, that you might have met somebody."

The two girls: "Uncle Jimmy has a girlfriend! Uncle Jimmy has a girlfriend!"

"Behave yourself," said Jimmy, and he got up and started tickling both of them, until they promised to stop.

"We'll see, Michele. It's been a while. I kind of forgot what it's like."

He finished his breakfast and gave the girls a kiss on the forehead. He was at the door, now, and Michele came over and gave him a long, hard hug, and looked in his eyes and said, "Thanks for everything. Thanks for being a friend and taking care of my Tommy."

And then, he was outside in the morning air, in the Jeep, and home.

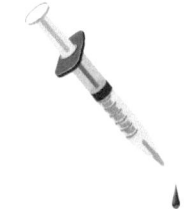

# Chapter 44

He *always* stopped at the florist on the corner of Woodhaven Boulevard and 68th Road, whenever he visited the cemetery. He'd buy the white cross, set in the green wreath, and come into St. John's through the side entrance, off Cooper Avenue. The five-foot, marble cross was set off a bit from the road. You could spot the azalea bush that was in front of it from a distance.

He pulled the Jeep over, got out, and then walked over and sunk the cross into the ground in front of the tombstone. His grandmother and grandfather were listed, as were the names of three of his aunts and uncles. His Mom and Dad were there, and now the most recent addition, his wife, Catherine, evidenced by the look of the etching. He bowed his head and said his prayers, and he finished up uttering, aloud, "May all the souls of the faithfully departed, through the mercy of God, rest in peace, amen."

The Woodhaven House was a couple of long blocks away on the Avenue. It was once called Kate Cassidy's, but a million dollars in renovations completely changed the look, so much so, that if you blindfolded an old patron and walked him in, he would never be able to tell it was the same joint. The new owners had done away with the square bar and added a fireplace and cozy nooks, to give the place a whole new feel. Jimmy was early, and grabbed a table off to the side and out of the way, and ordered a coffee. He was still dragging.

Meg came in, a couple of minutes later, in sunglasses, her hair pulled back in a ponytail with a bright, yellow, rubber band, and wearing white shorts and a blue blouse, tight against her body. She looked wonderful. He gave her a kiss on the cheek and then pulled out her chair. He was going to have some fun. Her little lie didn't bother him. He ordered up a couple more coffees.

"You look great, Meg. Work must really agree with you."

"Thanks, Jimmy," she said, with a big smile. "You waiting long?"

"No, not at all, first cup of Joe."

"Why'd you pick *this* place? I actually love it. I've been here before with my girlfriends."

"My people are over at St. John's, resting."

"Including your wife?"

"Yeah." He could sense her regret and said, "So, tell me, anything interesting happening over at Silver Cup?"

"No, not really. Long, boring days, the kind that define the word, monotony."

"My partner, Tommy, he's up on the latest. Tells me they're filming a new movie over there called *These Bells Toll*," and he almost burst out laughing. "He said the female lead had to put on some weight to get into character. Can you imagine?"

Meg couldn't resist saying, "I think I could." She was studying his face, now, intently, deciding whether or not to come clean, when Jimmy said, "He also said that it might be a role that would generate Academy Award consideration for her. What do you think of that, Meg *Cassidy*?" He was all serious.

She was looking right at him and blinking nervously. She didn't appear to know what to say, so he bailed her out. "No big deal, Meg. Lying to someone you're dating is not always an indication as to how the relationship will progress."

And then Meg, laughing and at ease, and coming right back at him, "Oh, we're dating, are we? I must not have gotten the memo." They were smiling at each other.

She gave him the short version of the little fib and the movie life, and he sat on the edge of his seat, all interested and understanding. There was a television on at the bar, turned to an all-news station, and it was updating the condition of the NYPD detective shot the day before in Harlem.

"I thought of you often, yesterday, Jimmy, when I heard about the shooting. Just horrible."

"I was up there. Tommy, me, and the boys. We were there when the perp got smoked. I know Alba well. She's the one that got it. Lovely gal." He went on to explain her condition.

"I'm so sorry," and Meg reached across the table and patted his hand.

He was easing into another subject and participating in a little lie himself. "Tommy says you got the same agent as Dexter Spencer from the Lions, and the guy from the TV show."

"Yep, Artie Levin. We actually dated a little, which is kind of funny, because when I look back at it, I can't help but ask myself why. Possibly, because he 'discovered me,' " and she used her fingers to signify quotation marks and started to laugh. " My Dad wasn't a fan. I saw him a couple of weeks ago. I'm on the phone often, but we've been playing tag. He's working with a new artist, and seems very excited."

"What, an actor?"

"No, a rapper. Supposed to be the real deal. Artie is very keen on this guy, which means he thinks he will be making lots of money off him."

They wound up having burgers, Meg telling him that they weren't as good as Donovan's. He grabbed the check, and they walked out onto the boulevard.

"Now that we're dating, Detective McTigue, I can expect to see and hear from you more often?"

"Certainly, Miss Cassidy, as long as you behave yourself."

"Maybe I don't want to behave" and she gave him a look that surprised him with its possibilities. Then she punched his arm and said, "Filming is just about done. The wrap party is on Friday at Silver Cup. You want to go?"

"Do I have to wear a tuxedo?"

"No, you silly goose. Very informal."

"Can I bring Tommy? He'd get a kick out of it."

"You most certainly can. I'll have my car, so I'll just meet you there."

"Okay. I'll be the guy in the shades, with the cigarette holder," and she punched him again.

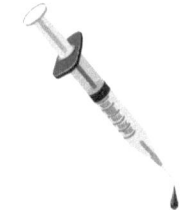

# Chapter 45

After the shooting of Alba Castro, there was such an overwhelming sense of sadness up at the Armory, that it reached epic proportions.

Bobby Washington came into the cubicle and said, "I don't know who's a bigger asshole, Obama, Donald Trump, or Colin Kaepernick" and no one laughed, or paid attention.

Charlie Defranco had switched up the feeding schedule for Rudy. He came walking through the office with a live mouse, everybody knowing what it was and what it meant, and nobody got up from their desks to come over and see the show.

The television was off and no music. There were computer keyboard and typing noises, and whispers but that was about it.

Captain Sink was up by the FOD taking down the Lodge A5-5, Original Finish Chuck Wagon Dinner Bell with a screwdriver. No one had a complaint. The Vicious Jim Carrey was dead, replaced at last by Inspector Norman Lucas, a "cop's cop" and a true gentleman. The bell went into storage.

Sgt. Quinn and Sgt. Lewis sat at their desks doing paperwork. All the boys, including Al Gavin and Jack Clint, were in the cubicle catching up on shit. Some were drinking coffee.

Jimmy had the set book on his lap, and was sitting next to Tommy, who was trying to catch up on two weeks' worth of DARs.

"I'm giving Earl a call, Tommy. Get all this information to the Feds. They're certainly better equipped to deal with it than us. Besides, it's going to be all-hands-on-deck when we begin to get some payback down at the Wagner Houses."

"Yeah, call him. I'd feel a lot more comfortable with just a steady diet of B and B and *Dinero Mandar* from now on."

He got up from his desk and plopped into the chair in front of the fish tank with the Maine lobster—back to living the good life after the kidnapping. He dialed Earl's number.

"Earl, it's Jimmy."

"What's up, pal? Funny, I was thinking of you."

"I need to talk to you about this whole thing."

"Give me a couple of minutes, and I'll call you from a landline. Reason I thought of you, didn't you mention something about a rapper and the location?"

"Yeah, I did."

"Get the *New York Post*, page eight. Little box in the ISIS article. I'll call you back in ten."

Wally was at his desk reading the *Post*.

"Wally, when you get a chance, can I get a look?"

"A minute, Jimmy. Let me finish reading *Hondo*."

Done, he passed over the paper, and Jimmy turned to page eight. Inside the box, from the AP:

"Washington, DC: Officials at the Pentagon have confirmed that a U.S. airstrike in Syria has killed French citizen, Pierre Lefitt. Lefitt, a one-time rapper, who went by the name of Snoop Dread, before converting to Islam, was a member of ISIS and had been instrumental in its propaganda operations. An unnamed spokesperson for the Pentagon put it simply: 'The plug has been pulled on Dread's mike, forever.' "

Jimmy folded the page back, pointed to the box, and handed the paper to Tommy.

Then, Earl called.

"Alright Jimmy, I'm all ears."

"Yeah, Earl. Honestly, I thought I'd be done with this, but it has taken on a whole new life of its own. With Alba getting shot . . . things are going to be real busy here. Anyway, one of the players sold a firearm to Bobby. We think the brother might have actually gotten the piece from the mosque. Couple of other things going on. Bottom line, this might be a little above our pay grade and—"

"Jimmy, don't *ever* sell yourself short," said Earl. "I know what kind of detective you are. There are agents here I'd go through doors with, guys I'd trust with the safety of my family, but there are also agents here who have never put the cuffs on anyone. Some of the shit we did in narcotics, stuff we accomplished with nothing more than our street smarts, this crew here has nothing on us."

"Thanks, Earl, but it's time I gave this to somebody there, the people who were looking into it in the first place."

"No problem, pal, but let me give you a heads-up on some shit. You got time?"

"Yep, go ahead, Earl"

"There is always going to be an edge in the relationship between the Feds and us—just the way it is. It didn't help that after Nine-Eleven, the FBI reached out to Kerik and asked about fresh intelligence, knowing he had Saudi contacts from his days in the private sector. Who *knows* what happened, but they say they were ignored—off on the wrong foot, right away. It really incensed the ADIC. That's the Assistant Director in Charge. So there was already a bit of a pissing match between the FBI hierarchy and the new three-star from our job, who came on board after our numbers went from about twenty guys to a hundred."

"Now, you got to realize that there are two major bones of contention between us and the Feds. Number one, the polygraph. I know you, Jimmy, and I know me, and I know a shitload of other guys. *We* never took a dime. We're honorable men, doing an impossible job to the best of our ability. But what, the Feds are going to hook me up to a lie detector and ask if I ever drank while I was working, or slapped the shit out of a guy who deserved it, or had a discounted meal—even though the waitress got the cash? We get to JTTF, we've been cops for years. Some of these agents get here, they just got out of law school. No history of doing *anything*, which means no problem sitting down for a polygraph. Bottom line—and you *know* how the union feels—we don't submit. You know what? When they strap up Hillary, or the head of the IRS to one, and start asking tough questions, I'm all, fucking in."

"Jimmy said, "Man, all that has *got* to cause a problem.""

"Yeah, because, now, some of the agents don't think we deserve national security clearance. Bottom line, some of the guys don't trust us, and they can be awfully stingy with information and access. Here's an example. This pretty much sums it up. Jimmy, you find a guy with actionable intel, you and Tommy jump in the car, go out, sign him up. Shit, no problem. I got a source I want to put on paper, I need an agent. Two agents got a guy, that's not a problem. But two NYPD detectives, by themselves, can't, and they are left with their thumbs up their asses. It sucks."

"It's all about *sharing*, right? I've been up here for some time now, and I *always* think the Feds are holding something back. They got access to dozens of different databases that we don't, and it sometimes feels like you need an Act of Congress to get them to take a look in there for you."

"You must be pulling your hair out."

"What little I have left. All right, you called, and I found out who's been looking into your location. The ASAC (Assistant Special Agent In Charge) is a guy by the name of William Hawthorne—*not* Bill—*William*, and he has reminded me of that on several occasions. He has time on, but I don't have a clue what he did to get here. I know he's got a Master's degree in accounting from Northwestern. The diploma is up in his office. I know he attended a seminar in DC, with terrorism expert, Steven Emerson. The guy founded "The Investigative Project," wrote *American Jihad*—knows exactly what he's talking about. The left's all over him, because he fucked up and said Birmingham, England was a totally Muslim city. But the *real* reason is that he knows the real deal, knows the savages are coming, and that they are here, and *nobody* wants to hear it. Thank God, he's on our side. Back to our boy, William. I went into his office, laid the groundwork, and told him you had some information. You reached out to me from our days in narcotics. I told him I knew what you were doing, but that I had notified the agent in charge—and I did. It looked to me like he was trying to blow me off, but he said he'd meet you in his office tomorrow at around one. That good for you?"

"Yeah, Earl, thanks. That's a weight off my shoulders."

"Just give me a call when you get close. I'll come down and get you."

"Ten-Four."

"How's Alba?"

"We're getting ready to go up and see her."

"Tell her everyone down here sends their love and prayers."

"Will do. I'll let you know when the Ten-Thirteen party is, too."

"Thanks, Jimmy."

"No, thank you, Earl, and I mean it."

\* \* \* \* \*

They took two vehicles down to see Alba—Wally and Bobby in the UC car, and the rest of the team crowded into the P van. They brought stuffed animals, sweets, and bakery goodies with them. There was a florist on the corner of 96th Street and Madison; Jimmy went in and grabbed a fruit basket from the team.

After the initial surgery, Alba had been moved to the recovery room: comfortable lighting, the soundproof ceiling, the walls painted in a soft, relaxing hue. The nurses checked on her condition continuously. When it was determined that she had fully recovered from the anesthesia, they shipped her upstairs to six, the Surgical Intensive Care Unit. There was a team of critical care specialists, who were on the case, and had taken a keen interest in her.

Her parents had been with her every step of the way, and, now that she had been moved to her own room, the visiting restrictions had been relaxed. Employee Relations had provided a team of guys from the office with a car to take care of Alba's Mom and Dad, 24/7. The members of the North were pulling duty at Alba's room, all day and all night, until she went home.

The boys beat Wally and Bobby to the hospital and headed up to four. They could see where Alba's room was, from a distance, when they came off the elevator. There were men and women standing around, detectives in business attire and dressed-down, uniformed cops, and civilians. Al Link was sitting in a chair outside Alba's room.

"How goes it, Al? How's she feeling?"

"Jimmy, she's amazing. You walk in, she puts you at ease. You know how cops are, some of these guys don't know what to say, but in a little while, she has them laughing. Inspector Carney is in there now with Lt. Bilge and Lt. Joyce. Erick Boltz is in there. He's taking it hard, still all shook up."

"Inspector Lucas been by?" asked Charlie Defranco.

""Yeah, God, what a change in that guy. He must have spent an hour with Alba's parents, and then told them it was important that they were eating properly, and took them to dinner with Captain Sink. Anything the family needs, they go right to him. They got his cell number. You boys want to go in now?"

"We'll wait a minute, Al, for Bobby and Wally," said Sgt. Quinn.

Erick Boltz came out of the room with his head down and a cup of coffee in his hand. He looked out of it. He nodded to everyone except Frank Martin, who was leaning up against the wall with his hands in his pockets. Erick went over to Frank and hugged him.

Right about now, Wally and Bobby came down the hall. Bobby was carrying a four-foot Snoopy that was wearing the

Manhattan North Narcotics sweatshirt, those words, and the city skyline underneath a cobra. Alba's room door opened and the place emptied out. Sgt. Quinn led the team in.

Her bed was up against the window, and already the room was filled with flowers and candy, and cards that the nurses had taken the time to hang about the place. Alba, with an IV hookup, had a big smile on her face. The sheets and blankets came all the way up to her chin, and, considering that she had taken a gut shot, she looked healthy. There was no indication on her face of the insidious disease that was killing her. But it was right about then that everyone in the room realized what Al Link had said earlier.

"Well, well, well. The boys are back in town. Hope you guys are here to invite me to another one of your rooftop barbecues, or one of those McTigue search warrants. I really felt proud, me being the only girl you asked."

"That's 'cause we love you, Alba. You are most definitely always welcome," said Sgt. Quinn.

Bobby Washington stepped up and placed the Snoopy to the side. In that moment, he completely lost the edgy look he sported and he looked at Alba and said, "You still look great," and grew silent, and put his head down and walked out of the room. There were a couple of moments of quiet, and then Alba said, "Look at that—Bobby Washington at a loss for words. And it only took me getting shot for you guys to experience it." Alba had them howling.

Charlie Defranco wanted to say, "Alba, you're killing me," but thought better of it. "We got some goodies here for you. Anything else you need?"

"I'll be honest with you, Charlie. I'm kinda missing Rudy."

"He'll be there when you get back. We'll have a special dinner for him, in celebration of your return."

A nurse came in, went to Alba, and took her temperature.

"Everything is perfect, honey. I'll leave you with these fine gentlemen."

Tommy Bell looked around for effect and then said, surprise-like, "I guess she's talking about us."

"She obviously doesn't know you boys like I do," said Alba, and there was more laughter.

"You're awfully quiet, Detective McTigue. Hangover?" and she started giggling.

"I find that you have again resorted to a little racial profiling, Miss Castro. You *know* how sensitive I am . . . please . . . any idea when you'll be going home, Alba?"

"Doc says about a week. Then, I get strong and come back to work. Get ready for the Ten-Thirteen party, too."

"I got it all hooked up, Alba," said Santos. "The good Marist Brothers up at Mount St. Michael's said we can have it up there in the gym. Plenty of room. It's going to be great."

"It will be a lovely time," said Frank

"Frank Martin has spoken. Wow!" yelled Alba, and then she got serious and looked at him and said, "Thanks, Frank. I owe you."

His face went completely red.

Al Link came through the doorway and said, "Let's go, boys. Me and Alba are splitting the take—five bucks per visitor. They're lining up in the hallway, as we speak."

Everyone said there goodbyes, and then Alba said, "Al, give me a minute with Detective McTigue."

Jimmy moved the chair up close that stood near her bed, sat down, and reached out and grabbed her hand.

"Funny, Jimmy, all those guys up there in the Armory making passes at me, and *you* were the guy I was looking to receive one from," and she smiled. "You don't have to say anything."

"That day at the Kinsale, Alba, I got close. But I still wasn't ready. It's not you, it's me," and he hid a smile, because he knew it was going to get a reaction.

"Take it easy, George Castanza. That's *my* routine," and Alba couldn't stop laughing.

"I knew you'd appreciate the line. That was a good episode."

"Yeah, Kramer was the ball boy, and Jerry was going out with the deaf lineswoman."

Then, Alba got a little serious and said, "We would have had some laughs together, though."

"We sure would have."

"Now don't be crying on me, McTigue. Jimmy, I got a favor to ask."

"Anything at all, my dear."

"My folks don't even know how close it is. I don't think anyone does, except the doctor and now you. I'm preparing. My Mom loves the sound of the pipes. I want you to promise me that you'll get a guy to play them at my funeral. It would mean a lot to her. It would be kinda special for me, too, hear them while I'm leaving. Promise me. In fact, promise me two things—*that* and you stop crying."

"I promise, Alba. You'll have your piper. I'm not sure about the other thing. You need anything else?"

"Nope, not at all. Home in a week, and you are certainly welcome to come by with the boys. I'll have my Mom whip up some chicken with some rice and beans. And, you can bet your life, I'll be at the Ten-Thirteen. You can buy me a beer, Jimmy."

"I'll be honored to, Alba," and he leaned over and gave her a kiss on the mouth.

Alba smacked her lips like she just had ice cream. "Mmmmmmmm . . . what's that, Coors?"

"You never miss an opportunity, do you? You're special, Alba."

"You know it, Jimmy boy."

Jake McNicholas

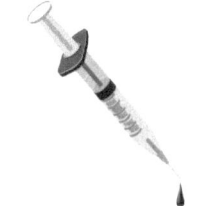

# Chapter 46

"**How about I drive, Jimmy?**" Tommy said.

"Wow, what's the occasion?"

"Give an old-timer a break."

"Don't go there, Bell, it's unsportsmanlike."

Tommy walked over to where Sgt. Quinn sat and asked him if he had the vehicle book for number 582. Quinn looked through the bottom drawer of his desk, then waded into the huge pile of paperwork, stacked on top, and found the green logbook with the soft cover, underneath overtime stats, buy operation closings, post-search warrant paperwork, "28s," kites, a week's worth of DARS, and a couple of menus—all this stuff, on the opposite side of the desk, where the pictures of his kids were. Stapled inside the book was a small zip lock bag with the keys.

"Figures," Tommy said, opening the book, "hasn't been filled out in over a week, and I know guys have been using it. I'm going to have to figure out some dates, times, and some mileage to write in here. Okay, Jimmy, let's make a move."

"Where are you guys going?" asked Frank Martin, who was sitting in the corner, staring at the fish tank with the Maine lobster in it, drinking a coffee and going through a package of Chips Ahoy. He looked tired.

"Down to JTTF at Eighty Five, Tenth Avenue," said Jimmy. "You need a ride somewhere?"

"If you could, I have to head downtown to the DEA Office. It's a bit out of the way, but I'll make my way back up. Appreciate it."

"Frank, we'll drive you there, and you give us a call when you're done. We shouldn't be that long. We'll come and get you," Jimmy said.

The car was parked in the vehicle lot, out back by the basketball courts, off the Harlem River Drive. Cal Bunnion, Sid Harwood, and some of the other guys from the Two-Eight team were down for the day, so they were playing a little three-on-three. Harwood had spotted them heading to the car, stopped mid-shot, an easy one from five feet, and then they all looked over and gave thumbs-up signs and waves, then went back to playing ball.

They took the Drive south, and Tommy *did* drive, with Jimmy riding shotgun, and Frank in the back. They had sports radio on, and today's topic of conversation was whether the Yankees were going to sign the latest pitching sensation from Samoa. Tommy and Jimmy exchanged small talk, and Frank remained quiet.

"You're okay, aren't you, Frank?' Jimmy finally asked, not sure the question was necessary, but going with it, nonetheless. The two had a good relationship. "You don't have to say anything, if you don't want to, Frank. Just making sure you're good."

They had just slipped past Gracie Mansion, when Frank took a deep breath. He was looking out the window, slouched down in his seat, when he told Jimmy, "Thanks for asking, boys." And then he began to speak in earnest.

"You know, it's funny. Lots of people ask the question, yeah, and I know I got some history, but I'll be honest with you, on all four occasions, I found myself at peace. I think it certainly has to do with my faith and my family, but it's more. Putting those guys away and then learning, in the aftermath, some of the pure savagery they participated in. Well, you know what, they had it coming."

He was quiet again for a while, and neither Tommy, nor Jimmy felt it was necessary to comment.

"I will tell you about an incident on the Job, though, that bothered me, really ate at me a couple of days, before it got straightened out. I was a young cop in the Three-Four, and I was walking a foot post on Broadway. There was this SRO hotel, and a job comes over for an unconscious female, and I pick it up and go over there. You couldn't even define the living quarters as rooms, more like a large, walk-in closet. Room for a bed and not much else. You'd put a Yale lock on the door, when you weren't inside. Anyway, I get up there, and the lady, I find out she was in her sixties, is in the bed and not responding. EMS shows and confirms that she's DOA.

"She's actually living in that little hovel with a guy, the common-law husband, he called himself, and, at the end of the day, I made him the notification. Only, I went home that night and I started thinking on it. The only thing that kept coming to mind was that both of them, being kind of transient, maybe the guy didn't know any real relations for her, and maybe if she does have next of kin, they wouldn't find out she had passed. And maybe that poor soul ends up alone, with no one ever knowing, in Potter's Field."

Tommy and Jimmy kept quiet.

"Anyway, I swung out, and, for two days, it was on my mind. I couldn't sleep. First one back, I'm doing a four-by, but I get in early and head up to the squad with that worried, rookie look on my face. An old-timer, Vic Pagon, sees that look and calls me over to his desk and tells me to sit down. Make a long story short, he did some checking and told me the squad had contacted a legitimate next of kin. No worries. What relief."

They left it like that for a while, gave everyone in the car time for it to seep in, and then, right after they exited at South Street, Tommy said," You know what, Frank?"

"What, Tommy?"

"You talk too much," and they were back to laughing.

Tommy rolled over to Broadway and pulled to the curb opposite 26 Federal Plaza. JTTF used to be housed there. They still had offices in the building, along with the GSA, Department of Labor, FEMA, and Office of the Inspector General, up on fourteen, ICE, you name it. It was a bastion of bureaucracy, pure and simple.

Thomas Street was just down the block. "You guys need anything? DEA cards, dental forms?" asked Frank.

"I'm good," said Tommy.

"Me, too. Give us a call, Frank, when you finish up. We shouldn't be long. We'll be down to get you," said Jimmy.

Tommy inched his way to Chambers, made the right turn, and headed west. He went north on Church to where it sliced into Sixth Avenue and then took a leisurely drive through the Village, and past the basketball courts on West Fourth. At Greenwich Street, he banged a left, continued to Eighth Avenue and north to Fifteenth Street, and then west toward the Hudson. He came around the block, grabbed a spot in front of the Old Homestead Steakhouse, and threw the parking plaque in the window.

The 10th Precinct covered most of Chelsea, and the neighborhood was booming. Cattycornered and opposite the restaurant was the Chelsea Market, the old home of the Nabisco Biscuit Company, the producer of Saltines and Oreos. It took up the whole block, bounded by Ninth and Tenth Avenues, and 15th and 16th Streets. There was everything you wanted in there, including topnotch eateries and the offices of Google and Major League Baseball. A couple of the *Food Channel* kitchens, too.

Jimmy and Tommy came in through Ninth Avenue and walked to the rear of the location and Tenth. When they exited, Earl's building was right in front of them.

Eighty-Five Tenth took up the whole block, as well. It was a massive edifice of forty-plus stories, the back of the building up close to Westside Highway with the Chelsea Piers sprawled out on the other side. Chef Mario Batale's *Del Posto* was on the ground floor.

They stood in front of the building with the High Line, the old elevated freight rail, which was now a park, overhead. Jimmy put in a call to Earl, and he met them in front of the location.

"Thanks again, Earl, we really appreciate it," said Jimmy. "I'll be glad to be rid of it. Things have really heated up in the North since Alba got shot."

"No problem, Jimmy. Hawthorne is in his office and expecting you. It is what it is. Don't let anything he says raise you up. We got some time afterwards, I'll buy you guys a beer at the Brass Monkey."

They took the elevator to eight and checked in with the FBI police, and, then, headed up to nine, where the Domestic Terrorism office was. Most of the PD guys, up there, were former Narcotics and OCID detectives. The boys with the heavy, squad experience, the first and second-graders, were, more often than not, assigned to IT, International Terrorism, located on another floor.

They got off at nine into a completely white hallway, and Earl led them to the door. He used his swipe card, attached to a ShugZ, and gained access to the office itself, laid out in a grid with small cubicles and carpet under the feet. This wasn't the Armory; there were plenty of office supplies, the latest in computer software but no TV—*and* definitely no ball breaking.

"This is it, boys. Home sweet home. It gets so, sometimes, all you want to do is go outside and get a breath of fresh air. I'm thinking of taking up smoking. Only kidding. Just the quiet and the noise of the computer keys gets to be too much. Nothing else up here. That's Hawthorne's office in the corner. Stay here. Let me look in and see if he's ready for you."

Earl walked to the doorway, looked in, gave a thumbs-up sign to the occupant, walked back toward Jimmy and Tommy, and motioned them over.

"See me before you leave. Good luck."

William Hawthorne sat behind his desk, 40—*maybe*—lean looking, with a full head of dirty blonde hair, and sparkling white teeth. Jimmy thought that he looked like he should have been on the tour, golfing. His accounting degree was up on the wall behind him, as well as some certificates and shield plaques from a few law enforcement entities in the Midwest. There were two chairs in front of his desk; Hawthorne was texting with one hand, took a quick look up, and then motioned to them to take a seat. The landline rang, he answered it, and he kept on texting. A little while later, he was off the phone.

"Hogan filled me in. Tells me he knows you guys from narcotics. This isn't narcotics. We're conducting real and important investigations here. Not looking to bag three guys smoking a joint."

Jimmy and Tommy looked at each other.

"We're just here to help you out, anyway we can, William. By no means were we ever looking to step on anyone's toes, or compromise any investigation," said Jimmy. "We fell into this. Everything I got is in this binder," and he got up and handed it across the desk. "Make copies for yourself, if you like. Hope it helps you out. We had one of our detectives shot the other day. We're *plenty* busy, uptown."

Hawthorne took the binder, placed it on the desk in front of him, and began turning pages with his free hand, the one that wasn't texting. He got another call and took it, placed his cell down, turned a couple of more pages, and then picked up the cell again and started fingering. Then he hung up the phone.

"Bottom line is this," said Hawthorne. "Thanks, but we got the location covered. I'd appreciate it if you forgot about it and stayed away. Go back to locking up crack heads, and leave the terrorism investigations to the professionals. We got this information," and he closed the book, without ever looking at its entire contents, and handed it back across the desk. "Take care, and good luck. Sorry about your detective. Tell Earl I want to see him, as you're going out the door," and he went back to texting.

Jimmy and Tommy left the office and went to Earl's cubicle, leaned over and looked down on him, as he was typing.

"That's a wrap, Earl. I don't think he was much interested, but we did what we had to do," said Jimmy. "Back to chasing the Kilo Fairy."

"Oh, yeah," said Tommy, "we have definitely been relieved of duty. He wants to see you, Earl."

"Rain check for the Brass Monkey. See you at Alba's."
They both said, 10-4.

\* \* \* \* \*

They were walking back to the car, when Frank called and told Jimmy he had finished up. He was going to walk south on Broadway and make a stop at the pension section; they could get him there, if they didn't mind. Tommy rolled up to Seventh Avenue and took another slow ride through the Village.

"That's done," said Jimmy. "The binder goes back in the bottom of the drawer, never to be seen again, thanks to William Hawthorne. Time for me to dust off some of those kites I got, a couple of weeks ago."

"You have to admit it, though," said Tommy, "he made it easy on us."

"Sure did. Now, all we got to worry about is tomorrow night."

"Oh, yeah, the wrap party. And Meg's good with it? Me coming?"

"Sure is. She's looking forward to meeting you."

"You know, Jimmy, really, who knows, I *might* get discovered."

"Oh, you'll get discovered, all right. I'm not quite sure what the discovery will be, but I'm sure Michele will be interested. Keep your eye out for Frank. We're coming up to the corner."

"Jimmy, there he is," said Tommy.

Frank Martin got in the back seat and said, "Thanks, boys. Let's go home."

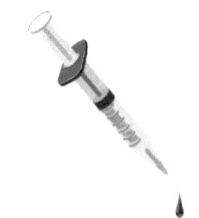

# Chapter 47

**Jimmy was on the phone.** "Tommy, listen. I'll get you in two hours. We're going in suits, regular suits. Forget the turtleneck and the three-quarter leather you wore last year to the DEA Christmas party."

"That's my John Shaft look," said Tommy.

"I know it is. Here's the problem. Thank God we watch old movies. *You* know who Shaft is, and *I* know who Shaft is. But I've got to be honest with you, I don't think too many *other* people know who Shaft is."

"I'll look around in the closet. But that's my man, Richard Roundtree. See you later."

Jimmy McTigue had two suits: the black, striped Stafford Executive he got from J.C. Penny, and the Elgara, Gray Sharkskin he bought from Men's Warehouse.

It wasn't like he was going places. He'd put on a suit for a retirement party; he'd put on a suit for a wake and funeral; and he'd put on a suit to testify—that was about it.

But he and Tommy were meeting Meg at the wrap party, and he was taking it seriously. He shined his black dress shoes, and found a nice, light green, Monterey Bay tie that he had purchased from a street vendor down in Chinatown. Five for ten dollars—couldn't go wrong with that. He was going with the Stafford, and he was taking his five-shot .38 in the black holster. It would be tucked inside his waistband.

Jimmy drove over to Tommy's house, left the Jeep out front, and gave a soft tap on the side door. Tommy opened up, half-dressed, and said, "Uncle Jimmy is here," and Bonnie and Britney came running out with hugs and kisses and said, almost in unison, "You look *so* handsome, Uncle Jimmy." Michele came in from the living room and scooted the girls back to the television. Jimmy took a seat at the kitchen table, and Tommy came walking in wearing his Michael Kols blue, slim-fit.

"You know, Jimmy, he still wanted to wear his Shaft outfit," said Michele. "Wore it on our first date. I'll never forget it. He comes to the front door, and my dad starts humming the Isaac Hayes theme song and saying 'Can you dig it?' I almost died of embarrassment."

"I think your dad was jealous," said Tommy. "I was looking fine that night."

Michele told them to stand next to each other. Then, she eyed them up and down, adjusted each one's tie, brushed the lint off the suits, and finally said, with much satisfaction, "My boys are certainly looking good. Now, behave yourselves."

"Listen, Michele," Tommy said, "knowing how irresistible I look, if Halle Berry is there and makes a play for me, I might be a little late."

"Tommy, dear," said Michele with a big smile, "if that happens, just make sure you give my number to Denzel." She gave them both a big hug, and they were on their way.

Meg had told Jimmy to meet her in front of the building. They found a spot across the street from the 5-Star Bar and Grill on 43rd Avenue and 21st Street, and came up 22nd Street.

The block had been completely cleared, closed down from each direction with the old, wooden police barricades. There were none of the usual trucks that would be lined up during the day: the Henry's International Cuisine, Chef's on Fire, and the Haddad's "Can do People" costume and equipment vehicles. Harry Suna Place, 22nd Street, so named for the real estate developer responsible for the studio, had been cleaned and scrubbed.

Halfway up the block, they could see Meg in front of the studio by the benches under the light. She was wearing a short-sleeved, V-neck, polka dot dress, and sandals. She looked stunning.

"Wow," said Jimmy.

"Wow, that's *more* than wow, partner," said Tommy.

They walked up to Meg, and she flashed her big smile and went to Jimmy and kissed him. He wrapped his arms around her, then retreated a bit and said, "Meg Cassidy, my partner, Tommy Bell."

"Hi, Tommy, real nice to meet you," and she gave him a firm shake.

He was a bit tongue tied, but he finally said, "Nice to meet you. You know, I told Jimmy, that first time, you looked familiar. Me and my wife saw you in *The ICE Men Cometh*. We *loved* that movie."

"Why thanks. Maybe you can get Jimmy here to watch it. You guys look good. You ready for a party?"

"Yeah, let's do it," said Jimmy. "Tommy thinks he might get 'discovered.' He told the missus he's on the lookout for Halle Berry."

"She won't be here," said Meg, "but Karen Slater *will*. Do you like her, Tommy?"

"I sure do. I saw her in *Magnum Lunch*. Thought she was great."

The head of Monarch Studios was 75-year-old Chauncey Wyatt, and the gentleman outdid himself setting up the party. The movie had come in under budget, thanks to the no-nonsense approach of Fred Meunch and Wyatt's friendly relationship with the unions, so he was happy to spend the money.

The original set, inside the studio proper, was still up, as were the classrooms and the fake pub, so you could go in there and check it out. There were food and drink at both locations, but the center of the celebration was the parking lot across the street from the studio itself.

They had cleared out the area completely of cars, blasted the old surface clean, and transformed it into an outdoor wonderland. A huge, white tent had been erected, with sidewalls and French windows off to the back, and you could hear the music from the street—*even* over the noise of the 7 train running up above. It was a beautiful night, with a cool breeze in the air, and it was magical.

"Let's take a walk into the tent," said Meg, and she led the way.

At the far end, under the chandelier, was the band, up on a two-foot-high platform, playing a mix of oldies and modern classics. They were called "Rocks," and the sign on the stage advertised them as "A Good Time Party Band." Jimmy wondered if they were the same guys who used to play at the Dublin Pub on Jericho Turnpike. Off to the left and the right, and off the dance floor, were tables crammed with food, and bartenders serving up drinks. Meg didn't know who was responsible for it, but it was someone's idea to dress the waiters and waitresses in Catholic school uniforms. The guys looked ridiculous, but the girls in short dresses, high socks, and saddle shoes, looked lovely. They made their rounds, with stuffed figs with goat cheese; roasted mushrooms caps; and almond, asparagus, and Brie pinwheels. By now, Meg had grabbed a glass of Rhone Valley red from a waiter with a tray, and a waitress approached with some mystery edibles and made an offer.

"Would you like to try some?" she asked.

"Sure," said Jimmy. "What is it?"

"They're petite polenta cakes finished with smoked Gouda and fresh mushroom."

Jimmy deadpanned, "Wonderful, that was my second choice." Then, he grabbed one, winked at Meg, stuck out his pinky, and took a tiny bite.

Tommy said, "Any chance somebody will be around with the little hot dogs?"

"Who writes your material?" Meg asked, laughing. "What are you guys drinking? I'm buying."

"Meg," Jimmy said, "just an ice cold beer of anything I've heard of."

"Me, too," said Tommy.

She walked off to a bartender, about twenty feet to the right, who had bottles lined up on the table.

"This is some shit," said Jimmy. "Who would believe it? I'll tell you one thing, Tommy. I'd pay money to have Bobby Washington here. Now *that* would be a reality show, funnier than anything they got on TV at the moment."

An older gentleman sidled up and homed in on Tommy. "Lovely party, isn't it?" A waiter walked by, and the guy grabbed two glasses from the tray. "Oh, you *must* try this. It is simply *brilliant. Cru Beaujolais Melaric Cabernet Franc.* The tiny pink bubbles are just *heavenly.*"

"Thanks, my friend," said Tommy. "I have a drink coming," and then Meg came over carrying two bottles of beer and handed them out. The "gentleman" moved on.

"Tommy was about to be discovered," said Jimmy.

"That's Marshall Van Ives. A money guy. He absolutely *loves* these parties. I must be honest, Tommy, he's partial to—"

"Just spit it out, Meg," laughed Jimmy. "He's fond of 'the brothers.' Play your cards right, Tommy, and you'll be able to vest out."

"Ain't this a bitch?" said Tommy. "I'm thinking Halle Berry, and I get hit on by a wrinkled old white guy. I'm sure no one in the office is going to hear about *this*, right, Jimmy?"

"My lips are sealed."

They were all laughing and taking it in. Jimmy checked his warm beer and didn't recognize the label—something from Belgium—and Meg could see the question coming. "I walked around," she said. "I couldn't find any *regular* stuff."

Jimmy smiled back at Meg, and found himself staring at her, every chance he got. She caught him doing it on more than one occasion, and when she did, she just gave him a playful punch in the arm.

The band kicked into Tommy James's "Money Money," which sent a whole bunch of people onto the dance floor.

Tommy went over to one of the tables and filled a plate with some Rosemary chicken skewers, Buffalo chicken wings, and jumbo shrimp cocktail.

"He's a nice guy," said Meg. "Thanks for coming," and she leaned into Jimmy, and gave him a kiss.

"It's our pleasure, Meg, though we are certainly not happy with your beer selection." Meg gave him a little elbow, and Tommy returned with the food. Jimmy spotted three, casually dressed guys, drinking sixteen-ounce Buds from the can, and took a walk over.

"You know, Meg," said Tommy, "you couldn't find a nicer guy or a bigger gentleman. It's been a long time for him. He's been denying himself happiness."

"Thanks, Tommy," and she patted his arm. "I've had good feelings about Jimmy ever since we met at the pizzeria."

The three stagehands were in a circle, admiring the waitresses in the Catholic school get-ups.

"Hate to bother you guys," said Jimmy. "You got to be the union boys. Know where the *good* beers are? Any suggestions?"

The huge, older guy said, "Guess you haven't been to one of these shindigs before. Always imported beers, and *always* warm for some reason. We got our own stash, in a garbage can behind the curtain. We saw you over there with Meg. We all love that gal. A real sweetheart. You a friend of hers?"

"Yeah, I am."

"You work for the city, don't you?"

"And *you're* retired from the Job," Jimmy laughed. "Me and Tommy work uptown in narcotics."

"I'm out ten years. Worked Brooklyn South Narcotics for a while. Retired from the Four-Oh. Moved upstate. Still the best job I ever had. Help yourself to our cache. Anyone asks, Big Mike said it was okay," and he winked.

"Thanks, Big Mike," and he grabbed two Buds and returned. There was still food on the plate. He handed Tommy a can, and then he nibbled. "Stagehands."

"They're a nice bunch of guys," said Meg. "How about we go outside. It's such a lovely night."

There were probably three hundred people under the floodlights, groups in semi-circles talking away. The music from the band, the noise of the train, and the overhead traffic to the approach of the 59th Street Bridge—it was an eclectic mix. They got their spot, and were taking it all in, when Meg spotted Fred Meunch and Karen Slater, walking through the crowd, and waved.

"Fred, Karen, nice party isn't it? These are two friends of mine, Jimmy McTigue and Tommy Bell. They're detectives with the NYPD," she said, like a proud parent.

Jimmy and Tommy both winced and stuck out their hands.

"Cops, eh?" said Meunch. "I got a lot of respect for you guys. A fucking, thankless job, excuse my French, ladies."

Tommy couldn't help himself, and said to Karen, "I saw *Magnum Lunch*. Me and my wife. We thought it was amazing. You were great in it."

Karen looked both of them up and down, and said, "Do you really enjoy working for a racist, occupying force, whose sole purpose is to deny the Black man his fundamental rights?" and she walked away.

Meg was horrified, but Meunch came to the rescue. "Don't sweat it, guys—and I *know* you don't. She lives in a bubble and doesn't have a fucking clue. Been drinking the *Kool Aid*. Told her, if she really thinks the cops are the problem, move from the Upper Eastside, stick her kid in public school, and start taking the train to work. Oh, yeah, and lose the bodyguard. She's been watching too much *MSNBC*. She and my daughter might be the only ones—according to the ratings."

Meg, still looking like she was about to cry, "I'm so sorry."

"Guess we're not getting an invite to Karen's Christmas Party, Tommy," laughed Jimmy.

"Yeah, what a shame," and things were good again.

Meunch said, "God bless you, boys, nice meeting you." He gave Meg a kiss, and walked away.

They had their backs to the entrance to the parking lot, where a couple of security guards were checking passes for admission. They were facing Meg, and were watching as she tapped her foot to the music, waving and exchanging pleasantries. She grabbed another wine off a passing tray, looked up, and called out, "Artie, over here!"

Jimmy and Tommy turned around to see super agent, Artie Levin walking across the parking lot, in a black sweat suit and crooked Yankees hat. He was in the company of Poon and Slice—dungarees and the white T-s.

Tommy and Jimmy looked at each other.

"Hey Artie, little late. How's it going? Want to introduce you to two of my friends, Jimmy McTigue and Tommy Bell. They're—"

Jimmy grabbed Meg's hand and squeezed.

"Garbage men," he said. "I'm a friend of Meg's from the old neighborhood," and he stuck out his hand.

"Yeah good. Nice to meet you," said Artie. "Here's Poon and Slice," and he nodded toward them. Neither one offered a hand. Slice eyed Jimmy up and down.

"Know you from somewhere . . ." and he was playing with a toothpick in his mouth. "You work with him, brother?"

"Yeah," Tommy said. "We pick up garbage."

"We're making the rounds," said Artie. "See you later," and they walked off.

And then, Meg, "How come you said that?"

"Meg, we're a little embarrassed to tell people we're cops. Kind of shifts the conversation onto us. Sometimes, it's better left unsaid. You know what I mean," and he grabbed her hand and gave it a kiss.

"Okay, it's our secret. Stay here. I'm going to use the ladies' room in the studio. I'll be back," and she was off.

"You picked up on it?" asked Jimmy.

"If you're talking about Slice and Poon being strapped, yeah."

"I wonder if William Hawthorne knows they're here?"

* * * * *

They hung around for a couple of more hours. Meg showed them the inside of the studio, where the classrooms and the fake pub had been erected, and introduced them to everyone. She had a few more wines, and Jimmy hit the stagehand stash twice more and thanked Big Mike for the hospitality.

They were about to make the move, when something slow came on by Rocks, and Jimmy grabbed Meg's hand and brought her out to the dance floor without saying a word; he wrapped his arm around her waist tight, snuggled his cheek up against hers and smelled the flowery scent of her hair—and at that moment, he was the happiest he had been in years. Meg pulled her head back to look at him, looked in his eyes and she said, "Thanks," and put her cheek back up against his. Then it was over and he kissed her on the lips, more noise from the 7 train off in the distance.

"We're going to make a move. We really appreciated it."

"Thanks for coming Jimmy. Tommy, it was wonderful to meet you, and I hope to see you again." She was about to shake his hand, but changed her mind and gave him a kiss instead.

"I'll call you tomorrow, Meg. You're okay to drive?"

"Sure, Jimmy," and she grabbed his hand again and squeezed.

Then, Tommy and Jimmy were in the Jeep, with the engine on. "Great time, Jimmy. She's a sweetheart. Some shit—with Poon and Slice."

"Tell me about it. Well, we're just following the instructions of William Hawthorne. We're out of it and we're staying away. Let me sit here a couple of minutes and make a couple of calls."

Tommy pointed up the block. "Isn't that Artie's Escalade?"

"Yeah, looks like it."

\* \* \* \* \*

"Nice party, isn't it, Artie?" said Meg. Then, she pointed off in the distance to Poon and Slice. "Which one is the rapper?"

"Yeah, that's my meal ticket, the one without the hat. The other guy's his *homeboy*. I'm chauffeuring these guys. You okay? Got a way to get home?"

"I was going to drive, but I don't think I should. I had a few too many glasses of wine," said Meg.

"I'll get you back home. Drop them out by the Airport." And then, with an annoyed look on his face, "You seeing that big guy?"

"Yes."

"A fuckin' *garbage man*? We're leaving now," and he gave the high sign to the brothers.

\* \* \* \* \*

"Okay, pal," Jimmy said to Tommy, placing his phone in the coffee cup holder, "let me get you home to your beautiful wife and kids." He was about to put it in gear, when he said, "What the fuck?"

Tommy looked up to see Artie, Slice, Poon, and Meg walking to the red Escalade.

Jimmy dialed her cell.

"She must be getting a ride," said Tommy.

"She's not picking up. *Shit*, she's getting in. We follow them, we could lose them. Something happens, I'll never forgive myself. We've got to stop them."

"Find a spot and we'll do it."

Slice was up front with Artie, Meg was behind Slice. The lights of the Escalade came up, and Artie pulled out onto 43rd Avenue.

"First chance we get, Tommy. A red light and some traffic would be the best thing." He tried Meg on the phone again, but it was still voicemail. He pulled out.

The Escalade made a right onto Crescent, going well above the speed limit. They were hoping for a red light at 47th Drive, but it was yellow when Artie went through, and Jimmy took it and checked his rear view mirror out of habit. Headlights, high off the ground and a little behind him, and not slowing down.

"Shit, "said Jimmy, "I hope he's not heading to the LIE."

The Escalade made the left on Thompson Avenue, and now they were driving over the Sunnyside Train Yards and past the entrance to the upper level of the 59th Street Bridge. They drove through another green light, with Artie driving obnoxiously, weaving in and out, and then the two vehicles shot past LaGuardia College. No chance for a stop. Again, Jimmy tried Meg's phone and *again* it went to voicemail.

"Queens Boulevard is coming up, Jimmy. Always a mess. We do the stop there."

Sure enough, the Escalade rolled onto the thoroughfare, the concrete rail line of the Number 7 train smack in the middle of the roadway, Artie still moving, Jimmy trying to keep close. Then, all of a sudden, Artie shot past 38th Street and went across two lanes of traffic to the right and pulled into a Citgo station just short of 37th. Artie pulled the car up to the pump, got out, and walked toward the Ameri Store in the back of the station.

They didn't have to say a word. Jimmy pulled up to the curb and took the driver's side, and Tommy the passenger's, with his Glock out in front. They dragged Poon and Slice out of the vehicle, had them spread-eagled on the floor, grabbed the .380s from both of them and had Meg out and off to the side, when a Range Rover and a black Impala roared up to the pumps. Out jumped William Hawthorne and three Feds.

"You couldn't leave it alone, could you?" screamed Hawthorne, as two agents came over to the Escalade, while another headed into the store for Artie.

Jimmy came around to the other side, where Meg was standing, and took her in his arms. He said to Hawthorne, "My friend, this is the last thing we wanted to do tonight. You told us to cease and desist and that's what we wanted to do. Now, do me a favor and have your boys cuff these two assholes—*if* they know how to. You *do* know they're carrying?"

"We know everything," Hawthorne said. "We are very familiar with Mr. Poon and Mr. Levin."

"And the other guy," said Jimmy, "you telling me you don't know who *he* is?"

"We'll sort everything out when we get to the base. Everybody is going with us, *including* the girl."

"I don't think so, Billy," said Jimmy. "She's coming with me," And William Hawthorne knew enough to *not* make it an issue.

"You letting these guys make phone calls?" asked Jimmy.

"Of course. They may be in custody, but they *do* have their rights."

They jumped into the Jeep, Meg still shaking, and Tommy explaining to her what had happened.

"I'm sorry," and she was almost crying, "I don't know what to say . . ."

"Meg, my dear, don't worry about anything. It will be a good story we can tell our kids when they get older."

Now Meg was tearing up.

"You got money for a cab on you?"

"Yes."

"I'm dropping you up the block at Sidetracks," said Jimmy. "Hand the bartender my card, tell him I'm your boyfriend, and have him call you a taxi." He pulled up in front, came around, opened the door, and gave her a kiss. "I'll call you tomorrow. Get some sleep."

"Where to now?" asked Tommy.

"You heard Bill. They have no idea who Slice is. He gets a phone call, I'm figuring he's telling the brothers he took a collar and to be careful. Might be time to move the merchandise from the mosque, if there is any. He has no idea what the Feds know.

See if you can get Charlie, Richie, and Frank. I'll try the Sarge and Santos."

"Yeah, Jimmy," said Quinn, when McTigue reached him on the phone. "What's up?"

"Long story, Boss. We need you to get out by that mosque on Atlantic Avenue. Me and Tommy are heading there now from Queens. You in the office? Anyone around?"

"Me and Santos just walked in. Still in the bag. Had an 'Occupy Wall Street' detail. Fuckin' terrorism is off the hook, and we're minding these *assholes*."

"That works," Jimmy said. "Stay in uniform. Come out here. What about the rest of the team?"

"Everybody else is end of tour."

"Ten-Four. See you out there."

"Any luck, Tommy?"

"Yeah, Charlie and Richie are on the way."

They decided that the spot they had set up when Basically Bill made his visit to the *Suleiman Masjid* was the place to be, so Jimmy pulled up in front of CURESMART Storage on Atlantic Avenue. It was dark, all right, but the streetlights provided enough illumination to see the front of the location. There were absolutely no pedestrians around, few cars parked on the street, and very little vehicular traffic.

"We sit here, Tommy, see what happens. They get spooked, they move the guns, *if* they're in there. We could be completely wrong about that. So what? We made a mistake and we head to breakfast."

"Charlie and Richie are on the other side of the location on Atlantic."

Jimmy's phone rang. "We're in the V/O, Jimmy. Want us anywhere particular?"

"Stay hidden. Don't want anyone to see you. Thanks again, Boss."

By now, the rest of the team knew what happened after the wrap party. They sat in the vehicles with the engines off, pissing in 7-Eleven, Big Gulp cups, and throwing the urine out the car window. Most times, they'd be "whacking it up." This time, everyone was awake.

Four hours in, and nothing was happening, and then at about an hour short of sunlight, a battered, old, cargo van covered in graffiti took a slow drive past the location. A couple of minutes later, it came back and parked in front of the mosque. Two male Blacks got out and looked around.

"Could be the security brothers," Tommy said.

Jimmy called Sgt. Quinn and gave him the heads-up. Charlie Defranco was already on the phone with Tommy. They watched, as the taller of the males unlocked the door of the location and both entered. A couple of minutes later, the tall brother came outside carrying an oversized duffel bag, and placed it in the van.

"Sarge, come over here, but don't drive by the front of the location."

Two minutes later, the second male Black came outside, carrying an identical bag. He placed it on the ground and began to lock the front door.

Jimmy told the Sarge to move in.

Tommy told Charlie to move in.

The two guys by the van were the A Team.

They were loaded for bear.

\* \* \* \* \*

The sun was up, by the time things settled down. The Feds had arrived, and they had a secret squirrel location in Red Hook, so they took the A Team over there with the van and the firearms.

Matt Quinn said, "Boys, this is for my cousin, Jimmy Berger!" and he stuck out his fist, and everyone gave him a bump. He and Santos were getting in the car, when Charlie looked over and said, "Don't miss the opportunity, Boss. You're in uniform and Santos could use a meal, as broke as he always is." Everybody was laughing.

Charlie and Richie pulled away, and now it was just Jimmy and Tommy with their backs on the Jeep looking out onto Atlantic Avenue. There was a little bit of traffic now; the City was awake. Jimmy wanted to hear Meg's voice very badly. He punched in her number, but the call went to voicemail. He listened to her message, then left one telling her he loved her.

"Let's make a move, Tommy."

"Ten-Four, buddy."

And then, just as they were about to get into the Jeep, a Subaru Outback slowly drove past the boys, heading west on Atlantic Avenue, with Junior Bishop driving and Rasheed Abdullah in the passenger seat, eyeballing them all he way.

Jimmy looked at Tommy.

Tommy said, "Giddy up."

The Outback started to pick up speed.

"I mean it, Tommy! You can't make this shit up."

They were five or six vehicles behind, by now, and could see the Outback weaving in and out of traffic. Past the Barclays Center, Junior Bishop took the light and made the right onto

Flatbush Avenue. Jimmy pulled out into oncoming traffic and managed to close the gap by the time they got near Junior's Cheesecake.

Tommy laughed. "You sure you don't want me to drive?"

Jimmy smiled. "I got this Bro'. It's all me."

They were still on Flatbush Avenue, heading for the Manhattan Bridge, and Junior Bishop was still weaving in and out of traffic, cutting off drivers, and looking like a Pakistani cab driver hunting for a fare. At Tillary Street, he made a hard left against the light, two wheels off the ground, and, now, he was putting some distance between himself and Jimmy. When the boys made the left off Flatbush Avenue, they got a fleeting glimpse of the Outback getting on the Brooklyn Bridge. They were losing them.

But God works in mysterious ways. It just so happened that on this particular morning, and at that very moment, the assholes from "Occupy Wall Street" were demonstrating at City Hall, and blocking vehicular traffic into Manhattan. Seems they were beside themselves at the mere thought of a middle class, fast food, franchise owner actually considering buying a robot to stuff the French fries into the French fry box, rather than pay some 17-year old, fifteen dollars an hour to do it.

So when Jimmy sped up in the middle lane of Tillary Street, and so avoided the red-light traffic forming up to go over, and then went around and got up on the span, he found himself, within seconds, just a couple of cars behind, Junior and Rasheed, smack in the middle of the Brooklyn Bridge.

Traffic was going nowhere.

Jimmy and Tommy could see the Outback. They saw the passenger door open, and watched, as Rasheed, dressed in street clothes, started running toward Manhattan.

"I got him, Jimmy. He's mine," said Tommy, and he was out the door.

Jimmy was out, too. He fumbled with his .38, and was right up on Junior Bishop, as he exited the Outback, with the Mission Craze Cross Bow he had taken a liking to and been practicing with. He squared off on Jimmy, who now was no farther than ten feet away.

Jimmy was still going for his five-shot .38, which was snug in the holster and tucked inside his waistband. He drew the weapon. Only problem was, it had been so long since he had taken the fucker out of the holster that when he lurched into his combat stance and drew down on Bishop, the holster was still *on* the .38, wrapped around it like a glove. So, Jimmy reared back and threw the holstered "off duty" at Bishop, beaning it off his big noggin and knocking him down.

He rolled Junior Bishop over, cuffed him, and sat him down with his back up against the Outback.

"Fuckin' Tommy was right," said Jimmy. "I *am* better off just throwing that thing."

\* \* \* \* \*

At the end of the day it turned out like this: the Feds had two sources operating at the same time: One was working the mosque and was providing just enough information to satisfy his handlers; the second source was a music guy who spent his time at the studio out at the airport. The Feds were on to Poon and Rasheed *and* to their efforts to assist the brothers here and overseas with the *Jihad*, through the music. No one had really taken an interest in Slice. And they didn't have a clue about the firearms in the mosque.

As for Artie, in an effort to become even more "gangsta," he had purchased a .45 from Slice. He got so "into" the thug mentality that he had a guy build a trap in his car for the piece.

Members of the NYPD Auto Crime Division found the trap.

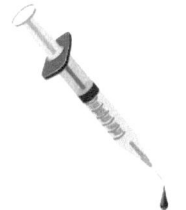

# Epilogue

**That old cavernous gym** at Mount Saint Michael's was fixed up, like it had never been fixed up before, for Alba Castro's 10-13 party. The place was huge, something out of the fifties and a sock hop. By the time the members of Manhattan North had finished, it looked magical.

They found out Alba's favorite colors, so they bathed the place in yellow, red, and blue ribbons, and papier-mâché hanging off the basketball rims and the scoreboard and decorating the folded-up stands, off to the side. There were balloons everywhere, and tables and chairs dressed in color.

By now, everyone knew the bad break that had befallen Alba. Friends of the police came out in force. Delis and distributors donated food and beer, prizes were furnished for the raffle, and a band volunteered to play for free. They said it would be an honor. Any money that was collected was secondary, really; Alba Castro would be taken care of for the rest of her life by the NYPD, regardless of the outcome. The party would be a testament to the love and respect the office and the police department had for one of their own. And, in many ways, it was as important for the cops working in Manhattan North as it was for Alba.

She was home now and had been receiving a steady stream of visitors. The P.C. had come by and had promoted her to

Second Grade. Jimmy, Tommy, and Frank had been in the living room when she got the bump. The look on the faces of her parents, the utter sadness, but the unbelievable pride would live with Jimmy McTigue for the rest of his days. Even then, with the PC honoring her, she looked over to them with a big smile on her face and winked.

Al Link had a buddy who owned a limo company, so, the night of the party, they sent Al, dressed like a driver, including the hat, up to get Alba and her parents. Every time she had talked about the party, she had referred to it as "Prom Night," so Inspector Lucas, riding shotgun, brought beautiful white carnations for Alba and her folks. Two, Highway cars, and a couple of motorcycle cops escorted them over to Murdock Avenue.

The men and women from Manhattan North Narcotics lined the sidewalk leading up to the entrance of the building. Everyone was hooting and hollering as they made there way in. Her parents lagged back a bit, so Alba could go through the double doors into the gym on her own. There were over a thousand people in there and more on the way. The noise was deafening.

"You know, Jimmy, I'm not getting cheated," she had said days before the party. So she walked into the gym, dressed in a black, flutter sleeve, beaded cocktail dress. It was her night. At about 9:30 PM, forty guys from the NYPD Pipe Band came marching in. Old Manhattan North Detective Dave McMahon was leading one of the columns. They circled up, and, at the end, had Alba and her mom and dad come in the middle and dance. There wasn't a dry eye in the house.

It was a night she would never forget.

Four months later she was dead.

\* \* \* \* \*

A .380 to the stomach wouldn't kill Detective Alba Castro. Digging at Ground Zero and looking for body parts on the conveyor belt at the Staten Island Landfill in the days, weeks, and months following September 11, 2001 would.

\* \* \* \* \*

It snowed the day Alba was laid to rest from St. Frances De Chantal on Tremont Avenue in the Bronx. Officially, it was a line of duty death; she had succumbed to the cancer from 9/11, *not* the gunshot wound from months ago. But that didn't change anything.

Historically, funerals for cops killed in the line of duty from other than, say, a gunfight, were less attended—but not *this* time.

Thousands showed up for the funeral.

The members of Manhattan North Narcotics came in NYPD school buses, dressed in uniform and white gloves. Bobby Washington and Wally Wong were still undercover detectives, still out there on the street buying drugs, but the two of them were adamant. They put their uniforms on and stood on the street and waited with everyone else, as the slow, steady beat of the drum brought the members of the NYPD Pipe Band up the street with Alba's body. She had gotten her wish. She had wanted *one* piper on this day—but she got *fifty*.

At the end of the service, the Pipe Band took her back again and sent her home to be with God. By now, the snow was coming down heavily, and looked beautiful on their yellow broths and blue tunics. They marched her away from the church, split in two, and the hearse came up between them. They played *Going Home.*

\* \* \* \* \*

Jimmy had driven his Jeep to the funeral and had brought Meg with him. He asked her if she minded making a stop, and she said, no, so he headed over to the florist on Woodhaven Boulevard and 68th Road. He bought the white cross, set in the green wreath, and then took Cooper Avenue to the side entrance and into St. John's Cemetery.

Meg stayed in the car, and he walked over to the azalea bush and the tombstone. He knelt down and said his prayers. And finally, after all these years, he was at peace.

"You okay, Jimmy?" she asked, when he got back in the car. He was looking straight ahead.

"It's all good, Meg. Really, it is. How about we go for a burger and a beer?"

"I shouldn't. I need to lose these twenty pounds."

"No you don't. You don't have to change anything. You're perfect just the way you are."

She gave him a punch in the arm.

# Acknowledgments

To Joe Perrone Jr of Escarpment Press for his unwavering assistance and support.

To the lads of the St. John's Rugby Old Boys and the NYPD Pipe Band, brothers all.

To the old neighborhood, the school and the church and the whole gang from that special place in Elmhurst, Queens.

To my partners, retired Detectives Anthony Amorese and Mike Zotto—wonderful investigators, but even finer men.

To retired Detective Jack Carney, my buddy from the "Paul's Place" days, who'd always ask me, "Jake, when are you going to write a book?"

To my dear family from here and from Ireland. Up Mayo (Balla)!

To the greatest police department in the world, the NYPD. Yeah, it was pure insanity on many occasions, and sometimes the things we saw and dealt with were unbelievably sad and soul-searching, but it was honest and rewarding work and, often, non-stop laughs; and at the end of the day, we can be proud to say that we made a difference.

# About the Author

Jake McNicholas is a former member of the NYPD, where he served for twenty-three years, retiring in 2007 as a First Grade Detective with the Terrorist Interdiction Unit of the Intelligence Division. Many of his years with the NYPD were spent in Manhattan North Narcotics. The events of 9/11 left an indelible impression upon the man, as did his entire career as a member of New York's Finest. He is currently working with the US Attorney's Office. He has been a member of the NYPD Emerald Society Pipe Band since 1991.

This is Mr. McNicholas's first book.

www.ingramcontent.com/pod-product-compliance
Lightning Source LLC
Chambersburg PA
CBHW051331250626
47155CB00007B/2547